Charles Duke Yonge, John Parker Anderson

Life of Sir Walter Scott

Charles Duke Yonge, John Parker Anderson

Life of Sir Walter Scott

ISBN/EAN: 9783337388195

Printed in Europe, USA, Canada, Australia, Japan

Cover: Foto ©Andreas Hilbeck / pixelio.de

More available books at **www.hansebooks.com**

LIFE

OF

SIR WALTER SCOTT.

BY

CHARLES DUKE YONGE

LONDON:

WALTER SCOTT, LIMITED,

24 WARWICK LANE.

CONTENTS.

—◦◦—

CHAPTER I.

CHAPTER II.

CONTENTS.

7

CHAPTER VI.

CHAPTER VII.

CHAPTER VIII.

CHAPTER IX.

CONTENTS.

CHAPTER XII.

LIFE OF SCOTT.

CHAPTER I.

WALTER SCOTT, the great glory of modern literature in England at least, if not in Europe, was born in Edinburgh in 1771, on the 15th of August, the same day which Napoleon afterwards assumed to have been his own birthday, and consecrated to a new Saint, whom he invented for a namesake. His father was a recognised member of a younger branch of the great Border family of Buccleuch ; his mother was a granddaughter of Sir John Swinton, the representative of another Scottish family of great fame as warriors in the early history of Scotland, of whose prowess he in some degree revived the recollection in his dramatic poem of Halidon Hill. His father, a Writer to the Signet, a class in the legal profession corresponding to that of attorney or solicitor in England, had a large family, and Walter was his third son. In an autobiographical sketch of his early years, he records that he "was an uncommonly healthy child" for the first year and a half of his life: when he was attacked by a teething fever, which settled in his right leg, permanently contracting the limb, and leaving a lameness which, though not severe, proved incurable. There are few evils without some compensation, and we may well regard this infirmity as fortunate for the patient himself, as well as for the whole nation, since it drove him to that devotion to literature which has made his name immortal, and has given a pure and lasting delight to thousands of readers in every part of the world. It is to this that we owe " Marmion " and " Waverley " ; as Spain is indebted to the wound that disabled Cervantes for the immortal record of the achievements of Don Quixote.

Not only was he thus led from his earliest years to cultivate a literary taste, but even, while still a child, he earned what, in some degree, may be termed a literary reputation. At nine years of age he was sent to the High School of his native city, where, as he had not been very well prepared beforehand, he was found to be a backward scholar in the classical languages ; but his mother, who, as he describes her, was "a woman of good natural taste and feeling," had inspired him with a fondness for poetry, accustoming him to read Pope's Homer to her, with which his own inclination had combined old ballads of border warfare, and legends of striking events in the annals of his country. Many such tales he got by heart, " almost," to quote his own words, " without intending it ; " and often, on a winter's evening, he would retail them to his schoolfellows, enlivening his narrative with the fertile vigour of a precociously ready imagination ; while, like the " noble youths who forsook the hunting of the deer " to listen to the strains of the Last Minstrel on the banks of Yarrow, they would sit around their dame's fireside, drinking in his stories with rapt attention, and looking up to the storyteller with as fond and proud admiration as if he had been the cock of the school at golf or football.

It was not a bad training for the future novelist, nor a deceitful omen of the judgement and feelings of future critics of maturer age ; and thus his schooldays passed by happily enough, and not without profit, though of a somewhat irregular kind, till, at twelve years of age, he was transferred to the college. There he extended his unacademical knowledge by learning Italian, becoming so enamoured of that rich and most melodious language as to give a somewhat whimsical proof of his love for it in an essay in which, to the indignation of the Greek professor, he maintained the superiority of Ariosto to Homer, "supporting his heresy," to quote once more his own words in after life, "by a profusion of bad reading and flimsy argument." But the legal studies for which the university afforded facilities were those to which his father attached greater importance than to classical scholarship, since he destined him for his own profession ; and, with this view, presently placed him in his own office to acquire the technical knowledge which would be indispensable to him, if he were to become a Writer, and very useful if he should prefer the more dignified position of a barrister. To adopt his own account of his legal studies during these elementary years, though he disliked the drudgery of the office, his affection for his father prevented him from crossing his soul like the clerk described by Pope, who "penned a stanza while he should engross"; but he contrived to mingle with his porings over Erskine's "Institutes," the perusal of more attractive volumes of "a most miscellaneous kind, reading them in his own way, which often consisted in beginning at the middle or end of a volume," and skimming them with what one of his brother clerks called "a hop-step-and-a-jump perusal," but contriving to know as much about them as the other acquired by the more methodical plan of beginning with the preface and plodding on to the "finis." Indeed, this desultory mode of reading, which has great attractions for many, and which, perhaps, is not without very considerable advantages of its own, seems to have been his habit through life ; and his son-in-law and biographer, Mr. Lockhart, has given some extracts from his note-books of 1792, when he had just been called to the Bar, which present an amusing idea of the variety of his studies, if they can be so called, and of the objects which attracted his curiosity and interest. One day he is delighted by the present of an old border war-horn, from a friend whose gardener had been profanely degrading it into a grease-horn for his scythe. Anon a page is occupied with the Norse original of " Vegtam's Kvitha, or the Descent of Odin," and the English poetical version of Mr. Gray. Next comes a page headed " Pecuniary distress of Charles I.," with the transcript of a receipt for some plate lent to the king in 1643 ; the verses of Canute on passing Ely ; then a translation, "by a gentleman from Devonshire," of the death song of Regner Lodbrog; after this an Italian canzonet in praise of blue eyes, which were much in favour with him at this time ; and extracts from an old journal about Dame Janet Beaton, the Lady of Branksome of the "Lay of the Last Minstrel," and her husband, Sir Walter Scott of Buccleuch, called Wicked Wat;

extracts about witches and fairies ; notes on the second
sight, with extracts from Aubrey and Glanville ; and a list
of ballads to be discovered or recovered, the whole completing as strange a medley as ever formed a relaxation
from closer studies. The last of these memoranda was undoubtedly that in which he took the keenest interest. Few
young lawyers have much practice to occupy them, and
Scott's business was not too great to hinder him from
making frequent excursions in the indulgence of his hunt
after relics of the olden time, among which ballads held a
principal place. The acquisition was the harder, since,
in many cases, no copies of them existed either in print
or manuscript, but they were preserved only in the
tenacious memory of old peasants, male and, still oftener,
female. Many passages in the novels are so many scraps
of biography : and the experiences and labours of which
Mr. Oldbuck boasts to Lovel, were, no doubt, records of
the author's successes in similar researches, and of the
means by which those successes were achieved. He, we
may be sure, would not have grudged " tobacco, snuff, and
the complete Syren," as the purchase of a bundle of
ballads two hundred years old : nor, more in harmony with
his jovial temper, " the drinking of two dozen of strong
ale," if such a compotation could have coaxed the proprietor of a similar treasure to bequeath it to him in
his will.

His fancy for this particular class of poetry was not
confined to specimens of it in his own language. He
set a judicious value on the acquisition of foreign languages, and had recently varied his legal studies by
attending a German class, which some letters of Mac-

kenzie, the author of "The Man of Feeling," had made
popular in Edinburgh; and his earliest attempt at verse
was a poetical version of Bürger's "Leonora," which he
executed in a single night to gratify a lady who, if not
the rose, had something of the perfume derivable from
proximity; or, in other words, if not the object of his
attachment herself, was in his confidence, as the friend of
her whose favour he was seeking, though unsuccessfully,
to win.   He read it to her at breakfast the next morning,
so greatly to her satisfaction, that it led her to venture on
a prophecy that "he was going to turn out a poet, something of a cross between Burns and Gray." A more
important work of the same kind was a translation of
Goethe's tragedy of "Götz von Berlichingen of the
Iron Hand ; " if at least the opinion, which seems to have
been entertained by Carlyle, be well founded, that it had
an influence on the translator, to which his adoption of
that line of literary composition, by which he made himself famous, may be traced.   "In his own country"
(Germany) " Götz, though he now stands solitary and
childless, became the parent of an innumerable progeny,
of chivalry plays, feudal delineations, and poetico-anti-
quarian performances. . . . And, if genius could be
communicated like instruction, we might call this work of
Goethe's the prime-cause of 'Marmion,' 'The Lady of
the Lake,' with all that has followed from the same
creative hand."[1] But such parentage seems very doubtful :
even in the love-scenes of the "Lay," or of "The Lady
of the Lake," there is no trace of the exaggerated senti-
mentality which was one besetting weakness of the German

[1] Carlyle's Essays, iv. 134.

novels and dramas of the day, and which was wholly alien from the manly disposition of our own poet.

With his translation of "Leonora" he himself was so well satisfied that it led him to try his hand at original composition of the same class; and, as he was soon afterwards made acquainted with "Monk" Lewis, an author, for the moment, of considerable fashion in London, he contributed four or five ballads of his own to a volume for which Lewis was making a collection of what he described in a letter to Scott, as an assemblage "of all the *marvellous* ballads which he could lay his hands on; ancient as well as modern." And, as the title of the volume was "Tales of Wonder," Scott bespoke the public favour for it by an "Apology for Tales of Terror," which was sufficiently ingenious, but which had a most disastrous effect on his subsequent fortunes, since it led him to form a connexion with a publisher named Ballantyne, whose unskilful management of his business eventually brought on Scott losses which nothing but his own strength of mind prevented from being absolutely ruinous. For the moment, however, the connexion promised a very different result, since it led him to open to his publisher a scheme for sending out a collection of his own, which in 1802 came out under the title of "Minstrelsy of the Scottish Border," prefaced by an elaborate Introduction, and enriched with a wealth of commentary which, in no feeble or uncertain manner, foreshadowed the novels of the author of "Waverley."

Meanwhile two all-important events in his private history had occurred. On Christmas Eve, 1797, he married, not the object of his first love, but a young English lady,

Miss Charlotte Carpenter, who, in addition to a fortune
of £200 a year, possessed, as he described her to Miss
Rutherford, one of his female relations, "very good sense,
with uncommon good temper, which he had seen put to
most severe trials." His previous disappointment had,
at the time, been felt most bitterly; so bitterly, that at the
first shock his friends were alarmed at his utter pros-
tration of body and mind; but he had good cause to be
now reconciled to it, since, in an union of nearly thirty
years, every one of them supplied proofs to a heart
willing and happy to acknowledge their validity, that the
good sense and good temper which he had praised to
Miss Rutherford, were sterling and lasting qualities, well
calculated to secure him, as they did, unbroken happiness
till it was cut short by his wife's death.

The other event was of a less sentimental character.
At Christmas, 1799, he received the appointment of
Sheriff-Depute of Selkirkshire, with a salary of £300 a
year; and this possession of an income which, though
moderate, was settled and permanent, was especially
welcome as placing him in a position of pecuniary ease,
which made him to a certain extent independent, and
left him at liberty to indulge his literary taste, in preference to wasting his talents on "the daily drudgery of a
precarious profession." From the first it had never
jumped with his inclination, and it had failed to grow on
him. His feelings towards it he compared to those
avowed by Slender to Miss Anne Page : " There was no
great love between us at the beginning; and it pleased
Heaven to decrease it on further acquaintance."

His first venture of the Border Minstrelsy had

been confined to two volumes. In the course of the next year he had a third ready, not quite identical in character with its predecessors, since many of the ballads were of no great antiquity; several indeed being originals of his own composition. In the summer of 1803, its publication took him to London, as the great publishing house of Longman had a share in it; and one of his letters on the subject to Ballantyne bids him add to the advertisement of it an announcement that there is "in the press, and speedily to be published, 'The Lay of the Last Minstrel,' by Walter Scott, Esq., Editor of 'The Minstrelsy of the Scottish Border.'"

All true Scots have a loyal reverence for the chief of their clan; and in Scott's breast that hereditary feeling received an additional impulse from his admiration for Lady Dalkeith, the young wife of his chieftain's heir. Her fancy had been caught by some of the "old wives'" tales of her new neighbourhood, and, among them, by the legend of a goblin, hight Gilpin Horner, whose pranks, as the tale ran, had in some bygone age been the terror of the district; and she had suggested it to him as a subject for his muse. Her request, or command, as he no doubt in his loyalty regarded it, went no further than for a ballad, and it is probable that he originally contemplated nothing more. But, while he was mentally sketching out a plan, the recital by a friend of a portion of Coleridge's as yet unpublished poem of "Christabel," led him to enlarge it, so as to work out a metrical romance, which, as it proceeded, grew under his hand, till it was finally expanded into an elaborate romance of six cantos. In Lockhart's opinion, "a single scene of feudal festivity in the hall of Branksome, disturbed by some pranks of a nondescript goblin," was possibly all that he had originally designed, till "suddenly there flashed on him the idea of extending his simple outline, so as to embrace a vivid panorama of that old Border life of war and tumult, and all earnest passions, with which his researches on the Minstrelsy had by degrees fed his imagination." If this surmise be correct, and it is highly plausible, no change of purpose was ever more felicitous. The principal female character in the "Lay" is the wife of the ancient chieftain, Wicked Wat, whom the superstitions of the district and the age had credited with a magical insight into things forbidden; but, wizard as she was supposed to be, she was never more amazed at the success of her own incantations, than the present lady of Branksome was at the power of the genius which her request had evoked. The gradual expansion of the poem had evidently delayed its completion far beyond the author's anticipations in 1803, for it was not till January, 1805, that it was published, when it at once attracted universal attention.

One of the most remarkable things in the history of a poem which now, above eighty years after its first publication, enjoys undiminished, it may perhaps be true to say increasing, popularity, is that, at its first appearance, it received a warmer welcome on the South than on the North of the Tweed. Some even of the poet's personal friends, to whom he read the opening stanzas of the first canto, pronounced a verdict on them so unfavourable, that he was half inclined to throw it aside. *The Edinburgh Review*, which had been recently started apparently on the rule of finding fault with everything and everybody, and which was edited by a man of very congenial disposition, the celebrated Francis Jeffrey, denounced the defective conception of the fable, "the great inequality in the execution," and especially condemned, with extreme severity, "the undignified and improbable picture of the goblin page, an awkward sort of mongrel, between Puck and Caliban," declaring that "the story of Gilpin Horner was never believed out of the village where he was said to have made his appearance;" the critic never suspecting that the story was, in fact, the cause of the poem having been written. With dangerous boldness he proceeded to venture on the prediction that "the locality of the subject was likely to obstruct its popularity," and that "even Scotchmen could not so far sympathise with the local partialities of the author, as to feel any glow of patriotism or ancient virtue in hearing of Elliotts and Armstrongs ; that the present age would not endure them, and that Mr. Scott must either sacrifice his Border prejudices, or offend all his readers in the other parts of the Empire." [1]

[1] In chap. xvi. of Scott's Life, Lockhart quotes a letter from a friend who, soon after the publication of "Marmion," met both Scott and Jeffrey at a dinner in Edinburgh. On literary subjects they were, as may be supposed, the two principal talkers ; and, says the letter-writer, "it struck me that there was this great difference between them—Jeffrey for the most part entertained us, when books were under discussion, with the detection of faults, blunders, absurdities, and plagiarisms ; Scott took up the matter where he left it, recalled some compensating beauty or excellence for which

The "other parts of the Empire" did not agree with Jeffrey. Among English readers the admiration was universal. Widely as the "Lay" differed from their own style, Wordsworth and Campbell were prompt and warm in their recognition of its excellence. The accomplished Sir Henry Englefield, who was generally so devoted to philosophical speculations that, as he said, he read but little poetry, read it three times through, and, even then, scarcely ventured to flatter himself that he had done justice to all its beauties. The political rivals, Pitt and Fox, vied with each other in its praise, the description of the trembling embarrassment of the aged minstrel, as he tuned his harp before the duchess, in particular, striking the great Minister as "a sort of thing which he might have expected in painting, but could never have fancied capable of being given in poetry." This is a singular criticism, since most people would think it far more likely that the greatest painter should prove unable adequately to reproduce the creations of the poet, than that the poet should fail to embody even the loftiest conceptions of the painter. But it is not therefore less valuable as the testimony of a man not only pre-eminent in practical ability, but also deeply versed in the works of the classical poets, to the truth and naturalness of the description ; qualities without which the most ambitious

---

no credit had been allowed, and by the recitation perhaps of one fine stanza, set the poor victim on his legs again." The very motto of *The Edinburgh* showed the bias of its founders : "judex damnatur cum nocens absolvitur;" and so, to save the judge from condemnation, every man or work that came before the tribunal was presumed to be *nocens* ; guilty, and to be lashed accordingly.

flights of the imagination fail to reach the heights to which they fain would soar.

Jeffrey had enumerated among the probable hindrances to the popularity of the poem, not only its intense nationality, but also the circumstance of its subject being confined to a delineation of only a section of Scotland, the Border district. It is not improbable that, on the contrary, this may at first have been among its special attractions, both from the novelty of the picture, and from the light thrown by it on the feelings and manners of the Borderers on both sides of the frontier. A stronger evidence of the difficulties which beset the rulers and statesmen of the two countries, so soon to be united under the sceptre of one sovereign, could hardly be found than in the anxiety with which, even in times of peace, the beacons were daily and nightly watched, lest isolated bands of marauders, or even the very Wardens of the Marshes themselves, might be arming for aggression, retaliation, or the more vulgar, but still dearer, objects of ravage and plunder. And when this singular feature of the manners of that age and district was illustrated, with life-like animation of action, and discriminating variety of portraiture, in the "courteous Howard," and the "wrathful Dacre" on one side, and, on the other, the stalwart Scott of Eskdale, the brave Thirlestane, and the poet's own more immediate ancestor, the veteran of Harden, prompt, as the youngest of his five stately sons, to don his helmet and hasten to Branksome to champion the lady whose rank and sex gave her a double claim to his devotion, it may surely be thought that genius thus brilliantly exercised had in it all the elements of a popularity as wide and enduring as it was immediate;

while the burst of patriotism with which the last canto
opens, though in the poet's own mind springing from his
deep love for Caledonia, not only as "meet nurse for a
poetic child," but still more as the "land of his sires,"
strikes a chord which can never be called local, but to
which, on the contrary, every manly and honest heart will
ever respond "from China to Peru."

Another quality, which greatly contributed to the
popularity of the poem, was its unflagging energy and liveliness, which presented a striking contrast to the character
of the general mass of poetry, or verse it may be more
fitting to call it, which the last generation had produced.
Scotland had indeed given us Burns, but the homely
Scotch dialect of his songs had prevented them, as in a
great degree it still prevents them, tender and impassioned
as so many of them are, from being fully appreciated, or
even widely known below the Border. Coleridge too had
written "The Ancient Mariner;" and more than one ode
of manly tone had shown of what Campbell was capable.
But, of the other strains in which the Muse had been
wooed since the death of Goldsmith, the prevailing
character was a level tameness and insipidity. Cowper,
indeed, and Crabbe, who had lately published "The
Village," and Southey, and Wordsworth, may not be
classed with tl e poetasters of the Della Cruscan School,
who would probably have willingly adopted the boast
which the author of the Baviad put into their mouths—

> "We want our sire's strength, but we atone
> For that and more, by sweetness all our own "—

though a vigorous criticism can find as little of real
sweetness as of strength in their lucubrations. But the

best works of Crabbe, Wordsworth, and Southey were not yet published, and of all the other elaborate poems of the previous thirty years scarcely one rose above that dead level of mediocrity, which neither gods nor men can endure.

To a generation that had been thus fed on Hayley, Rogers, and " Laura Matilda," the manly vigour and un-flagging vivacity of the " Lay," must have seemed like a resurrection of the Muse from the dead, the more so as every canto showed that energy and fire were not incom-patible with the most exquisite tenderness and delicacy, though the former may be supposed to have been the qualities at which, in this instance, Scott principally aimed, since the poem was avowedly, to some extent, an imitation of the spirit of the " old ballad or metrical romance ; " and since, in his introduction to the Border Minstrelsy, he had enumerated " rude energy," mingled at times with "natural pathos," as the special characteristics of that poetry, in which he at the same time warned his readers not to look for "refined sentiments," still less for " elegant expression." Not indeed that these graces, if unknown to or rare in the ancient ballad, were not as conspicuous as its sustained animation and spirit in the " Lay." The opening stanzas of the different cantos, the courteous, or, more than courteous, the kind sympathetic condescension of " the Duchess and her daughter fair," the pictures of Margaret, now in "wild despair " weeping "o'er her slaughter'd sire," now meeting her own true knight,

> " When love scarce told, scarce hid,
> Lent to her cheek a livelier red "—

are as instinct with delicacy and tenderness as Deloraine's "swift speed" to Melrose o'er moors, beds of flint,
and through the swollen torrent of Aill, or his "dire
debate" with Lord Cranstoun, briefly as it is told, are
instinct with the "rude energy" of the ancient minstrels.[1]

Nor, in all probability, was the metre, as Scott employed
it, a slight addition to the fascinations of the poem. It
had all the appearance of novelty, though, in fact, it was
by no means new to the language. To say nothing of
earlier and less-known instances of its use, Milton had
adopted it in his "L'Allegro" and "Il Penseroso"; Butler
in "Hudibras"; Gay in his "Fables"; and Swift in more than
one of his semi-satirical efforts; but a certain sing-song
monotony had seemed inseparable from it, and had prevented it from meeting with general favour. And no one
had ever conceived the possibility of making it the vehicle
of animated description of warlike enterprise, or of the expression of powerful passion, till Scott, suddenly triumph-
ing (to quote Byron's expression) "over the fatal facility
of octosyllabic verse," enriched it with every variety of
rhythm, and proved that no metre yet devised was
better adapted to every variety of subject, to fiery rapidity

---

[1] It may be supposed that his descriptions of Margaret, though few
and brief, were worked up with especial care, since we are told by
Lockhart, that, for his picture of the daughter of Buccleuch, he
was indebted in a great degree to the impression left on his heart by
"the form and features of his own first love," to whom, nearly ten
years before, he had devoted himself with so enthusiastic a passion
that, when he learnt that the lovesuit of a rival had been preferred
to his own, many of his friends (as has been already mentioned)
were alarmed for the effect which they feared his disappointment
might produce on him.

and force of action, to vivid and truthful delineation of character, to noble sentiment, to exquisite tenderness, and to the deepest pathos. On this subject it may be remarked as somewhat singular that, great as he must have been conscious was the charm of the diversity, which in this poem he gives to the metre,—in the varied length of the verses, lines of four syllables at times alternating with others of eight or even twelve, and in the arrangement of the rhymes, generally connected, as in the couplets of Pope, but at times alternating like those of the old ballad stanza, or diversified in other modes which will occur to the memory of every reader,—he adopted it to the same extent in none of his subsequent poems, except "The Bridal of Triermain;" and in "The Lady of the Lake" discarded it altogether. But, to whatever causes the popularity of the poem was owing, or whatever share may be attributed to each cause separately, of the completeness of its success there was, from the very moment of its publication, no doubt whatever, and, as Lockhart records it, that "success at once determined that literature should form the main business of Scott's life."

CHAPTER II.

SCOTT did not, however, at first entirely relinquish his profession, since the retention of his name on the roll of Advocates was necessary to qualify him for the lucrative appointment of one of the Clerks of Session, the reversion of which, in the summer of 1806, he secured by an arrangement with Mr. Home, an old friend of his family, who was its present holder. It had long been the custom to allow a clerk, whom age or infirmity might dispose to retire, to select a successor who, while doing all the work, should receive but a share of the emoluments : and Scott, going rather beyond the ordinary conditions of such a bargain, now agreed to take all the work on himself, but to allow Mr. Home to retain the entire income during his life. Six or seven years elapsed before, under this arrangement, he derived any profit from the appointment, but it was secured to him for the future ; and so saved him from any necessity of relying on his pen for an income. Without such a certainty he would hardly have felt at liberty, with a young family coming on, to consult his literary taste so exclusively. With this, law being "a staff," he could make literature his "crutch"; but, though so to use it was his original view of the duty imposed on

him by prudence, we cannot wonder that the substitute
gradually superseded the more regular support, and that
his attendance in the Law Courts grew less and less frequent every succeeding year.

Other circumstances also made even the emoluments
of his legal appointments of less importance to him.
In his case Fortune had shaken off her proverbial
blindness, a bachelor uncle who had died in June,
1804, while the "Lay" was in the press, leaving him a
small estate, with a share in other property, a bequest
altogether exceeding £5000 ; so that, by the beginning
of 1805, his own and his wife's fortunes, with the emoluments of his sheriffship, gave him a fixed income of
about £1000 a year, independent of the profits of any
literary work which he might undertake.   From this time
forth, therefore, we may regard him almost exclusively as
a literary man ; but it seems strange that the popularity,
daily increasing as it was, of the "Lay," did not at first lead
him to a fresh work of the same kind.   It might almost
seem as if he feared that a second attempt might fail,
and so tarnish in some degree the fame he had achieved
by his first.   He wrote to his great friend Mr. G. Ellis :
"As for riding on Pegasus, depend upon it I will never
again cross him in a serious way, unless I should, by
some strange accident, reside so long in the Highlands,
and make myself master of their ancient manners so as
to paint them with some degree of accuracy in a kind
of companion to the 'Minstrel Lay.' "   During the
year which followed the publication of the "Lay," he
occupied himself partly with a series of critical articles
for *The Edinburgh Review*, which had not yet taken that

subsequently strong political colouring as the organ of the Whig party, which eventually caused him to break off his connexion with it. But his chief employment was an edition of Dryden's works, which he introduced with an elaborate biographical memoir, which has ever since held its place as the best account of "glorious John." That Dryden was an especial favourite with him, we may perhaps infer from the pride with which Claude Halcro, in "The Pirate," boasts of his recollections of him, and which, we may be pretty sure, reflects some of Scott's own feelings. And it is worth noticing that this admiration led him to reject absolutely the advice of his friend Ellis to produce what in modern phrase would be called a "Family Dryden," an edition, that is, which should omit the works or the passages in which the great poet had made his genius too subservient to the licentiousness of his age. He did not deny that it might be very "proper to select correct passages for the use of boarding schools," &c. But he was "making an edition of a man of genius's works for libraries and collections; and he must give his author as he found him, and he would not tear out the page, even to get rid of that blot, little as he liked it." He believed, too, that the harm which was done by such works, passages, or expressions, was exaggerated or misunderstood. And, "in fact, that it is not passages of ludicrous indelicacy that corrupt the manners of a people." As he said truly, he did not like the blots. Dryden's offences were chiefly committed in his comedies, many of which Scott found "very stupid as well as indelicate"; though in some "there is a considerable vein of liveliness and humour, and all of them present extraordinary pictures of the age in which he lived." Accordingly, his " Dryden " was given to the public with all his "blots," as Cromwell insisted on Lely not leaving out a wart in his portrait. And scholars in general will think that he judged rightly; though the fever of "expurgation" is daily spreading, till even "The Merchant of Venice" cannot escape the pruning-knife.

His work drew him also into a correspondence with Wordsworth, with whom, as well as with Southey, he had recently become acquainted. The letter from Words-worth, which Lockhart prints at length, gives, it will probably be thought, a fairly impartial estimate of Dryden, even though he denies him a poetical genius, explaining his denial by an expression of his opinion that "the only qualities he finds in him, that are *essen-tially* poetical, are a certain ardour and impetuosity of mind, with an excellent ear." He "does not add to this, great command of language, because, though he cer-tainly had it, it is not language that is, in the highest sense of the word, poetical, being neither of the imagina-tion nor of the passions." " Dryden had neither a tender heart nor a lofty sense of moral dignity." He gives him, however, the credit of having often " strikingly improved Boccacio," in the translations from the "Decameron," which he regards as the best, at least the most poetical of Dryden's poems ; though even in them he points out in-stances in which the poet has "fallen below his original, and degraded some of the personages by his ignorance of the real character of love—of which, as purifying and ennobling those who feel it, Dryden had no idea."

The intimate acquaintance with the ancient manners
of the Highlands, for which Scott had declared he must
wait before again coming before the world as a poet, was
not yet acquired. But we can hardly doubt that he had
begun to plan another poem, since " Marmion " was not
only conceived, but published, before the edition of
" Dryden " was completed ; and, judging by his account of
his system of working in subsequent years, we may believe
that he regarded his articles in reviews, his labours in
biography and annotations, as a rest from original composition. He evidently was one who could not be idle ;
but he believed that a change from one kind of work to
another was in itself a rest, or, if not an absolute rest, at
least a relaxation equivalent to it. He called it "a
refreshing of the machine." " Poetry " he pronounced
"a scourging crop : one that must exhaust the land if not
alternated with something lighter, as wheat is followed by
turnips."

He had one relaxation also of a wholly different
class. As his sheriffship required his residence in Selkirkshire four months in each year, he had taken the
lease of Ashestiel, a country-house on the Tweed belonging to a cousin who was in India. But the remainder
of the year he passed in Edinburgh, and he would have
missed the benefit to his health of the invigorating air
and pursuits of a country life, if he had not found a safety-
valve in a new occupation which had no connexion with
the law ; though the experience of another kind which
he then acquired may have unconsciously been of service
in some of his subsequent literary works, just as Gibbon
declared that he had derived a more correct insight into

the operations of the Roman armies, from his own campaigns as a captain in the Hampshire Militia. One of the first schemes of the Directory in France had been an invasion of these islands; the general who was to conduct it was even named, if not formally appointed; and in every part of England preparations were set on foot to resist it successfully. Scott felt that his own country should not be behindhand in so patriotic a movement, and, at the beginning of 1797, he had stimulated a body of his friends to make the Government a formal offer of their services to embody a corps of Volunteer Cavalry. As one of his friends described the part he took, and the spirit that influenced him, there was in them a degree of anticipation of some of his literary work; as if he were but "rousing the spirit of the moss-trooper, with which he readily inspired all who possessed the means of substituting the sabre for the musket." His proposal was warmly taken up by the leading gentry of the district, and gratefully accepted by the Government. An efficient body of cavalry was speedily raised, of which he himself was appointed quartermaster; and the duties of that office have seldom been discharged with more genial efficiency. The same friend testifies that, while no fatigue ever seemed too much for himself, his zeal and animation served to sustain the enthusiasm of the whole corps; while his unfailing liveliness and wit kept up in all a degree of good humour, and reconciled them to the toils and privations of the daily drill. "At every interval of exercise, the order 'Sit at ease!' was the signal for the quartermaster to lead the squadron to merriment. Every eye was intuitively turned on 'Earl

3

Walter,' as he was familiarly called by his associates, and his ready joke seldom failed to raise the ready laugh."

Meanwhile, he kept himself before the public, if such a thing were needed, by one or two publications, which it is hardly worth while to mention; and, by the end of 1806, he had settled down to the composition of a new poem. I have ventured to surmise that he must have been revolving the plan of it for some time, as it has a more regular "plot" than the "Lay;" and the surmise is to some extent borne out by an introduction which many years afterwards he prefixed to the poem, when engaged on the publication of all his works in one grand body. "I had formed," he says, "the prudent resolution to bestow a little more labour than I had yet done on my productions; and to be in no hurry again to announce myself as a candidate for literary fame. Accordingly, particular passages of a poem, which was finally called 'Marmion,' were laboured with a good deal of care by one by whom much care was seldom bestowed." "Whether the work was worth the labour, he was no competent judge." That, however (says Lockhart), is a point on which the whole world has long pronounced a tolerably unanimous judgement; and the first knowledge that such a poem was in hand, was productive of a remarkable proof how high a reputation his previous publications had made for him, in the offer from an Edinburgh publisher, named Constable, of a thousand guineas for the copyright before a single canto was completed : and in the eagerness with which Mr. Murray, a rising London publisher, then engaged in founding what has become one of the first publishing houses in the world, embraced Constable's offer of taking

a share in his venture, Murray thanking him for the proposal because he regarded it as " honourable, profitable,
and glorious to be concerned in the publication of a new
poem by Walter Scott."

At last, in February, 1808, " Marmion " was published. That he had taken greater pains with it than
with the " Lay," is shown by the circumstance that nearly
a year and a half elapsed between its beginning and its
publication ; and the labour was fitly recompensed by the
reception given to it by all except the never to be satisfied
or silenced editor of *The Edinburgh Review.* Among
the first criticisms received by the author were letters from
Southey and Wordsworth ; both do credit to the writers,
who are equally warm and cordial in their praise, though
both agree that it hardly rivals the " Lay " in the estimation of the public. Southey, on this point, confesses his
agreement so far with the popular voice, since "as a
whole it had not pleased him so much, though in parts it
had pleased him more." And he selects for especial
commendation "the death of Marmion," as not only
surpassing anything in the " Lay," but as being such that
"there is nothing finer than its conception anywhere."
Another friend, on whose critical judgement he set great
value, Mr. George Ellis, agreed with them both that the
"Lay" was the more general favourite; though he admitted that "the fable of Marmion was greatly superior,
that it contained a greater diversity of character, inspired
more interest, and was by no means inferior in poetical
expression." He himself "would rather be the author
of ' Marmion ' than of the ' Lay,' because he thinks its
species of excellence more difficult of attainment." But

if he regarded it, as it will presently be attempted to show it may be regarded, as an epic poem, this estimate of Mr. Ellis seems rather at variance with his strange opinion, "sincere and sober" as he declared it to be, "of all the epic poems he has ever read, the Odyssey perhaps excepted, that they ought to have been written in prose." It may be a proof of my own deficiency in imagination, but I confess myself wholly unable to conceive what kind of work Herodotus or Livy, the most lively and powerful word-painters of their respective nations, would have made of the Iliad or the Æneid; or what Macaulay, though, as his "Lays" abundantly prove, himself imbued with no slight degree of poetic fire, would have made of "Marmion," or the "Lord of the Isles."

Jeffrey would have been false to his nature if he had not exercised all his ingenuity in finding fault. He even began with the second title: "Marmion, a Tale of Flodden Field"; of which he denounced the impropriety, since "it was no more a tale of Flodden Field than of Bosworth Field," a singularly captious criticism of a poem which opens with the despatch of Lord Marmion to the Scottish Court, on an embassy designed to avert the war which resulted in that stern conflict; while the latter half is occupied with King James's preparations for war, and his defiance of Henry, and the last canto with the battle itself. When he passes on to "the incidents," he pronounces the majority of them "unsuitable for poetry," and he is especially severe on "the paltry device of the forged letters," expressing his positive conviction that "an accuser, who was as ready and willing to fight as Marmion, could never have condescended to forgery in support of his accusation," and that the author "has greatly diminished our interest in the story, as well as needlessly violated the truth of character, by loading his hero with the guilt of that most revolting and improbable proceeding." His coadjutor in the establishment of the *Review*, Sydney Smith, who had been also his fellow student in the Edinburgh College, once explained the scantiness of Scotch scholarship by saying that " Greek was a witch, and, as such, could not cross running water, nor ever get beyond the Tweed." And it must be presumed that Latin lies under a similar disability, or otherwise Virgil and Ovid might have taught Mr. Jeffrey that Ulysses, whose hand was as prompt as Marmion's to defend his head, procured the condemnation of Palamedes by a crime precisely similar to that which, for a time, brought disgrace upon Wilton. Yet even Jeffrey was constrained to depart from his general rule,—to change his tone when he came to the last canto, and to admit that the description of the battle is beyond all praise, and that "certainly of all the poetical battles which have been fought, from the days of Homer to those of Mr. Southey, there is none at all comparable for interest and animation, for breadth of drawing and magnificence of effect, to this of Mr. Scott."

As a sort of prelude or preface, Scott had prefixed to each canto a poetical epistle to some valued friend, not on any subject connected with the poem, but touching sometimes on recent events, such as the national loss of Nelson at Trafalgar, the deaths of Pitt and Fox, and the fall of the Duke of Brunswick, the brother of the Princess of Wales, at Jena ; and in other passages on some of his own,

or his friends', private occupations and feelings. All his
correspondents, though they allowed that these epistles
were excellent in themselves as detached pieces of poetry,
objected to them as interruptions to the fable; and he
seems subsequently to have admitted the objection to be
well founded, by alleging, as an excuse for his "loquacity,"
that he was still "young, light-headed, and happy; and
that '*out of the abundance of the heart the mouth speaketh.*'"
It is at all events clear that the introduction to the "Lay,"
with its incomparable picture of the aged minstrel, affords
no parallel or resemblance to these epistles. That was
not only an exquisite, but also an indispensable frame, so
to say, to the picture; but not one of these have the
slightest connexion with the poem to which they are
attached: and, though certainly not devoid of a beauty
of their own as detached poems, they will probably
always be regarded as inappropriate excrescences in the
position he gave them.

One passage in the first of them brought an attack of a
different kind on him: a charge that he displayed a degree
of political venom in his mention of the great Whig leader,
Fox, whose death it deplores. It was not the first time
that he had been accused of injustice to Fox. The Tories
of Edinburgh had naturally taken a keen interest in the
impeachment of their fellow-citizen, Lord Melville, and
had celebrated his acquittal by a public dinner, at which
a song was sung which had been composed by Scott, and
which, in one stanza, was regarded as exulting over Fox's
broken health. Every one knew that Scott was an ardent
champion of the Tory party; he had been a busy canvasser
at elections, an earnest speaker on the hustings, and in

every way a zealous and effective adversary of the Ministry, absurdly known as that of "All the talents," which had succeeded to office on the death of Pitt. But the news of the state of Fox's health had not reached Edinburgh when he penned the offending stanza, nor had the poet the least idea that the great Whig Secretary of State was so near his end. The song, and the angry feelings which it had excited, had probably been forgotten, when the latter were renewed by a line urging that in Westminster Abbey at least prejudice should depart,

> " And, partial feeling cast aside,
> Record that Fox a Briton *died*."

And this was construed or perverted into an expression of opinion that he had not *lived* a Briton, that patriotism had not been the first and guiding principle of his political life. If those letters of Fox had then come to light in which he exults over Burgoyne's surrender at Saratoga, and, later, over the defeat of the Austrians by the French, solely because the former were our allies, and their disasters would be a severe blow to Pitt, whom he professed to hate (though in 1804 he was willing to join him as a colleague), we may well suppose that some of that first epistle would not have been written; but the passages which would be absent would be not this single line, but those which dwell kindly on the "talents untimely lost "—

> " When best employed and wanted most ; "

and those which seem to place not only his talents, but his patriotism on a level with those of Pitt. But it is

surely well that the lines should stand. Of Fox's general
kindliness of heart there is no more question than of the
brilliancy and solidity of his talents. And the letters
above mentioned may be regarded, not so much as an
expression of the poet's deliberate opinions and feelings,
as an instructive warning to all those concerned in public
affairs to beware, lest the keenness of their political attach-
ments may tempt them, for a moment, to hold even the
honour and welfare of the country second, as a motive
of action, to their allegiance to their party.

Of the peculiar and prominent qualities of genius displayed in Scott's poems, a fitter time will come to speak
when the last has been reached ; and when, therefore, the
entire set can be examined together. But the question
to what class of poetry "Marmion" and its predecessor, the
"Lay," belong, may fitly be discussed here. It is one on
which critics are not agreed. Some have spoken of them,
and of all their brethren, as romances. Mr. Conington, in
one of the Oxford essays, styles " Marmion " a minor epic,
the epithet apparently referring merely to its length, in
which it falls short, not only of the Iliad and the Æneid,
but of " The Jerusalem Delivered " and " Paradise Lost."
But it does not seem very reasonable to regard the class to
which a work belongs as depending on its length. The
Romans never refused the title of epic to the Æneid,
though consisting of only half the number of books of the
Iliad ; and it seems far more natural to consider the subject
and the mode of treatment as the criteria according to
which any work is to be classified. Johnson,[1] following in
some degree the principle which guided Horace in his com-

[1] " Life of Milton."

ment on the Iliad,[1] where he pronounces Homer superior as a moral teacher to the most rigorous of the Stoic, or the most subtle of the academic philosophers, has laid it down that "Epic poetry undertakes to teach the most important truths by the most pleasing precepts, and therefore relates some great event in the most effective manner." And, judging by this rule, we must refuse to place "Marmion" in the same class with its predecessor, the "Lay." That must clearly take rank as a "romance," according to Scott's own account of "the ancient romances of the metrical class," that "they were composed for the express purpose of being recited, or, more properly, chanted to some simple tune or cadence, for the amusement of a large audience."[2] But, in spite of its comparative shortness, "Marmion" fulfils all Horace's and Johnson's definitions of an epic poem. Like the Iliad it shows the disasters which follow in the train[3] of licentious love, it relates the failure of wise counsellors to appease the fury of a reckless king, and shows how the people suffer for the madness of their[4] rulers. It is founded, too, on one of the most momentous events in the history of the poet's nation, the war wantonly provoked by James, and its result in his disastrous overthrow and death ; and therefore, even if no account be taken of the varied felicity of the execution, it may well claim its place as an epic poem in that division of the art to which all critics agree in assigning the honour of being the noblest exercise of poetical genius.

---

[1] Epist. I. 2.   [2] Scott's Essay on Romance.

[3] Scelere atque libidine et irâ Iliacos intra muros peccatur.—Hor. Ep. I. 2.15.   As James is led by Lady Heron, v. 10.

[4] Quicquid delirant reges, plectuntur Achivi.—*Ibid.*

CHAPTER III.

MORE "refreshment for the machine" was required before "Marmion" could be followed by a third poem, and certainly it was not stinted. Mr. Ellis stood aghast at hearing of the number of "literary enterprises, some of them of immense extent," in which his friend was engaged. And certainly they were enough to have amazed and daunted any one. Scott, tempted in some degree, we may suppose, by the price offered (£1,500), but also by his admiration for the author, had undertaken, on a scale to correspond to his edition of Dryden, an edition of Swift, which was published a couple of months after "Marmion." He had also undertaken an edition of the State Papers of Sir Ralph Sadler, who, both as soldier and statesman, bore so important a part in the affairs of Scotland in the reigns of James V. and his unhappy daughter; another, of the vast body of tracts collected by Lord Somers. "The Memoirs of Captain Carleton," and those of Cary, Earl of Monmouth, must be added to the list. And the year had not expired, before we find him engaging, heart and soul, in the promotion of Murray's scheme of a new review, as a rival and antagonist of *The Edinburgh*, the vehemence of whose Whig partisanship, which had already alienated Scott, had seemed to the Tory leaders in London to require an antidote. Yet this immense accumulation of work had, in his own opinion, at least for the time, a beneficial effect on him. As many years afterwards he described it to Lockhart, " it was enough to tear me to pieces, but there was a wonderful exhilaration about it all; my blood was kept at fever pitch; I felt as if I could have grappled with anything and everything; then there was hardly one of all my schemes that did not afford me the means of serving some poor devil of a brother author. There were always huge piles of materials to be arranged, sifted, and indexed; volumes of extracts to be transcribed; journeys to be made hither and thither for ascertaining little facts and dates; in short, I could commonly keep half-a-dozen of the ragged regiment of Parnassus in tolerable ease."

His untiring eagerness to aid his less fortunate "brethren of the quill" was so generally known, that he was inundated with applications for assistance of one kind or another. Some entreated his recommendation of a manuscript to a publisher; others solicited his interest with the patron of some appointment; and few met with a refusal. Hogg, the Ettrick shepherd, whose poetical talents were beginning to meet with the appreciation which they deserved, failed indeed to induce him to back his application for a commission in the militia; but he did "endeavour to have him made an Excise officer," though "that station, with respect to Scottish geniuses, was the grave of all the Capulets, witness Burns, Adam Smith, &c."

Amid all this work his life went happily on. Few men have ever had a greater capacity for enjoyment, or found pleasure in a greater variety of the circumstances of ordinary life. His family deservedly occupied the first place in his affection and attentions, and Lockhart gives a delightful picture of him surrounded by his children :—

" No father ever devoted more time and tender care to his offspring than he did to each of his, as they successively reached the age when they could listen to him, and understand his talk. Like their mute playmates, Camp and the greyhounds, they had at all times free access to his study ; he never considered their tattle as any disturbance ; they went and came as pleased their fancy ; he was always ready to answer their questioning, and when they, unconscious how he was engaged, entreated him to lay down his pen and tell them a story, he would take them on his knees, repeat a ballad or a legend, kiss them, and set them down again to their marbles and ninepins, and resume his labour as if refreshed by the interruption. From a very early age he made them dine at table, and ' to sit up to supper ' was the great reward when they had been ' very good bairns.' In short, he considered it as the highest duty as well as the sweetest pleasure of a parent to be the companion of his children ; he partook of all their little joys and sorrows, and made his kind, informal instruction to blend so easily and playfully with the current of their own sayings and doings, that, so far from regarding him with any distrust or awe, it was never thought that any sport or diversion could go on in the right way unless *papa* were of the party, or that the rainiest day could be dull if he were at home."

Camp was a favourite dog, to be succeeded hereafter by the still more celebrated Maida; for, first among his sources of healthy enjoyment out of doors was every kind of field sport, his skill in his favourite one of coursing being so celebrated, that when a friend one day jestingly asked one of his children what it was that made "papa's" society so generally sought for and valued, the answer was that "it was commonly he that saw the hare sitting." And in a letter of this date to the celebrated female dramatist, Joanna Baillie, he gives as his answer to the question he expects, "what are you doing?" "Why I am very like a certain ancient king, distinguished in the Edda, who, when Lok paid him a visit,

‘ Was twisting of collars his dogs to hold,
And combing the mane of his courser bold.’ "

Dogs indeed were such pre-eminent favourites with him, that on a subsequent occasion a shrewd lawyer, insisting on the identity (as yet unavowed) of the author of "Waverley" with the poet of the "Lay," pointed, as one of the strongest proofs of the soundness of his conjecture, to the persistent ingenuity with which, in both novels and poems, every opportunity was seized for their introduction; whether sleeping on Branksome floor; running down a stag single-handed like Lufra; recognizing a long-absent master like Elphin; protecting his mistress through the wood like Bevis; or binding himself round the heart of the rude swineherd like Fangs, while even Mr. Oldbuck, hostile as he avowed himself to sport and sportsmen, could not find in his heart to look with lasting disfavour on the "female dog with a Pantheon kind of name," though she had broken his lachrymatory and devoured his buttered toast.

A better relaxation than the task of editing half a dozen works of different characters was a visit to London, with which he indulged himself at the opening of the next year, 1809. Even that was partly on business, as being connected with the starting of *The Quarterly Review*, to the first number of which he contributed no fewer than three articles; and which introduced him to new friends, Gifford, the editor; Frere, the author of "Whistlecraft"; Croker; and, above all, Canning, not less lovable as a man than delightful as a social companion and wit, and admirable as a statesman. And Scott was not so much a seeker of such men, but rather was sought by them. One gentleman of rare accomplishments, and of a congenially antiquarian taste, Mr. Morritt, of Rokeby, whose acquaintance he had recently made in Scotland, and of whom, during this visit, he saw much at Morritt's house in Portland Place, records in his journal that "the homage paid him would have turned the head of any less gifted man of eminence; but it neither altered his opinions, nor produced the affectation of despising it. On the contrary, he received it, cultivated it, and repaid it in its own coin. 'All this is very flattering,' he would say, 'and very civil; and, if people are amused with hearing me tell a parcel of old stories, or recite a pack of ballads to lovely young girls and gaping matrons, they are easily pleased; and a man would be very ill-natured who would not give pleasure so cheaply conferred.'" One of his female admirers (it may be doubtful in which class she should be ranked at this time) was the celebrated Miss Lydia White, a clever, kind-hearted woman, who, as she was rich enough to give good dinners, found it easy to collect a pleasant society around her, her "lions," as she called them,—though Scott, in one of his letters, describes her as herself "what Oxonians call a lioness of the first order, with stockings nineteen-times-nine dyed blue, very lively, very good-humoured, and extremely absurd."

The duties of his legal offices would not permit a long sojourn in London ; but, before the end of the summer, he found time to treat himself to another excursion, its direction being the Highlands, which, as has been recorded above, he had declared to be an indispensable preliminary to any fresh poem. In fact, he had already begun "The Lady of the Lake," and his principal object was to re-examine some of the spots which he had once before seen while a boy, but of which he now needed a greater accuracy of knowledge than could be derived from such early reminiscences. So careful was he on such points, that one day he rode from the shore of Loch Vennachar to Stirling, to ascertain that he should be warranted in ascribing a similar gallop to FitzJames. Even while occupied with what, to any other man, would have been the engrossing labour of completing a poem on the preparation of which he had bestowed such pains, he gave himself what he seems to have considered the relief of a variety of other occupations. He excuses to

Mr. Morritt some remissness in correspondence, to which he pleads guilty, by the explanation that "he has been Secretary to the Judicature Commission, which sat daily during all the Christmas vacation. He has been editing 'Swift,' and correcting for the press at the rate of six sheets a week. He has been editing 'Somers' at the rate of four ditto ditto. He has written reviews—he has written songs—he has made selections—he has superintended rehearsals; and all this independent of visiting and of his official duty, which occupies him four hours every working day except Monday."

But, in spite of this multitude of distractions, "The Lady of the Lake" was finished and published in May, 1810. It brought him one important proof of the steadily increasing solidity of his reputation, since he sold the copyright for double the price that "Marmion" had produced. A relation, whose nervousness of affection for him surpassed her judgment, had tried to dissuade him from giving "Marmion" a follower. "He stood high," she truly said, and she entreated him "not rashly to attempt to climb higher, and incur the risk of a fall; for he might depend upon it a favourite would not be permitted even to stumble with impunity." But no sort of timidity could find a place in Scott's breast. He had replied in the words of Montrose—

> " He either fears his fate too much,
>   Or his deserts are small,
>   Who dares not put it to the touch
>   To win or lose it all."

And now, while the last sheets were passing through the

press, he writes to Morritt, " If I fail, as Lady Macbeth gallantly says, I fail ; and there is only a story murdered to no purpose. And if I succeed, why then—as the song says—

> ' Up with the bonnie blue bonnet,
> The dirk and feather and a'.' "

Up, then, with the blue bonnet ; since not for even a moment was the success in doubt. The eagerness for the poem for weeks before the publication had been unprecedented, and the general approval and admiration went beyond the most friendly anticipation. They were shown in a singular way. Crowds from all parts of the kingdom set off to view the scenery of Loch Katrine, till then but little known. Even the most prosaic of offices, the Exchequer, bore evidence to the general feeling, since it is stated, on competent authority, that "the post-horse duty in Scotland rose in an extraordinary degree, and continued to rise for many years ; the author's succeeding works keeping up the enthusiasm for the Highland scenery which he had thus originally created."

Even Jeffrey was vanquished. He preferred the new poem to either of its predecessors. "The diction," he says, " is more polished "—indeed he compared it at times to the " careless richness of Shakespeare " ; "the versification is more regular ; the story is constructed with infinitely more skill and address ; there is a larger variety of characters more artfully and judiciously contrasted. There is nothing perhaps so fine as the battle in ' Marmion,' or so picturesque as some of the scattered sketches in the

' Lay,' but there is a richness and spirit in the whole
piece which does not pervade either of those poems ; a
profusion of incident, and a shifting brilliancy of colouring that reminds one of the witchery of Ariosto ; and a
constant elasticity and occasional energy which seem to
belong more peculiarly to the author." And he predicts
that it will be oftener read hereafter than either of its
predecessors.

Parts of this criticism may perhaps be regarded as a
kind of palinode, or retractation of the critic's former
disparagement of those predecessors. It cannot be
denied to be a candid and discriminating judgement ; and
the prediction on which it ventures—that the poem would
be a greater favourite with future generations—is, I venture
to think, borne out by the fact. That it is so with readers
of the softer and fairer sex is unquestionable. And this
is easily accounted for. For there is no want of fire
in the mission of the Fiery Cross ; the rising up of
Roderick's clan from its ambush in the heather ; the
combat with FitzJames ; and the victories of Douglas
and Lufra over all competitors. On a smaller scale, the
" full power of song," which soothed Roderick's dying
moments with the tale of his clansmen's gallant stand at
Beal'an Duine, breathes no little of the spirit which had
animated the grand account of Flodden. And last,
but by no means least, there is also that exquisite picture
of the heroine Ellen Douglas, to which more particular
allusion will be made hereafter.

Mr. Ellis, who had reviewed the poem in *The Quarterly*,
had tempered his general praise of its beauties with
a disapproval of the metre, which he contended was

unsuited to serious continued narrative; and his criticism drew a letter from the poet, in which he defended his use of it, as "more congenial to the English language, more favourable to narrative poetry at least, than that which has been commonly termed heroic verse." He pointed out that in the poems of Pope, the most accomplished master of that metre, there are "many lines out of which two syllables may be struck without injury to the sense." He particularly instances the translation of the "Iliad," "the first lines of which have been repeatedly noticed as capable of being cut down from ships of the line to frigates, by striking out the said two-syllabled words.

> ' Achilles' wrath, to Greece the *direful* spring
> Of woes unnumber'd, *heavenly* Goddess, sing ;
> That wrath which sent to Pluto's *gloomy* reign
> The souls of *mighty* chiefs in battle slain ;
> Whose bones unburied on the *desert* shore
> Devouring dogs and *hungry* vultures tore.' "

And he contends that, as scarcely one of the epithets in italics is more than merely expletive, "the structure of verse which least requires this sort of bolstering is most likely to be forcible and animated." He confines his defence of his favourite metre to narrative poetry : "In descriptive poetry" he admits that "the case is different, because there epithets, if they are happily selected, are rather to be sought after than avoided, and admit of being varied *ad infinitum*." "Besides," he presently adds, "the eight-syllable stanza is capable of certain varieties denied to the heroic. Double rhymes, for instance, are congenial to it, which often give a sort of Gothic richness to its cadences. You may also render it more or less rapid by retaining or dropping an occasional syllable. Lastly" (which he thought its principal merit), "it runs better into sentences than any length of line he knows; and finally, he thought he had somehow a better knack at this 'false gallop' of verse, as Touchstone calls it, than at more legitimate hexameters; and so there," he concludes, "is the short and long of my longs and shorts."

If modesty had not restrained him, he might have referred to his own works in that metre as irresistible evidence of its suitability to the most vivid narrative; for not even in Dryden's master-piece, "Palamon and Arcite," is the combat between the heroes told with a spirit and power equal to the description of the tournament in "The Bridal of Triermain," to say nothing of the splendid pictures of Flodden and Bannockburn; while, on the other hand, Dryden's description of "the glorious theatre" raised by "Royal Theseus" for the lists, might perhaps be quoted as a proof of the soundness of Scott's judgment in making an exception in favour of the heroic metre for descriptive poetry. But, on the other hand again, the picture of Loch Katrine and its surrounding scenery, which filled Fitz-James with rapture and amazement as he contemplated its fitness for every kind of abode or tenant, seems a proof that, in the hand of such a master in descriptive poetry, the octosyllabic metre can hold its own against all rivals, and is deficient in neither picturesqueness nor power. A few years later he might have called Byron into court as a witness in favour of his chosen metre. For though, as has been mentioned before, Byron, on one occasion, pro-

nounced a triumph over its "fatal facility" to have been
achieved by Scott alone, he himself adopted it with
scarcely inferior success in "The Giaour," and a great
portion of "The Bride of Abydos;" and, though he for a
moment deserted it, and in "The Corsair" adopted the ten-
syllable couplet, he returned to it in many of his subsequent
works, in "Parisina," "The Prisoner of Chillon," "The
Siege of Corinth," and "Mazeppa"; and therefore may
fairly be supposed to have been in practical agreement
with Scott as to its superiority, alike for pictures of the most
vehement action, and of the most impassioned tenderness.

That the general public sided with Scott, was sufficiently
proved by the great and increasing sale of all three poems,
so great as "to induce him for a moment to conclude that
he had at last fixed a nail in the proverbially inconstant
wheel of Fortune;" and his success had its natural
consequence in prompting him to take advantage of the
tide while it was in the spring flood, with a fourth poem.
He hesitated as to the subject, his first fancy being to
cross the Bay of Biscay, and "take a peep at Lord Wellington and his merry men in Portugal," thinking he should
"be able to pick up some curious materials for battle
scenery;" but he abandoned that idea out of consideration for the fears of his wife. The lameness of Tyrtæus
had not prevented him from sharing in "the rapture of
the strife," and she reasonably feared that Scott's warlike
ardour might lead him to forget that he laboured under
a similar impediment to rapid motion; or that, even if he
consented to keep in the background, and contented himself with viewing the deeds of arms from a distance, no

amount of caution could ensure perfect safety to the most
manifest non combatant.[1]

Once more, then, he fixed his attention on such materials
as his own country could supply, and accepted an invitation
from the Laird of Staffa to visit that and the adjacent
islands. He was delighted with all he saw; with a poet's
eye and delight he pronounced the wonders of Staffa as
" exceeding every description he had ever heard of them."
And the keen eagerness with which he surmounted every
obstacle which threatened to hinder his nearer scrutiny
of the different objects of beauty and wonder so charmed
the boatmen, that they christened a great stone seat, in
one of the caves, by the name of "The Poet's Stone."
The ceremony, as a letter to Miss Baillie describes it, " was
consecrated with a pibroch, which the echoes rendered
tremendous, and a glass of whiskey, not poured forth in
the ancient mode of libation, but turned down the throats
of the assistants. The head boatmen," he adds, " whose
father had been himself a bard, made me a speech on the
occasion; but, as it was in Gaelic, I could only receive it
as a silly beauty does a fine-spun compliment, bow and
say nothing."

---

[1] His interest in the achievements of our great General, of whom
he boasted that he had discovered the genius and predicted the glory
ever since Vimeiro, was not wholly unproductive. When, in the
spring of the next year, a committee was formed for the relief of those
Portuguese who were exposed to bitter distress by the movements
of the hostile armies, whether of friends or foes, alike fraught with
misery to the inhabitants of the seat of war, he wrote what he called
" a few wild stanzas," in other words, a short poem, to which he gave
the name of "The Vision of Don Roderick," and sent the profits
derived from it as his subscription to the fund.

The excursion produced its most welcome fruit, one which will last as long as the Poet's Stone itself, in the magnificent "Lord of the Isles." But that was not to be gathered yet, nor till he had found a new field for his genius, which he eventually cultivated with greater diligence, and perhaps, in the judgement of the world at large, with still more triumphant skill than he had wooed the Muse.

It was hardly to be expected that popularity such as his should not provoke attempts to pull it down. The first of which, and the only one of which the authorship was avowed, came from that contemporary who alone was destined to rival him in fame. Byron, in his "English Bards and Scotch Reviewers," sneered at him as "Apollo's venal son," writing "Marmion" "for just half-a-crown a line," because he had sold the copyright for 1,000 guineas. It was the only attack that seems to have caused him even the most momentary irritation, though, even then, it was but a good-humoured notice of it, when he wrote to Ellis, that "it was funny to see a whelp of a young Lord Byron abusing him, of whose circumstances he knew nothing, for endeavouring to scratch out a living with his pen. God help the bear, if, having nothing else to eat, he must not even suck his own paws." And all feelings of ill-will, however provoked, were too foreign to his nature to abide long in his bosom. Indeed both critic and poet were of too fine natures to cherish lasting malevolence. It was not long before Byron frankly acknowledged to Scott his repentance for "the evil works of his nonage," which Scott as frankly forgave, and then mutual admiration for one another's genius led to their becoming as fast and firm friends as men could be who had so few opportunities of meeting.

Other attacks had taken the form of parodies—"The Lay of the Scotch Fiddle," and "The Goblin and Groom," titles that showed their spite, which the stupidity of the works themselves made harmless ; and his comment on which was borrowed from Benedick, that "a college of such witmongers should not flout him out of his humour." Some were charges of plagiarism, though in more than one instance the poem from which he was accused of borrowing was of a later date than his own. One, sent to Scott himself in a letter with a Cambridge post-mark, and signed " Detector," contained a Latin couplet, which the writer asserted to be manifestly the original of Marmion's most pathetic address to Clare, which I cannot refuse myself the pleasure of quoting :

> " O woman ! in our hours of ease
> Uncertain, coy, and hard to please,
> And variable as the shade,
> By the light quivering aspen made ;
> When pain and anguish wring the brow,
> A ministering angel thou."

In Vida, " Detector " declared that he found—

> " Cum dolor atque supercilio gravis imminet angor
> Fungeris angelico sola ministerio."
> *Ad Eranen*, ii. 21.

But the lines are not in Vida, nor in any poem with such a title, and the couplet was probably the composition of some waggish undergraduate, thus anticipating the witty translation, by which, in the next generation, Father

Prout humorously pretended to rob Mr. Wolfe of the credit
won by "Not a drum was heard," while regarded as an
original composition.

One parody was of a different character. It was in the
purest good humour that the brothers Smith gave a place
to "the Burning of Drury Lane," among the "addresses"
supposed to have been "rejected" by the theatrical committee ; and it was with at least equal good humour that
the poet thus travestied expressed to his imitators his conviction that he must certainly have written it himself, only
that he could not recollect the occasion.

CHAPTER IV

THE year 1812 was one to be marked with a white stone in Scott's calendar. The death of Mr. Home had placed him in the enjoyment of the salary of the Clerkship of Session, of which till now he had only had the work ; so that he was able to reckon his income, without taking the profits of his literary labour into account, at £2,000 a year. He felt, therefore, that he could indulge a desire,—which we cannot doubt that he had long entertained, for a house of his own. His lease of Ashestiel was on the point of expiring, so that some move was unavoidable; and in 1811 there came into the market a farm of one hundred acres, extending, as he described it to his brother-in-law, Mr. Carpenter, along the banks of the Tweed for about half-a-mile. Its name was Abbotsford, having in former times, with the greater part of the adjacent territory, belonged to the great Abbey of Melrose ; of which the farm commanded a view. The farmhouse was small and in bad condition ; but many spots on the land offered favourable sites. The price was moderate, about £4,000, and not beyond his means ; so he purchased the land, with the intention of building a house for himself. At first his

idea did not go beyond an ornamental cottage, in the
style of an English vicarage; and, as he pressed the work
on with eager rapidity, it was completed sufficiently to
allow of his removal to it in the summer of 1812. He
and Mrs. Scott, as he described their feelings, were not
a little proud of being greeted as the *Laird and Lady of
Abbotsford*, and he celebrated their occupation of their
new abode by a "gala to all the Scotts in the country,
from the duke to the peasant, who were to dance on the
green to the sound of the bagpipes, and drink whiskey-
punch. We are very *clannish* in this corner." But
the "flitting from Ashestiel," though so full of delight
and pride to themselves, was a sad one for the poorer
neighbours they left behind them; for they had been the
kindest of friends to all whom poverty or sickness reduced to need aid or counsel; Mrs. Scott having even
some knowledge of the treatment required for ordinary
ailments; so that she had been a Lady Bountiful of the
most useful kind; and the sorrow of the peasantry of the
village was universal, though to the younger portion of it
relieved by the amusement caused by "the procession of
the furniture from the old to the new dwelling. Old
swords, bows, targets, and lances made a very conspicuous show. A family of turkeys was accommodated
within the helmet of some *preux* chevalier of ancient
Border fame. And the caravan, attended by a dozen of
rosy peasant children carrying fishing-rods and spears,
and leading ponies, greyhounds, and spaniels, would, as
it crossed the Tweed, have formed no bad subject for the
pencil, and really reminded one of the gipsy groups of
Callot on their march."

To lovers of literature and admirers of genius the same year is scarcely less memorable, as that in which Scott and Byron became acquainted. In his " Satire," as has been already mentioned, Byron had included Scott, not so much for faults in his poems, as for selling them ; as if that had not been the ordinary practice. But the irritation which Scott had for the moment expressed at such an absurd and uncalled-for attack on his management of his private affairs, had long passed away, and when, in the spring of this year, the first cantos of " Childe Harold " came out, no one was more prompt or cordial than Scott in the recognition of " their extraordinary power," though his admiration was modified by a disapproval of the tone of " misanthropical *ennui*" that marred their beauty. Murray, who had published " Childe Harold," as he had formerly published " Marmion," was not ignorant of the high opinion Scott had expressed of the genius of the younger bard, and was not unnaturally anxious to promote a better understanding between two such men ; and now he fancied he saw an opportunity for effecting his judicious and benevolent object in an incident which had lately occurred in London.

Byron, to quote his well-known account of the effect his poem had produced, "awoke one morning and found himself famous ; " and one result of his fame was that at an evening party the Prince Regent had desired the poet to be presented to him ; and had held a long conversation with him, in which Scott and his poems had formed one topic of discussion. Byron had mentioned this to Murray, apparently with the intention that Murray should report it to Scott, who regarded it as an excuse for opening a communication with Byron himself, in which, after paying him high and not undeserved compliments on the " vivid and animated description mingled with original sentiment " of the "Childe," and " thanking him for the flattering communication he had taken the trouble to make to Murray in his behalf, which could not fail to give him the gratification which he was sure was intended," he took the opportunity of "putting him right as to the circumstances connected with the sale of 'Marmion,' which had reached him in a distorted and misrepresented form." For "the poem was not written upon contract for a sum of money," as "The Satire " seemed to imply, " though it was too true that it was sold and published in an unfinished state." And he only mentioned the matter at all as " he might well be excused for a wish to clear his personal character from any tinge of mercenary or sordid feeling in the eyes of a contemporary of genius."

The promptitude of Byron's answer showed his eagerness to stand with his correspondent on a friendly footing. As has been mentioned already, he expressed with all sincerity his regret for his Satire ; and after thanking his correspondent for his praise, he proceeded to relate his conversation with the prince :—

" After some sayings, peculiarly pleasing from royal lips, as to my own attempts, he talked to me of you and your immortalities ; he preferred you to every bard, past and present, and asked which of your works pleased me most. It was a difficult question. I answered, I thought the 'Lay.' He said his own opinion was nearly similar. In speaking of the others I told him I thought you more

particularly the poet of *Princes*, as they never appeared
more fascinating than in 'Marmion' and 'The Lady of
the Lake.' He was pleased to coincide, and to dwell on
the description of your Jameses as no less royal than
poetical. He spoke alternately of Homer and yourself,
and seemed well-acquainted with both ; so that (with the
exception of the Turks and your humble servant) you
were in very good company."

With as little delay, Scott replied in a mirthful and
facetious tone, quoting the saying of some unknown
" wise man," that there is no surer mark of " regard than
when your correspondent ventures to write nonsense to
you." And from this time forth the great poets kept up
a tolerably frequent correspondence, though more than
two years were to elapse before they met.

Scott at this time was occupying himself with two
poems at once, of which the longer, " Rokeby," appeared
first, being published before the end of the year. Rokeby
was the Yorkshire seat of his friend Morritt, with the
extreme beauty of which, with its romantic variety of
glen, torrent, and copse, and two most beautiful rivers,
the Greta and the Tees, which join their currents in the
demesne, he had been greatly struck when he paid his
friend a visit two or three years before. And he now
made it the scene of a poem, whose action was laid in
the civil war of Charles I. It was not perhaps a poetical
time, and I confess to a feeling that, though by no means
destitute of vivid description, and characters well kept
up, it falls very short of the earlier poems. His own
description of it to Mr. Ellis was that of " a pseudo-

romance of pseudo-chivalry. He had converted a lusty
buccaneer into a hero with some effect, but the worst of
all his undertakings was that his rogue, always in despite
of him, turned out his hero." But, in spite of this per-
version or conversion, "he hoped the thing would do,
chiefly because the world would not expect from him a
poem of which the interest turned upon *character*." "If it
was fair for him to say anything of his own poems, he
would say that the force in the 'Lay' is thrown on
style; in 'Marmion,' on description; and in 'The
Lady of the Lake,' on incident."

The expectation of a new poem from him could not
fail to be eager and general: though, as it was understood to have no reference to Scotland, less keen
in Edinburgh than in London. The whole edition of
3250 copies was sold off within a week. Those were
glorious days for authors when first editions were tall
quartos, selling for two guineas. But the demand was
sooner satisfied than that for "The Lady of the Lake"
had been; and, though Lockhart is warm in his praise
of many incidents and passages, of "the whole contrast
of the two rivals for the love of the heroine, of the
inimitable descriptions of scenery, and the splendid
vivacity and thrilling interest of several incidents," he is
"compelled to confess that it has never been so much a
favourite with the public at large as any other of his
poetical romances." Moore even ventured to raise a
good-humoured laugh at it, as if it had owed its existence
to the circumstance of Rokeby being the abode of a
friend; hinting that if Scott had any friends equally valued
in the more Southern counties, their seats might come

to be celebrated in the same manner. "Mr. Scott," he wrote—

> " Having quitted the Borders to seek new renown
> Is coming by long quarto stages to town ;
> And beginning with Rokeby (the job's sure to pay),
> Means to do all the gentlemen's seats by the way."

With the other poem, "The Bridal of Triermain," he tried to practise a hoax—not only on the general public, but on his own most intimate friends. It was published anonymously at the beginning of 1813. It was copied out by a strange hand, that the printers might not recognise the writing ; he had even, as he afterwards confessed, " tried to mix something that might resemble (as far as was in his power), the feeling and manner of a friend who was more than suspected of a taste for poetry, Mr. Erskine." And, though Lockhart thinks it (as all must) next to impossible that many should have been deceived, the reviewer in *The Quarterly* was taken in—though it was probably Scott's own intimate friend, Mr. Ellis. In Lockhart's opinion it was for Jeffrey that " the trap had been set"; but he had gone to America a short time before it was published, and so escaped the hunter's toils. But Mr. Ellis spoke of the poem throughout his review as " an imitation of Scott's style ;" one which, " if inferior in vigour to some of his productions, equals or surpasses them in elegance and beauty ; and is more uniformly tender." The diction undoubtedly " reminds him of a rhythm and cadence he had heard before ; but the sentiments, descriptions, and characters have qualities that are native and unborrowed."

The subject was taken from the very oldest of our national legends—the achievements of King Arthur— though this particular incident in his history was due to the poet's own invention; and the combatants in the tournament are gallants known to all students of those romances as the Knights of the Round Table. In comparison with the other poems, "The Bridal" has one fault, undeniable and incurable; it is shorter by more than half. Like Goldsmith's "Traveller," or "Deserted Village," it is but a cabinet picture; and therefore, at least in the judgement of those who estimate a work of art by the amount of canvas it covers, not entitled to be put on a footing of equality with "Marmion" or "The Lady of the Lake,"—which again, if judged by the same standard, would be placed on a lower level of dignity than any poem in twenty-four or even twelve books or cantos. But, except in length, it will be difficult to point out any quality of excellence or attraction in which it is inferior to its stouter predecessors. The Valley of St. John, in which the scene is laid, was especially endeared to Scott, since it was at a ball in that neighbourhood that he first met his wife; and if in "Lyulph's tale" he puts before us the most striking features of the country itself, it may perhaps not be too violent a stretch of fancy to believe that in the vision of beauty which presented itself to the sleeping knight, he was describing the charms of her who for thirty years was the ornament and happiness of his home.

Once more, and once only, did he again court the judgement of the public with a poem; and before he did so he had tempted it with a composition of a different

5

class, the reception of which led him for the future to devote himself wholly to prose as a vehicle for his fictions. But it will be more convenient to close the examination of his poems, before proceeding to speak of him as a novelist.

The scenery of the Western Isles had impressed his fancy as full of poetical suggestion on his visit to the Laird of Staffa, which has been previously mentioned. The impression had never worn off, and "The Bridal of Triermain" had scarcely been completed, before he began to carry out an idea, which had struck him, of connecting it with the triumphs of the great champion of Scottish independence, the heroic Bruce. And in the spring following the publication of "The Bridal," an attempt, as it may almost be regarded, was made to bind him to the continuance of his poetical labours by the offer of the post of Poet-Laureate, which proceeded from the express direction of the Prince Regent himself. He was somewhat embarrassed by it, since he saw some difficulty in declining what the Prince, "of his own free motion," had undoubtedly intended both as a compliment and a service. But, as he truly said to a friend to whom he mentioned it, "the office was a ridiculous one." If it was, it had not been made less so by the manner in which it had been generally filled since the days of Dryden. Pope's indignation or envy at Cibber's appointment had excited him, most undeservedly, to brand the author of "The Careless Husband," by placing him in his intellectual pillory—the throne of the Dunces; but Scott had no reason to fear a similar result. He anticipated indeed that, if he accepted the post,

he "should be well quizzed;" though, if ever the
holders of it had been solemnly crowned, as in other
countries, the custom had been so long disused that it
was nearly forgotten.[1] That, however, he should not
mind; but he did fear lest, "favoured as he had been by
the public, he might be considered, with some justice, as
engrossing a petty emolument, which might do real service to some poorer brother of the Muses." All the friends
whom he consulted approved of his disposition to decline
the honour. The noble head of his clan, the Duke of
Buccleuch, pronounced that the title "would stick to him,
and all his productions, like a piece of *Court-plaster;*"
and, fortified by the general opinion and wish, he
declined it; and was the more satisfied with his decision
when he had succeeded in procuring the offer of it to
Southey, certainly the man next in literary reputation to
himself at the time, and one who was unfortunately not
in such circumstances as made him equally indifferent to
an increase of income.

Interrupted, as it necessarily was, by his new occupation
as a novelist, the "Lord of the Isles," for that was the title
on which he fixed for his new poem, was not completed
till more than two years after the first canto had been
sketched out. As he meant it to be his last effort of the
kind, he took especial pains with it, and, in the summer
of 1814, revisited several of the islands to refresh his
recollection of the most striking features of the scenery.

---

[1] D'Israeli ("Curiosities of Literature," vol. i. p. 457) mentions
that "Selden, after all his recondite researches, is satisfied with
saying that some trace of this distinction is to be found in our
nation."

It was published in January, 1815. The principal
reviews coincided in warm praise of its "glow of
colouring," its "energy of narrative," and its ampli-
tude of description, at the same time tempering their
eulogies with a suggestion of "defects," which, it must
be confessed, seem dictated by a spirit of hypercriti-
cism. *The Edinburgh Review* denounced the title as "a
misnomer," because the ostensible hero was, from the very
first, not the Lord of the Isles, but "King Robert Bruce,"
and found defects in the scantiness of the narrative, the
want of sufficient connexion in the story, and of diversity
of scene and character. That the Bruce is the real hero
will of course be admitted ; but Scott, in more than one
instance, avowed his opinion that too taking a title was
injurious to a work, as raising too high the reader's
expectations. The accusation of scantiness of incident
will meet with little sympathy from those who remember
the banquet at Artornish, with its interruptions by the
arrival, first of the Bruce and his party, and after them, of the
Abbot, and the noble prophecy, with which, "like the
Midianite of old," he was constrained to foretell Bruce's
triumph and undying glory ; the flight of Edith ; the
perilous voyage of the bark which bore Bruce and his
fortunes ; and the great battle itself. While the want of
"diversity of character" is a strange charge to bring in
the face of the portraits of Bruce, of his brother Edward,
of Lorn, of Argentine, of Edward the King ; and of the
unintentional rivals in Lorn's affections, Isabel and Edith.
Nor less does the critic seem to have overlooked the
glowing pictures of the varying scenery of the islets—

  "That guard famed Staffa round ; "

and of Staffa's " wondrous dome "—

> " Where, as to shame the temple deck'd
> By skill of earthly architect,
> Nature herself, it seem'd, would raise
> A Minster to her Maker's praise."

The Quarterly too was equally unfavourable, seeing "certain violations of propriety," which it, however, forebore to particularise, "both in the language and in the composition of the story ; " and complaining of the poet's neglect to bestow on his work "that common degree of labour and meditation, which it is scarcely decorous to withhold,"—a charge which is at once disposed of by the assertion of Scott himself, which has been mentioned above, that he had bestowed especial pains on the poem, because he meant it to be his last work of the kind.

Neither critic, however, denied that Bruce himself was delineated with unsurpassed power; that, if the description of the battle of Bannockburn does not quite equal that of Flodden Field, it has no other superior, nor even equal, in the whole range of modern poetry; and that the heroines, for it may almost be said that there are two, are painted with the most exquisite delicacy as well as diversity of character. But, though the first edition was sold off at once, the demand was not kept up as had been that for the former poems, a falling off which must probably be attributed mainly to the popularity of the Eastern tales, which Byron was throwing off with unexampled rapidity, and which, by their novelty, as pictures of countries and peoples as yet unsung by English bards, and still more by the intensity of passion which they created, put forth as they were with an unrivalled mastery of language, a most exquisite melody of rhythm, and an apparently inexhaustible richness of imagination, took the fancy by storm, and for a time made all competition hopeless.

"The Lord of the Isles," then, was Scott's last poem. And, before proceeding to speak of his subsequent works, the present seems a fitting place for an endeavour to point out what were the prominent features of his genius which pervaded, and lent their charm to, each and all of the works which have been mentioned. First among their most characteristic excellences (which as will be seen hereafter are also among the distinguishing beauties of his novels) are the animation, the spirit, the Homeric fire and sustained energy of the action. This is not confined to descriptions of battles and feats of high emprise, but displayed with equal fulness in such episodes as that of Deloraine's ride to Melrose, of the transmission of the Fiery Cross, of the "sweeping by" of Lord Ronald's fleet, "streamer'd with silk and tricked with gold," or of Bruce's lonely bark now "o'er the broad ocean driven," now dragged overland across the isthmus,—a wondrous exploit foretold by "many a mountain seer" of old, as a sign that the time was come when

> "Old Albyn should in fight prevail,
> And every foe should faint and quail,
> Before her silver cross."

Such vigour, perhaps the grandest fruit of the highest poetical genius, has been given to few. If it is not without poetical justice that Dante represents Homer as marching at the head of the band of poets, sword in hand,

as if he were their king,[1] Scott might in like manner be
portrayed " with spear and glaive, with targe and jack," so
far beyond all modern rivals are his descriptions of all
deeds of manly daring, courage, and toil.

Secondly, in no degree inferior in the variety of its excellence, nor in its influence on the taste of the reader,
may be pointed out the equally Homeric delicacy of his
female portraits. In the consummate purity and tenderness with which he draws maiden or matron, whether
noble or peasant, Christian or infidel, (to anticipate for
a moment the praise shared by the novels), if he does not
surpass Homer and Shakespeare, he is without compeer
among all the other masters of the lyre. It is no ex-
aggeration of the importance of a single gift or faculty, to
contend that not one is more indispensable to warrant a
claim to a place in the highest class of poets, than a per-
vading sense of the respect, the affectionate respect and
reverence, if I may say so, due to the female character.
And, as it is among the most precious, so it is among the
rarest distinctions of poets. Among the ancients it was confined to Homer and Sophocles, whose Antigone may almost
be placed by the side of the earlier bard's Helen and
Andromache. It was so alien to the Roman idea of the
sex, that even Virgil fails in it. And among the moderns
the proportion who can claim it in any high degree is no
larger. Among the French, though Racine, and occasionally
Voltaire also, aimed at it, their want of success proves that

---

" Mira colui con quella spada in mano,
Che vien dinanzi à tre sì come sire."
        Inferno iv. 86.

the feeling which they laboured to express found no echo
in the nation. Tasso's admirably diversified delineations
of Clorinda and Erminia, more even than the Laura of
Petrarch, save the more chivalous Italians from the same
imputation. But I fear it must be owned that, in the
seventeenth and eighteenth centuries, the due recognition
of woman's highest attributes, and right to the most respectful consideration, now justly considered inseparable from
the character of an English gentleman, was nowhere less
apparent than in English poetry. With the exception of
Shakespeare, who has been already alluded to, and whose
Lady Constance, Rosalind, Imogen, Desdemona, and
others, show him to have been equally endowed with this
as with every other faculty requisite to form the most
consummate and perfect genius, the Lady in " Comus " is
probably the only female portrait, worthy either of the
subject or the author, which was produced in that long
period ; and the exception is the more remarkable, since
certainly few poets ever showed in their own conduct less
of chivalry, or even of ordinary respect for the sex, than
Milton.

But Scott's mind was cast in the best mould of the
ancient chivalry, one of the most distinguishing features
of which was that which ranked undeviating respect and
deference to woman among the most powerful mainsprings
of action to every one who aspired to the character of a
perfect knight. And accordingly there are few of his
works in which at least one woman is not a conspicuous
and important character, and is not portrayed with the
most loyal care to justify the prominence assigned to her
by every feminine grace of person and mind, as well as by

the respect in which she is held even by the rudest of
the opposite sex. Margaret of Branksome, Clare, Ellen
Douglas, Edith of Lorn, Isabel Bruce, even Gwendolen
and Constance of Beverley may be added (though their
treatment was one of greater difficulty)—all, however
widely different, are equally objects over which the poet
might gladly linger, for which a champion might cheerfully
encounter death itself.

And somewhat akin to this excellence of female portraiture is his appreciation of the parental feeling,
in which again Homer and Sophocles almost alone
had preceded him. It has been seen how Pitt pronounced Scott to have surpassed all his ideas of the
painter's power in his portraiture of the old minstrel
tuning his harp, and seeking to refresh his memory
in the presence of the Duchess and her ladies. And
even Canova failed to realise the exquisite pictures of
Astyanax and his parents, when the boy, beauteous as a
star, fell back affrighted on his nurse's breast, and the
god-like Hector laid aside his helmet, with its awfully
waving plumes, and kissed and dandled his child, while
he prayed that the infant hope of Troy might hereafter
surpass even himself in renown, and in the joy with which
Andromache would greet him, returning home in triumph
laden with the spoils of slaughter'd enemies.[1] The
"blind old man's" picture is still unequalled ; but it was
a spirit akin to his that showed to the Scottish minstrel
the stern Lady of Branksome, standing with dry eye beside
her husband's bloody bier, while

[1] Il. vi. 476.

" Vengeance, deep-brooding o'er the slain,
  Had locked the source of softer woe,
And burning pride, and high disdain
  Forbad the rising tear to flow.
Until, amid his sorrowing clan,
  Her son lisped from the nurse's knee,
' And, if I live to be a man,
  My father's death revenged shall be.'
Then fast the mother's tears did seek
  To dew the infant's kindling cheek."

Lay, i.

It was that spirit that taught him that nature did not confine the feeling to the softer sex, but exerted the same sway over the rudest barons of the Middle Ages as over Cornelia, whose sons were the only jewels she desired.

" Some feelings are to mortals given
  With less of earth in them than heaven ;
And, if there be a human tear
From passions dross refined and clear,
A tear so limpid and so meek
It would not stain an angel's cheek.
'Tis that which pious fathers shed
Upon a duteous daughter's head ;
And as the Douglas to his breast
His darling Ellen closely pressed,
Such holy drops her tresses steep'd,
Though 'twas a hero's eye that weep'd."

Lady of the Lake, ii. 22.

The skill with which, in all the poems, the perfect consistency of each character is throughout preserved, may not be passed over, nor the rare picturesqueness of painting with which the beauties of every variety of scenery, rock, wood, meadow, or torrent, separately or mingled, are brought before the eye, with a vivid fidelity, which, if subsequently equalled in " Childe Harold," has never, I think, been surpassed. As a crown to the whole, the entire mass of poems is instinct with a cheerful, genial, healthy spirit, beyond any rules of art to catch, but implanted by Heaven in the breast of the author as among the most priceless of gifts.

With such qualities, if I have not erred in asserting them to be conspicuous in these poems, it cannot be thought strange that they should have been received on their first appearance with unanimous admiration ; nor that they should retain a great measure of their original popularity, though nearly three quarters of a century have elapsed since the publication of the latest.

We must pass on to the novels, in which also much of the same qualities will be found, in their degree, to be equally manifest.

CHAPTER V

A S has been already mentioned, before the publication of "The Lord of the Isles," Scott had
broken new ground as a novelist. When his cousin had
tried to dissuade him from tempting fortune, and the
judgement of the critical public, by a third poem, lest the
fame achieved by the "Lay" and "Marmion" should
be dimmed, as she feared it might be, if a new work of
the same kind should be thought, in ever so slight a
degree, to fall short of their excellence, he comforted her
for turning a deaf ear to her warning, by declaring his
resolution, if "The Lady of the Lake" proved a failure,
" to write prose for life." And he had begun to carry out
that resolution even before the diminished sale of "The
Lord of the Isles," in comparison with that of its predecessors, seemed a proof that his poetry had been superseded in popularity by that of his younger rival, Lord
Byron. He himself was not disposed to quarrel with the
general verdict. On the contrary, he frankly avowed his
conviction of Byron's superiority in poetical genius,
telling Ballantyne that "Byron hit the mark, where he
did not even pretend to fledge his arrow," while (for the
disposition of both poets was too noble to admit a feeling
of the most passing jealousy or envy) Byron, with

equally sincere modesty, continued to avow his opinion of Scott's pre-eminence; and, in spite of the present popularity of his own poems, foretold that the day would come when the public would return to its earlier love. He had sent Scott a copy of "The Giaour," with an inscription on the fly-leaf that it was "an offering to the Monarch of Parnassus from one of his subjects;" and every mention of him in his published works, or private correspondence, shows that his opinion, as honourable to himself as to its object, knew no change.

However that might be, and whether the balance of sterling merit was on the side of the elder or the younger poet, it was indubitable that the taste of the public for the time gave a preference to the latter; and Scott, recognising the correctness of the judgement without a murmur, at once decided on clothing his inspirations for the future in a new dress, and on making the experiment whether the same intellectual qualities, which had been admitted to characterise his poetical fictions, might not be found almost equally attractive in the more sober garb of prose. And, with this view, in July, 1814, he published "Waverley: or 'tis Sixty Years Since."

It was no new idea; and, in one point of view, this work was certainly not open to the charge of having been hurried, since a portion, nearly one-third of it, had been written nine years before. It had then been laid aside, partly in consequence of the doubts of its success expressed by some friends to whom he had shown the earliest chapters, but partly, too, and no doubt more, because, as he himself explains in the preface to the entire series of the novels, "as he had some poetical reputation,' (acquired by "The Lay" in the beginning of the year), "he was unwilling to risk the loss of it, by attempting a new style of composition." The same feeling had its share in suggesting the course he now adopted of publishing "Waverley" anonymously, though not blind to the drawback that, "as the title-page was without the name of the author, it was left to win its way in the world without any of the usual recommendations." Mr. Morritt, who, almost alone of his friends, was taken into his confidence, remonstrated against the appearance of secrecy, which he foretold would be vain, since the veil was sure to be seen through; but Scott adhered to his determination, alleging first, as his chief reason, that, "if he owned 'Waverley,' it would deprive him of the pleasure of writing again"—an argument which it is not easy to understand; and secondly, that "he was not sure that it would be considered quite decorous for him, as a Clerk of Session, to write novels. Judges being monks" (we have certainly seen some who had little of the monastic character), "clerks are a sort of lay brethren, from whom some solemnity of walk and conduct may be expected." So whatever he may do of this kind, "he 'will whistle it down the wind, and let it prey at fortune.'"

But the first month had not elapsed before he found Mr. Morritt's prediction verified, and that his incognito was seen through. David Hume, nephew of the historian, told him that "the author must be of a Jacobite family and predilections, a yeoman-cavalry man, and a Scottish lawyer," and desired Scott himself to guess in whom these happy attributes were united; and the reviewer in

The Edinburgh, mindful perhaps of the mystification which
had been attempted with "The Bridal," more than hinted
his suspicion, when he closed his notice of the book with
the suggestion that, "if it were indeed the work of an
author hitherto unknown, Mr. Scott would do well to
look to his laurels." While, as has been mentioned before,
Wilson, the author of "The Isle of Palms," but better
known, perhaps, as Christopher North, reproached a
company of pundits who were discussing the claims of
possible candidates for the honour of the authorship, by
reminding them of the notes to "The Border Minstrelsy,"
as amply sufficient to prove the identity of the novelist
with the editor. The disguise, such as it was, however, Scott
persisted in maintaining long after he knew that it had
ceased to be such, but had been universally penetrated;
a perseverance for which "he could render little better
reason than by saying with Shylock that 'such was his
humour.'" Nor was it till the ruin of Ballantyne's affairs
rudely tore off the mask, that novel after novel was issued
with any other description of the writer than as "the
author of 'Waverley.'"

The entire series may be divided into three classes : [1]

[1] CLASS I.—" Guy Mannering," " The Antiquary," " Rob Roy,"
" The Black Dwarf," " The Heart of Midlothian," " The Bride of
Lammermoor," " The Pirate," " St. Ronan's Well," " Chronicles
of the Canongate," ser. i. ; Do. 2, " Fair Maid of Perth."
  CLASS 2.—" Ivanhoe," " Kenilworth," " Fortunes of Nigel,"
" Peveril of the Peak," " Quentin Durward," " The Talisman,"
" The Betrothed," " Woodstock," " Anne of Geierstein," " Count
Robert of Paris."
  CLASS 3.—" Waverley," " Old Mortality," " The Legend of
Montrose," " Redgauntlet," " Castle Dangerous."

those illustrative of Scottish life and manners ; those
of which the scene is not laid in Scotland, but which
turn on some well-known event or character in history—
Scottish, English, or continental ; and, thirdly, those
which combine the two previously-mentioned features,
being both Scottish and historical.

Scott's original aim in his new character of a novelist was
" to attempt for his own country something of the same
kind with that which Miss Edgeworth had so fortunately
achieved for Ireland—something which might introduce
her natives to those of the sister kingdom in a more
favourable light than they had hitherto been placed, and
might tend to procure sympathy for their virtues, and indulgence for their foibles." For his success he placed
some reliance " on the intimate acquaintance with the
subject which he could claim to possess, as having tra-
velled through most parts of Scotland, both Highland
and Lowland ; having been familiar with the elder, as
well as with the more modern race ; and having had,
from his infancy, free and unrestrained communication
with all ranks of his countrymen, from the Scottish peer
to the Scottish ploughman." As he was reducing his ideas
to a definite plan, it seems to have occurred to him that
" Waverley," his " essay-piece," would have a better chance
of being acceptable to the public, at least on the southern
side of the Border, if he connected his delineation of
Scottish manners and feelings with some well-known
event with which the people of both England and Scotland were in some degree concerned. He was the more
inclined to such a course, since from his childhood his
familiarity with " the songs and tales of the Jacobites had

imbued him with a very strong prejudice in favour of the
Stuart family." And certainly no event in their modern
history afforded a more tempting opportunity for placing
them in an attractive light than the gallant attempt of the
youthful prince, Charles Edward, to replace on his father's
head the crown which, having been worn by his ancestors,
he regarded as their inalienable right.

"Waverley" may be said to belong to the third of
the classes by which I have ventured to distinguish
the novels. And it may be regarded in some degree as
belonging to the first also. Scotchmen, it is probable,
looked on it primarily, as Scott undoubtedly desired, as
a powerful and truthful description of the manners and
feelings of the Highlanders when this second opportunity
was afforded them of showing that their ancient hereditary loyalty to the heirs of the great Bruce burnt as
warmly and steadily as ever. English readers, taking
another view, welcomed it chiefly as a novel with a wholly
new kind of subject, commemorating a great historical
enterprise in prose fiction, as, two centuries before, Shakespeare had portrayed the prowess of the Conqueror of
Agincourt. In whichever light it was regarded, it well
deserved the universal admiration it excited. As illustrative of Scotch manners and feelings, the Lowland laird,
whose hospitable feast was nearly having a termination,
which, if not unusual, was very inconsistent with the
joviality of its commencement; and the Highland chieftain, the devotion of whose clan was nobly represented
by his foster-brother's offer to bring up the six best men
it could boast to die in his stead,— are portraits of which
even those who have no personal acquaintance with Scot-

land, cannot fail to recognise the truth. While regarded
in its historical aspect, it gives as lively, and at the same
time as correct, an idea of the brilliancy of the first
successes of "The Chevalier," and of their transitory
and delusive character, as can be gathered from the grave
and more detailed narrative of the professed historian.
Not less characteristic is the foray which spoilt the
baron's breakfast, and Evan's indignation at Waverley for
regarding the plunderer as " a common thief," when "to
take a tree from the forest, a salmon from the river, a
deer from the hill, or a cow from a Lowland strath, is
what no Highlander need ever think shame upon." Again
the war-cry of Fergus at Preston, " Forward, sons of Ivor,
or the Camerons will draw the first blood !" exhibits one
of the most striking characteristics of the clan system
and feeling, in the mutual jealousy with which the clans
regarded one another, and which, if it was sometimes
the parent of deeds of admirable gallantry, was more
frequently the source of disaster, and at all times
made the task of commanding a Highland army one
of peculiar difficulty. Byron had described Scott to
the Regent as especially the poet of princes; and that
the power which had made the Jameses appear so fascinating in "Marmion" and "The Lady" was in no
way weakened by prose having become its vehicle, was
now shown in the portrait of their descendant, not
untruly invested with that chivalrous courtesy, genuine
kindness of heart, patience, high courage, and princely
tact, which no one ever needed more if he were to have
the least chance of surmounting the manifold difficulties
which surrounded him at every step of his enterprise.

The battle of Preston, the skirmish of Clifton, are told with a spirit akin to that which had celebrated the battle of Beal'an Duine. It may be added that this new class of composition brought out one talent, for the exhibition of which the poems had afforded no similar opportunity—that of humour. The Baron is no very unequal successor to Uncle Toby, as a veteran with a fond reminiscence of the feats of arms in which he has borne his part, though more fortunate than King William's soldier, as not being disabled from future service if occasion should offer; prouder also in the dignity of his free barony, and consequent right to pull off his sovereign's boots, while Uncle Toby was little concerned by the bar-sinister on the Shandy arms, and would have exulted equally at William's reproof of Count Solmes, whether his Majesty had worn boots or brogues, or charged at Steinkirk as barefooted as Cameron at Killiecrankie. How great a value Scott set on pathos may be seen in his praise of Otway in "The Essay on the Drama." The description of the death of Constance Beverley had shown that he himself was not destitute of it; but neither that, nor perhaps any passage in the language, surpasses in truth and power the agony of Flora at her interview with Waverley, while her fondly-loved brother is awaiting his miserable doom, and she is wrought up by misery to self-reproach, as if "the strength of mind on which she prided herself" had contributed to his ruin.

The week after the publication of "Waverley," Scott had gone on the two months' trip among the Western Isles which has already been mentioned in connection with the "Lord of the Isles"; and on his return he was met

by the welcome intelligence that two editions had already
been exhausted, and that a third was in the press.
Before the end of the year a fourth also was required;
and it is not strange that a success so wholly unprecedented should have decided him to lose no time in
following it up. " Guy Mannering, or the Astrologer,"
was instantly commenced, even before the " Lord of the
Isles " was finally dismissed from his desk; and it was
completed with a rapidity which seems hardly credible,
but which shows how just had been his claim to an
intimate acquaintance with every class of Scottish society;
even gipsies not being excluded. We may also, perhaps,
see in the tale traces of a lurking fancy that there was
somewhat more foundation for the claims of astrology
to be reckoned among the sciences, than was generally
admitted; and the novel would have an interest attaching
to no other, if we were to adopt the notion of the poet
Hogg that Colonel Mannering, whether by design or not,
was an unmistakable likeness of the author himself. But
Hogg's critical judgement does not seem to have equalled
his poetical talent. Certainly no features in the character of the Colonel resemble any idea which Lockhart's
biography leads us to form of Scott himself; and, if any
one of the personages can be supposed to reflect any of
his own lineaments, his tastes or habits, they may, one
would think, rather be found in the shrewd old Scottish
lawyer, Mr. Pleydell : drawn with a sly humour which
did not even spare himself, if we may suppose, as no
doubt we may, that he in his time had borne his share in
the " High Jinks "—"anciently, O Themis, the sport of
thy Scottish children." From his subsequent preface

to "Guy Mannering," in the edition of his collected
novels, we learn that the principal incidents, the astrolo-
gical predictions delivered at the birth of the infant, with
their eventual accomplishment in the recovery of his
property and station, had a foundation partly on well-
known fact, and partly in a story, if not true, at least
very generally reported as such ; and that many of the
characters, Meg Merrilies, the Dominie, and even Dirk
Hatteraick, had their prototypes in real persons ;—in Jean
Gordon, in the "tutor in the family of a gentleman of
considerable property," whose name is not given, and in
a Dutch skipper named Yawkins, long "a terror to the
officers of the revenue on the coast of Galloway": the
last-mentioned identity being so commonly recognised
that a cave near Rueberry, in which Yawkins used at times
to store his smuggled goods, has ever since been known
as Dirk Hatteraick's cave. That "Guy Mannering" was
wholly Scotch proved no obstacle to its success. Again
the printers could hardly keep pace with the demand for
fresh editions. Nor is the popularity, thus satisfactorily
attested, difficult to account for. Whether Colonel
Mannering resembled Scott himself or not, it is clear
that the colours in which he was painted must have
been regarded as most attractive for the idea to have
occurred to any one. And, besides him, we have the
gossipping, amiable, but weak Squire, as pleased as "the
King himself, honest gentleman," at his commission of
Justice of the Peace ; the long-lost heir, with his vicis-
situdes of fortune ; the lively, impulsive, but faithful
mistress of his affections; the honest yeoman with his
"Ailie," his bairns, his Dumple, and Mustard and Pepper,

whose descendants were soon to find a domicile at
Abbotsford; the shrewd and benevolent lawyer; the
pompous Baronet with his "triads"; the Dominie, drawn
with infinite humour; the old gipsy-woman, with her firm
belief in her own power of learning the secrets of futurity
from the stars, and her unfaltering loyalty of affection to
the House of Ellangowan; and, as the piece does not lack
the contrast of villains, the ruffianly smuggling skipper,
and the still more odious, because more contemptible,
agent; the whole forming a gallery of portraits not less
admirable in their diversity than in the truth to nature and
harmonious keeping with which each, gentle or simple,
male or female, honest or infamous, is conceived and
set before us.

CHAPTER VI

I F more "refreshment to the machine" was needed, none could deny that it had been handsomely earned. And that which Scott now felt entitled to give it was of a more healthy kind than a mere transition from one kind of work to another. The large returns from the two novels had given him, as he reckoned, a hundred or two to spare, which he resolved to devote to a visit to London, which he had not seen for several years. It was a visit which was looked forward to with great eagerness by all who were aware of his intention. Miss Baillie wrote to him to warn him "that he must make up his mind to be stared at only a little less than the Czar of Muscovy, or old Blücher," who, the year before, had startled the metropolitan world out of its propriety, as it crowded to gaze on the warrior who, next to our own great general, was regarded by us as having the principal share in pulling down Buonaparte from his throne. Scott had grown to be a greater lion than he had been before, and more than ever was the object of attentions enough to turn any head less strong than his own.

Probably the most gratifying of all the events that befell him was the opportunity of making the personal acquaintance of Byron. They met almost daily, each occasion of their intercourse increasing their respect for each other's talents and, it is hardly too much to say, personal character. Like the heroes in the Iliad, they exchanged gifts, in which Scott himself, in his own opinion, "played the part of Diomede"; since, in return for a gold-mounted dagger, "which had been the property of the redoubted Elfi Bey," Byron gave him a large sepulchral vase of silver, filled with bones which might have belonged to some of the greatest warriors or philosophers of antiquity, since they had been recently found in some ancient sepulchres within the long walls of Athens. It may well be believed that it was cherished among the choicest treasures of Abbotsford, its value being infinitely augmented in Scott's eyes by his real regard for the giver. Others whom he now met were Sir Humphry Davy, the great chemist ; and Rogers, known as Rogers the poet, but the excellence of whose breakfasts far surpassed the merits of his verses.

Among those, if it be not more proper to say, first of those, who looked forward to his visit, was the Prince Regent. He had desired Croker, of whose previous acquaintance with Scott he was aware, to give him the earliest notice of his arrival, that he "might get up a snug little dinner that would suit him." And, as soon as he had been presented at Court, as etiquette required before he could with propriety be the object of the royal notice, the dinner took place. The company, as the Prince proposed, was to be "just a few friends of his own, and the more Scotch the better;" and, as among the half-intellectual, half-social gifts of the Prince was the same faculty of story-telling for which Scott had been distinguished from his childhood, they, both being, as Croker afterwards described the events of the evening, "aware of their *forte*," exerted themselves to the utmost and with delightful effect, so that the company could not really decide which of them had shone the most. To whom the world was indebted for "Waverley," was still unavowed, though it is hardly too much to say that it had ceased to be unknown. And the Prince thought he could make a custom, which in those days still prevailed at dinner tables, available to extract a confession of the truth. The company had not yet risen from table, when the Regent filled his glass, and called for "a bumper with all the honours, to the author of ' Waverley.'" An old Borderer and an old lawyer was not a person to be taken by surprise, and Scott was equal to the emergency. He, too, filled his glass, and, since "His Royal Highness looked as if he thought that he had some claim to the honours of this toast," explained "that he had no such pretentions ;" but promised "to take care that the real Simon Pure should hear of the high compliment that had now been paid him." But neither was the Regent a man to be baffled in his purpose. Once more he filled his glass, and demanded "another of the same to the author of 'Marmion ;' and now, Walter, my man," he added, "I have checkmated you for *once !* "—the "checkmate" being an allusion to an anecdote that had just before been told by Scott of a well-known Scotch judge. Other dinner parties followed, not less lively or less flattering to the guest. And, as a lasting memorial of his visit, the Prince gave him a golden snuff-box, set with diamonds, and further embellished with his own portrait on the lid.

Scott had hardly returned home when he was irresistibly tempted to a second " outing " by the great event which has made 1815 a landmark in history, the crowning victory of Waterloo. To express his feelings in his own words, the intelligence " set him on fire." It has been seen how, for some years, his attention had been rivetted on Wellington's career, how he had even thought of repairing to the Peninsula to witness the exploits in which he took so deep an interest, but had been induced to abandon the scheme. But now he could be restrained no longer, and with a small party of friends, whom he inspired with his own ardour, he at once crossed the Channel, repairing first to Brussels, to satisfy his eyes with an examination of the scene of action, and then proceeding to Paris to feast his patriotism with a sight of the once proud city, no longer sending forth armies to seize upon all the other capitals of the Continent, from Madrid to Moscow, but now herself captured and in the possession of an English army, and its not unworthy Prussian ally. He proposed too to make his countrymen sharers in his exultation, and in the details which he did not doubt to gather, by publishing an account of all he might see and hear. And with this view, before he quitted England, he arranged for the publication of a volume, in the form of letters to his friends in Scotland. Immediately after his return they were issued, under the title of " Paul's Letters to his Kinsfolk ; " the letters being in reality those which he had written almost daily to his wife, and which, after being circulated among the members of his family, were at once

almost without alteration, transmitted to the printer.
They would not be his if they were not lively, animated,
and often shrewd, though like most of the early visitors
to the field, he was imposed upon by a cunning Flemish
peasant, who, according to his own account, had been
pressed into the service of Napoleon, as his guide for the
day, and was consequently able to describe the great Emperor's movements, orders, and occasional sayings ; even
how he had himself excited Napoleon's laughter by duck-
ing his head at the whistle of the cannon balls, which the
Emperor told him " would hit him all the same," while
the truth was that the man had been in a secret hiding.
place ten miles from the battle-field the whole day.   But
people were too eager for news to scrutinise vigilantly all
the tales that might be told them.

From Waterloo he proceeded to Paris, where he was
presented to the Czar, and, as he was wearing his volunteer uniform, was cross-examined, as to his military
service ; and also to Platoff, the celebrated Hetman of
the Cossacks, who, a day or two afterwards, leapt off his
horse in the middle of the street to kiss him on both
sides of the face ; and, above all, to the Duke of
Wellington himself, whom he had always regarded with
a respect bordering on enthusiasm, steadily maintaining
that the talent requisite to form a general of the first class
was of a far higher order than that of any poet or
philosopher.   His acquaintance was also sought with
eagerness by many of the Frenchmen most eminent
for literature or science ; but it was not without great
disgust that he found that among those introduced
to him had been the infamous David, the Jacobin

and regicide artist, whose portrait by some unaccountable, and, I must think, not creditable oversight, has been allowed to disfigure the Albert Memorial.

After some weeks spent in such interesting scenes and company, he returned home, the price he received for " Paul's Letters" being not the only, nor perhaps the most valued profit he had derived from the excursion. Mrs. Rawdon Crawley[1] had not so entirely exhausted the memorials of the great battle for the behoof of her aunt-in-law, but that there were still some relics to be gleaned. Indeed, at all the neighbouring villages, a regular mart had been established for the sale of such articles, and he was able to enrich his museum at Abbotsford with cuirasses, caps of the Imperial Guard decorated with the Imperial Eagle, Crosses of the Legion of Honour, and, more curious still, with a MS. collection of French songs, found in the pocket of a French officer who had fallen, among which was that now so widely known as *Partant pour la Syrie*, which caught his fancy so much that he clothed it in an English dress, and,

"It was Dunois, the young and brave,"

was presently sung in many a Scotch and English draw-ing-room, and applauded by companies ignorant of the history of its discovery. Another fruit of his excursion was "'The Field of Waterloo," a short poem written that its profits might go to swell the fund which a grateful nation was raising for the relief of those whom the great victory had left widows or orphans. That purpose it answered, since it had an enormous sale, but it cannot be regarded as worthy of his poetical renown ; and

[1] " Vanity Fair."

perhaps a battle in modern times, not depending on the
personal prowess of the champions, or presenting such
romantic features as those fought on the fields of Troy,
of Latium, or Stirling, is not calculated for a minute detail
in verse, but can only be effectively treated in a sketch,
such as that presented to Childe Harold's eyes and mind
as he traversed the same field.[1]

After some weeks so spent, Scott returned to Abbotsford, where he now found occupation almost as congenial
in adorning the outside with judicious plantations as in
decorating the inside with antiquarian relics. From
time to time he had been extending his boundary by the
purchase of outlying farms, which fortunately came into
the market, till the estate was approaching the dignity of
a domain ; and no little space in many of his letters is
taken up by discussions on the comparative merits of larch,
birch, mountain ash, and oak, and of the distances to be
allowed between the young trees, so as to give them
sufficient room for growth, with a clear regard to an
undergrowth of sweetbriar, honeysuckle, and other shrubs
of colour and fragrance, not forgetting to leave space for
a bowling green, that he might " have a game at bowls
after dinner every day in fine weather."

His bailiff, or *grieve*, Tom Purdie, was something of a
" character," whose acquaintance he had originally made
under circumstances not calculated to win much sympathy
from any one in whom benevolence and shrewd judgement were less combined than in himself. Tom had been
brought before him, as Sheriff, on a charge of poaching,
but, as Lockhart relates the incident, " he gave such a

[1] " Childe Harold," c. iii.

touching account of his circumstances, a wife, and I know
not how many children depending on his existence, work
scarce, and grouse abundant, and all this with a mixture
of odd sly humour, that the Sheriff's heart was moved.
Tom escaped the penalty of the law, and was taken into
Scott's own employment as shepherd, in which capacity
he showed great zeal, activity, and shrewdness; and his
master never had any occasion to repent the step he
soon afterwards took in promoting him to the position of bailiff, and entrusting him with the management of his farm and plantations." Tom's personal
appearance cannot have been attractive, since he sat
for the picture of Cristal Nixon in "Redgauntlet," but
he took the most faithful interest in all that concerned
his master, not only speaking of the plantations as "our
woods," but of the novels, as they proceeded, as "our
baiks." As the "odd sly humour" remained with him
to the last, there were few whose conversation afforded
greater amusement to his master and his friends ; and,
when he died in 1829, Scott erected a modest monument
to his memory, and himself wrote the epitaph, "In grateful remembrance of his faithful and attached service of
twenty-two years, and in sorrow for the loss of a humble
but sincere friend."

These, however, were relaxations. His business was
the completion of a third novel, the commencement of
which he thus announced to Ballantyne, his printer —

"Dear James, I'm done, thank God, with the long yarns,
    Of the most prosy of Apostles, Paul,
And now advance, sweet Heathen of Monkbarns,
    Step out, old quiz, as fast as I can scrawl."

It need not be said that the "sweet Heathen" was Jonathan Oldbuck, "the Antiquary." With that title the new novel was published in the following May. To one of his friends Scott himself described it as "wanting the romance of 'Waverley,' and the adventure of 'Guy Manner-ing;' but yet having some salvation about it, for, if a man will paint from nature, he will be likely to amuse those who are daily looking at it." In Lockhart's belief, he eventually regarded it with greater favour than any other of his novels, a judgement which to this day is shared by not a few of his readers. An old family friend would perhaps have explained his preference by the likeness the Laird himself bore to one of the most valued friends of the author's father. But it is possible that the attraction might have been found still nearer home, since few shared the tastes or entered into the pursuits of Mr. Oldbuck with greater keenness than Scott himself. And it may even be that the traps into which the Antiquary occasionally fell, and which afforded such humorous amusement to old Edie, were drawn from some of his own mis-adventures.

His rapidity of composition was something marvellous, when it is considered that it was not purchased by any carelessness in the execution of his work. "The Anti-quary" had not been published till May, but before 1816 passed by, two more novels were completed, bound together by one title of "Tales of my Landlord." The landlord in question is the innkeeper at Gander-cleugh, a town strangely overlooked by the hydro-graphers, and his name, according to the account of the schoolmaster of the parish, is Mr. Jedediah Cleish-

botham. Like mine host of the Tabard, in Chaucer's
"Prologue," he is "a pleasing and facetious man," one who
seemed fitted by these qualities to perform to the Tales
the part which the aged minstrel had played to the
" Lay." The " tales " were two in number, " The Black
Dwarf " and " Old Mortality "—the former a cock-boat
in comparison with the gallant first rate, in whose wake it
sailed. " Old Mortality " was the name, or rather nick-
name, of a small farmer of Dumfriesshire, who, inheriting
no little of the Cameronian fanaticism of the preceding
century, neglected his farm, and his family, and devoted
the latter years of his life to visiting the graveyards of the
different parishes in which those whom he regarded as
martyrs for their religion, had died from the hardships
brought on by long imprisonment, or from injuries sustained in attempts to escape ; the object of his visit
being to keep in repair the monuments and gravestones
designed to preserve the memory of their virtues and their
fate.

" Old Mortality," in the eyes of Lockhart, a critic by
profession, since he was the editor of *The Quarterly
Review*, is " the ' Marmion ' of the novels." He calls it
Scott's first attempt to repeople the past by the " power of
imagination working on materials furnished by books."
For in " Waverley," he had but revived the dreams of
his own boyhood, and had drawn upon the artless oral
narratives of aged friends. " The story," Lockhart adds,
" is formed with a deeper skill than any of the preceding
novels ; the characters are contrasted and projected with
a power and felicity which neither he nor any other
master ever surpassed."

The praise is hardly exaggerated. But "Old Mortality" is also entitled to special notice as being the first instance in which the author's principal object was to delineate a great historical character, and indeed to do justice to one who had been undeservedly traduced. His indignation had often been excited by the libellous accounts of Graham of Claverhouse, which had obtained circulation and belief in many districts. Scott often complained that "no character had been so forcibly traduced," that thanks to Wodrow, Cruikshank, and such chroniclers, "he who was, every inch, a soldier and a gentleman, still passed among the Scottish vulgar for a ruffian desperado, who rode a goblin horse, was proof against shot, and in league with the devil." Scott's own grandfather had been a Killiecrankie man. Dundee's picture was the only one in his own library; and, as if he had foreseen the bitterness with which Macaulay gave a lasting and wider currency to the falsehoods of those annalists of the Covenanters, he now, by a happy anticipation, set the gallant warrior in his true light, as one who, though he confessed sympathy with Froissart,—whose "beautiful expressions of sorrow are confined to the death of the gallant and highbred knight, of whom it was pity to see the fall, such was his loyalty to his king, pure faith to his religion, hardihood towards his enemy, and fidelity to his lady love,"—saw nothing in these knightly principles, which Claverhouse had indeed adopted for his own rule of life, inconsistent with unsparing severity towards "the villain churls" whom he found in open insurrection.

The taste of the public coincided with that expressed by Lockhart, as was shown by the sale, which exceeded

that of any of the former novels. Before the "Tales"
had been out two months, Scott could estimate the profit
at £2,500. And, confident in his ability to follow up this
success by similar efforts for many years, he began to
enlarge his views, and to aim at becoming himself the
founder of a new branch of the great house of Buccleuch.
His purchases of land around Abbotsford had already
extended his estate to near 1000 acres, much of the
land thus acquired proving also of greater value than he
had anticipated ; and the house was growing in corresponding proportions, till it gradually became a mansion
suitable for the entertainment of the visitors of all ranks
and all nations, who flocked thither in numbers constantly
increasing, as his fame spread more and more widely, to
enjoy his society, or to do homage to his genius. In a
burlesque poem, with which he had recently amused himself and the readers of *The Saleroom*, a weekly paper
which was one of Ballantyne's speculations, he had
represented Sultan Solimaun of Serendib on a voyage
for the discovery of "a happy man," but coming to the
conclusion that, wherever else one might be found, Scotland was not the country, so full of grumbling were the
natives at the high price of tea, pepper, and nutmegs;
and, though meal also was dear, at the fall in the price
of "grain that wadna' pay the yoking of the plough."
But, if the mighty prince had prosecuted his search on
the author's side of the country, he would have found as
happy a man on the banks of the Tweed as any who
"jested, sang, or capered fair and free" on those of the
Liffey or the Shannon ; so complete and pure was Scott's
enjoyment while directing Tom Purdie's planting, drain-

ing, and top-dressing with " marle," of which he reports
to Mr. Morritt he has discovered wealth in a newly-
purchased bog; and which was so invaluable for his
purpose, that already, " in his mind's eye," he saw all the
bluebank, the " hinnybee, and the other provinces of his
poor kingdom, waving with deep rye grass and clover,
like the meadows at Rokeby." An envious critic, one of
the class whom the sight of virtue or genius, especially
when successful, seems to provoke rather than to tran-
quillise, has found matter for grave reproach in Scott's
ambition to acquire an estate and found a family, as
if it were a prostitution of genius to the sordid and unworthy object of mere acquisition. But such an attack
shows rather the unreasoning meanness of the critic than
of the author. Wealth and high position are legitimate
objects of pursuit, so long as the means employed are
honourable. Of the noblest families in the British
peerage many owe their origin to the professional ability
of a learned or eloquent lawyer, not a few to the judicious
enterprise of a merchant or a manufacturer. And, if few
such houses can be traced back to authors in prose or
verse, the reason is to be found in the rarity of pre-
eminent literary genius; but certainly not in the disdain
of poet, novelist, or historian for riches, which, it must
be borne in mind, can never be acquired by them, except
as the reward of the pleasure, combined with instruction,
which they have afforded to thousands upon thousands
of readers, not confined, as Scott's are not, to one country
or one generation.

CHAPTER VII

SCOTT could not afford to be idle, nor had he the inclination. Appetite is said to be sharpened by eating, and the fondness for composition is not less stimulated by indulgence. As usual, he had more than one other work in hand, which may be passed over without any special notice. But the last sheets of " Old Mortality " were hardly out of the printers' hands, before he began to plan a fresh novel, though the execution of his idea was delayed by different circumstances; one of which was of a melancholy character, being a severe attack of illness, beginning with cramp in the stomach, which, though at first it was subdued for the moment, recurred continually for the next year or two, often with an increased violence, which quite incapacitated him for work. At last, however, in December, the new novel came out, under the title of " Rob Roy," the name of the chief of the broken or proscribed clan of McGregor, who, at the beginning of the century, had enjoyed a somewhat equivocal reputation from the diversity of his occupations : at one time as a peaceful dealer in cattle, at another as a levier of black-mail, not infrequently as a political agent in the confidence at once of Jacobite

lairds and chieftains, and, at the same time, so singularly
adroit were his machinations, of their most active and
influential enemy, the Duke of Argyll; and, once at
least, as the captain of a well-armed body of clansmen,
sufficient to have turned the scale at Sheriff Muir, if he
had not, in spite of many a command to act, obstinately
preferred the part of a spectator to that of an actor in
the conflict.

From one point of view "Rob Roy" was composed
on a new plan. The novelist was not the narrator of the
story. In "Guy Mannering" much of the private history
of Colonel Mannering and his daughter Julia had been
explained in letters of their own to distant friends; and
in "Rob Roy" the incidents in the life of Mr. Francis
Osbaldeston, on which the story turns, are throughout
related by himself in a series of letters, though the flow
of the narrative is not interrupted by any epistolary
commencements or conclusion, and the reader is only reminded of the fact by the occasional recurrence of the first
person. But the public did not care about the form. In
a letter to Mr. Morritt, Scott expressed a fear that the book
"smelt of the cramp." But that fear was only suggested
by the pain in which much of it had been written; and
that it had no other ground was proved by the universal
favour with which the tale was at once received, and
which it still retains without much diminution. Nor is
it strange that it should do so, since, in addition to the
animation with which the different incidents are related,
and which was indeed among the most inseparable characteristics of the author's genius, it contains one character,
the Baillie, conceived and drawn throughout in a vein of

the richest humour ; and one of his most exquisite
female portraits in Die Vernon, the winner of all
hearts in her own circle then, and of all readers now,
who cannot but rejoice at her extrication from the toils
of Rashleigh, the villain of the piece, and from the
threatened miseries of a convent, to find the rest and
happiness her beauty and virtues deserve in her union
with her cousin Francis, also, like her, victorious over
the machinations of his enemies.

So steady had been the rise in the popularity of the
novels, that the publishers of " Rob Roy" had begun with
an edition of 10,000 copies, a number which no work of
any kind ever published in the kingdom had reached
before ; but which only met the demand of a single
fortnight. It was a natural consequence of such success, that Scott at once began to make arrangements for
another novel, which was to be called a second series of
" The Tales of my Landlord," though, in fact, it contained
but one, " The Heart of Midlothian." It was the tale of
what had nearly been a painful tragedy, the execution of
a girl for the murder of a child who was still alive. To
the citizens of Edinburgh it was commended by the
circumstance of their own city having been the scene
of the principal incidents described, and especially of
the singular riot organized for the murder of Captain
Porteous : to Scotchmen, in general, for the amiable
light in which the Duke of Argyll was represented—
that Argyll celebrated by Pope as

> " The state's whole thunder born to wield,
> And shake alike the Senate and the field ; "

and, of whom, though so long dead, Lowlanders, as well as Highlanders, still cherished a proud and fond recollection. While it is endeared to Englishmen and Scotchmen alike, by the sympathy so skilfully excited by the weakness and perils of one sister, the unswerving truthfulness and courage (for which heroism would not be too strong a word) of the other,—a picture of virtues, which leads many readers, especially those of the softer sex, to place it in the very front rank as one of the most interesting of all the stories which ever proceeded from the author's pen.

Nothing in literary history is more extraordinary than that, though the works with which Scott was delighting the world were by themselves sufficient to occupy the entire time, and engross the whole attention, of ordinary writers, they were but a portion of his work. A list of his writings, which Mr. Lockhart gives in an " Appendix to his Memoirs," enumerates no fewer than ten other compositions belonging to this year, elaborate reviews, ballads, and one series of essays on the provincial antiquities of Scotland, which, though no doubt a labour of love, must have made a serious demand on his leisure. And all this was undertaken in spite of the frequent recurrence of the illness of the preceding year, which more than once disabled him from the performance of the duties of his legal office ; and even on one occasion brought him, in his own opinion, so near death's door, that in his agony he called his children round his bed, and took leave of them as a dying man, seasoning his farewell with affectionate advice,—his own rule of life being not the least practically valuable

of his admonitions, when he said that he was unconscious of ever having done "any man an injury, or
omitted any fair opportunity of doing any man a benefit,"
such being the best guide for their own conduct that any
father could leave his children, and one that they might
well cherish as their best and proudest legacy.

Another of his "refreshments," in 1818, was a second
"labour of love," akin to that which has been mentioned above. His earnest solicitation had induced
the Prince Regent to issue a commission to search for
the Regalia of Scotland, which, in spite of a clause in
the Treaty of Union, strictly forbidding their removal,
were commonly understood to have been transferred to
the Tower of London, though the chest in which they
had certainly at one time been kept was still at
Holyrood. Indeed a crown had been shown to Scott
himself in the jewel-room of the Tower, which was stated
by the keeper of the room to be the identical crown
which had been placed at Scone on the head of the
great Bruce, and worn by all his descendants till the
sixth James quitted his native land to receive the still
nobler crown of England. The Duke of Buccleuch was
the President of the Commission, but Scott was the
working member. The keys of the chest had long been
lost, but the Regent's warrant authorised the breaking
open of the lid, though so stout was its double cover of
oak and iron, that it was no easy or speedy task. At
last, however, it was accomplished, and to Scott's great
joy the regalia were found in all their completeness.

In June, 1819, exactly a year after the second series
of "The Tales of my Landlord," a third was completed,

containing two stories of the most opposite character,
but both of an excellence calculated in no degree to
lower his fame, but rather to enhance it, if by this time
it had admitted of any increase, by the fertility and
variety of genius displayed in dealing with subjects so
widely different in character. "The Bride of Lammermoor" is a tragedy of the deepest pathos, founded on
an event which had really occurred in the family of
Dalrymple. "The Legend of Montrose" is a sketch of
the great marquis, who so long and gallantly upheld the
royal cause in his native land, and whose victory over
Argyll, at Inverlochy, crowns the story. Yet, deservedly
dear as is the hero's memory to all Scots worthy of the
name, and admirable as are the discrimination and fire
with which he is presented, it is not the portrait of the
commander which most engrosses the attention, but
rather that of the officer whom he enlists in the king's
service, the inimitable Dalgetty. The major's previous
career, as he describes it to Lord Monteith, closely
resembles that of the cavalier whose imaginary memoirs
were the firstfruits of the invention of Defoe. But the
humour with which it is set forth is Scott's own, and
keeps the reader in an unbroken state of amused
delight, from the major's first explanation of why, at the
supper at Darlinvarach, "he eats so very fast and so
very long," his evasion of the offers to relieve him of
the partner of his campaigns, his gallant grey, his
suggestion to Sir Duncan to erect a sconce upon
Dramsnab, by which Ardenvohr is in some degree
"overcrowed"—from all these, to the "exquisite dex-
terity" with which, as "an accomplished cavalier," he

gives Argyll a lesson in the treatment due to " valiant soldados " who may fall into his hands, and effects his own escape from the Inverary dungeons.

Persons who desired to pose as patrons of literature (for I do not think any scholar or author had ever condescended to complain) had frequently expressed surprise and dissatisfaction that literary genius was overlooked in the distribution of honours, such as were at times conferred on men of science.[1] The fact was certain; but the dispensers of those honours might, perhaps, have pleaded as their excuse the difficulty in late years of finding any literary man of sufficient merit to justify such distinction.[2] But the Regent (for the act seems to have been his own), as has been seen, had conceived a strong personal regard for Scott, and felt justly that his genius entitled him to be regarded as the representative man of the literary body. To honour him, therefore, was to honour literature in his person; and with this feeling the Prince proposed to the Prime Minister, Lord Liverpool, that an offer of a baronetcy should be made to him, and the proposal was warmly agreed to. Had the offer come at an earlier date, Scott would have been inclined to doubt whether his means were such as would have justified his acceptance of it. But his novels were now producing him a steady income of £10,000 a year, and, as he was still in the prime of life, he made no doubt of being able to find fresh

[1] Sir W. Herschell and Sir H. Davy had been made baronets in this reign.

[2] Gibbon and Hume had given too much room to objection, on the score of the scepticism which taints their otherwise great works.

subjects for his invention for many years. He had also
lately received intelligence of the death of his brother-
in-law, who had for many years held a lucrative
appointment in India, and who had left the reversion
of his property, after the death of his widow, to his
nephews and nieces at Abbotsford. He, therefore,
might now fairly think that such obstacles as might
have existed a few years before had passed away.
And, though, as he wrote to his friend Morritt, on
the 7th of December, 1818, "he would not have gone
a step out of his way to have asked, or bought, or
begged, or borrowed a distinction, which, personally,
would rather be inconvenient to him than otherwise, yet,
coming as it did directly from the source of all feudal
honours, and, as an honour, he was really gratified by
it. He anticipated the jest, 'I like not such grinning
honour as Sir Walter hath';[1] but after all, 'if one
must speak for themselves,'[2] he had his quarters and
emblazonments free of all stain but Border theft and
high treason, which, he hoped, were gentlemanlike
crimes,[3] and he hoped 'Sir Walter Scott' would not
sound worse than 'Sir Humphry Davy,' though his own
merits were as much under the latter's in point of
utility, as could well be imagined. But a name is
something, and his own was the better of the two."

[1] Shakespeare, "Henry IV.," part i. v. 2.

[2] A singular piece of English.

Die Vernon had expressed the same opinion to Frank
Osbaldeston :—

" 'And so it is high treason then, and not simple robbery, of
which I am accused.'

" 'Certainly ; which, you know, has been in all ages accounted
the crime of a gentleman '" (" Rob Roy," c. vii.).

Up to this time Scotland had been the scene of all
his novels; but he was now about to take a wider range,
and to attempt a description of the great feudal hero,
Richard I., and of the condition of England in his
time. The adoption of such a subject was dictated
by prudential reasons, which are explained in the
preface to "Ivanhoe," the title fixed on for the new
work. Great as had been the popularity of the novels
hitherto published, it was plain, he conceived, that
frequent publication must finally wear out the public
favour, unless some mode could be devised to give
an appearance of novelty to subsequent productions.
Nothing could be more dangerous for the fame of a professor of the fine arts than to permit (if he can possibly
prevent it) the character of a mannerist to be attached
to him, or that he should be supposed capable of success
only in a particular and limited style; he felt also that,
in confining himself to subjects purely Scottish, he was
not only likely to wear out the patience of his readers,
but also greatly to limit his own power of affording them
pleasure.

No one is likely to dispute a train of reasoning which
bore so splendid a fruit. The name, he tells us, was
"suited to his purpose, first, because it had an ancient
English sound," [1] and secondly because it conveyed no

---

[1] An old rhyme recorded the names of three Manors as forfeited
by an ancestor of Hampden, for striking the Black Prince a blow
with his racket, on a quarrel in the tennis court.

> "Wing, Tring, and Ivanhoe
> For striking of a blow,
> Hampden did forego
> And glad he could escape so."

Preface to Ivanhoe.

indication whatever of the nature of the story ; a quality
which he presumed to think of no small importance to
the author, with whose interests those of the publisher
are in this instance at variance, the latter preferring a
taking title as calculated to further his object of an early
and quick sale ; while "whatever raises high expectations of a work before its appearance is disadvantageous
to the former (the writer), if the execution of the work
is thought inferior to the expectation thus raised of its
excellence."

" Ivanhoe," however, is a tale which had nothing of
this kind to fear, since no anticipation could surpass,
nor even equal, the universal admiration that it excited.
I will not go so far as to say that it is the best of all
the novels, though that praise has often been bestowed
upon it, because it seems imprudent, and not wholly free
from the imputation of arrogance, to pronounce a judgement which, as it were, claims an authority to dictate
to all the world on what must after all be a matter of
taste. But there can be no presumption in asserting that
it stands high even among Scott's master-pieces. From
the preface we learn that, among the reasons which had
influenced him in adopting the reign of Richard I. for
the period of his narrative, one was that it abounded
with characters whose very names were sure to attract
general attention, and another, that it afforded a
" striking contrast between the Saxons by whom the
soil was cultivated, and the Normans, who still reigned
in it as conquerors, reluctant to mix with the vanquished,
or to acknowledge themselves of the same stock."
And it is not going too far to say that he has availed

himself with something more than mere artistic skill, with the most brilliant genius, of both these advantages. Richard himself is indeed the only character known to real history, so that his name was calculated to attract general attention; but Robin Hood and Friar Tuck also play such active parts in many of the old ballads, that they may be looked on as having at least a semi-historical character. And the contrast between the haughty Norman and the Saxon not less unbending, though with a different pride, is worked out with great skill and consistency; as is a second contrast, not men-tioned in his enumeration of advantages, that between the Jew and the Christian of either race; and on this the attention is attracted and rivetted by one of the noblest of his female portraits, the grateful, generous, and every-way high-minded Rebecca.

Of the power with which the other leading characters are drawn, and the most striking incidents described, a time will come to speak when we compare the poems and novels together. But, high as "Ivanhoe" was placed by universal acclamation, complete justice to the author could not be done by the general public, who were not aware that the two years in which that and its predecessors, "The Bride of Lammermoor" and "The Legend of Montrose," were composed, were years of severe and almost uninterrupted suffering. For months Scott was unable to hold a pen, and was forced to em-ploy an amanuensis to take down the chapters from his dictation, a process which most authors would find a great dragchain on their invention. Often he was con-fined to his bed, and even in that place of rest was

attacked with paroxysms of such violence as to be
unable to proceed, while his scribes, thus reduced to
inaction, sat silent and marvelling at the grace and
vigour of his thoughts and language, which no pain
seemed able long to subdue. It would probably be
difficult in the entire history of genius to find another
such instance of the supremacy of the mind over the
body.

Nor were these admirable tales the only objects for
which he nerved himself to exertions almost inconceiv-
able in his state of health. A variety of causes, a depression of trade and consequent distress of the working
classes being the most influential, had led not only to
wide discontent, but to violent demonstrations of it in
many of the Northern Counties. A formidable riot at
Manchester had not been quelled without a lamentable
loss of life; and in the latter part of 1819 serious fears
were entertained that the colliers of Northumberland
might unite with the weavers of Paisley and Glasgow
in some outbreak of a similar character. In Scott's mind
the call of duty to his country was at all times paramount
to every other consideration, and no duty ever was held
by him to be equally imperative with that of the maintenance of law and order. Ill as he was, he set himself
to work to organise a company of sharp-shooters for the
defence of the district, prepared, though still unable to
hold a pen, to march at their head in case of emergency.
As is often the case, the knowledge of the preparations
to resist violence rendered them apparently unnecessary.
Tranquillity was preserved. But that in such a state of
health he should have made such exertions, and have

been ready to make more, affords an additional instance of Scott's indomitable resolution and strength of mind, under the most discouraging circumstances. And some of his arrangements for the organisation of the force are not without interest at the present day, in so many particulars do they foreshadow those of the noble army of volunteers, whose efficiency, if ever hostile invasion should render their services necessary, would prove one great defence of the kingdom, as the feeling of loyalty to which the force not only owes its origin, but which, still more admirably, brings it around its standards in yearly increasing numbers, is an honour to the whole nation.

In a letter to his steward, to whose care he was forced to entrust the carrying out of many of the details, he tells him, " the dress is to be as simple, and, at the same time, as serviceable as possible. A jacket and trousers of Galashiels grey cloth ; and a smart bonnet with a small feather, or, to save even that expense, a sprig of holly. And we will have shooting at the mark, and prizes, and fun, and a little whiskey." In these instructions we might fancy we were reading a description of the uniforms yearly to be seen at Wimbledon, and of the competition for prizes ; though, with all his powers of imagination, even Scott had never pictured to himself the unerring skill, aided by greatly improved weapons, with which bullet after bullet is sent at the target from distances till recently thought out of the reach of the largest cannon.

CHAPTER VIII.

IT is curious that, in spite of the reasons which, in the preface to "Ivanhoe," Scott had alleged for the selection of scenes and events out of Scotland, and of the approval of them unmistakably manifested by readers of all classes, in his next two works he should have returned to Scotland. The second, "The Abbot," is a sequel to the first, so far that the youth who in the first, "The Monastery," raises himself from the rank of a peasant to that of a knight and to be the husband of an heiress of noble birth, is also to a certain extent a prominent character in the second, his more peaceful brother being, moreover, "The Abbot," who gives it its title. It may be that in "The Monastery," a tale of pure invention, Scott proposed to avoid the imputation of "mannerism" by a recourse to the supernatural world, in the introduction of "the White Lady," and, to a different style of speech in "the Euphuist"; but, in the opinion of Mr. Lockhart, of which Scott himself subsequently admitted the correctness, neither novelty was much relished, and the combination contributed to the comparative coldness with which the tale was received. It was admitted that the picture of the White Lady was

poetical in its conception, but the idea of spirits influenc-
ing the fortunes of a race or family was not familiar to
the English mind. It was also objected that her appear-
ances were too frequent, and that some of the modes in
which she exerted her influence savoured of the tricks
of a conjuror rather than of the dignified proceedings
of a supernatural being. The romantic language of
euphuism also, though, even in so grave a drama as
Hamlet,[1] Shakespeare had condescended to adopt it,
when it fell in with the humour of the day, had long
been forgotten ; and was generally regarded as an incon-
gruous absurdity. Lockhart, indeed, whose critical judgement is commonly biassed a good deal by his feelings of
nationality, expresses a belief that the exquisite descriptions of woodland scenery, and the sterling Scotch
characters and manners, will ultimately secure it greater
favour. He might have added, the judgement and
historical truth displayed in the delineation of Murray's
character, and of the difficulties by which as Regent he was
beset, not more from the grasping turbulence of Barons
like Morton, than from the manœuvres, intrigues, and in-
consistencies of Elizabeth, "a sovereign as moody and
as fickle as her humorous ladyship [Dame Fortune]
herself." But his prediction has not been fulfilled ; the
merits which he finds in it have probably not been denied
in any quarter ; but the very popularity of its predecessors,
whose excellence was the standard by which it was

---

[1] Osric's fine language seems evidently meant for a modified
euphuism, though Don Armado, in " Love's Labour's Lost," is the
example referred to by Scott in his preface to " The Monastery" in
the collected edition.

measured, injured it, and certainly it has never held the same place in the general estimation as is occupied by them.

But Scott was justly too confident in his powers to be discouraged by finding that in a single instance he had failed to hit the public taste. And, before the end of the year, "The Abbot," which, as has been mentioned before, was, to a certain extent, a sequel to "The Monastery," was universally accepted as a proof that his powers had suffered no diminution. The subject is the imprisonment of the beautiful but most unfortunate Mary in the castle of Lochleven, her romantic escape from it, and the almost instant overthrow of all the hopes she had built on that escape by the crushing defeat of Langside. The story is full of stirring incidents, the visit of the fierce Barons to extort the Queen's signature to the deed of abdication, the escape from Lochleven, the fatal battle. All are told with the author's characteristic animation. But the great beauty of the work is the portrait of Mary herself, and the considerate grace which distinguishes her under every vicissitude of fortune, and abundantly explains the empire she established over all hearts which were not steeled by religious fanaticism, and of her queenly courage, worthy of her royal race. While the union of lively wit with enthusiastic loyalty, and that unswerving courage which inspires all who approach the possessor with similar feelings, are set forth in all their attractiveness in Catherine Seyton, a high-born damsel, not unworthy to match with Die Vernon, and well deserving her place in the favour of her royal mistress.

Scott was always of opinion that his best things were

those which he threw off the most easily and swiftly; and the idea may be thought to be supported by "Kenil-worth," which was published within four months of "The Abbot." The author has told us, in the preface subse-quently prefixed to it in the collected edition of his works, that the subject was suggested by that of its predecessor, since the success with which he was considered to have presented the character of the beauteous Scottish queen, "naturally induced him to attempt something similar respecting ' her sister and her foe,' the celebrated Eliza-beth." We are therefore bidden to regard them as designedly companion pictures; and in one respect it may be said that Elizabeth is, from the outset, placed in the more disadvantageous light, since the chief incidents in the tale relate to one of the most discreditable passages in her career, her infatuated passion for one of the most worthless of her subjects, the every way contemptible Leicester. And the manner in which Scott has dealt with it brings to light a difference between the mode of dealing with historical subjects adopted by him and by his only superior in that class of composition, Shakespeare. The satisfaction which the great delineator of Henry V. and Richard III. gave the Duke of Marlborough, as an authority on history, was not shared by Die Vernon, who complained that his Lancastrian partialities, and a certain knack of embodying them, had turned history upside down, or rather inside out. She herself would hardly have claimed to be an impartial critic; and it would prob-ably not be difficult to show that, wherever Shakespeare's representations are inconsistent with the more accurate knowledge which the researches of modern historians have opened to us, his mistakes, such as they are, were caused by a reliance on ancient chronicles or traditions which he accepted as authentic.

But Scott evidently considered that the class of composition which he adopted, and the object which he partly proposed to himself, permitted him a license which the great dramatist forbore to claim. He did not, indeed, when dealing with historical events or persons, disregard the duty of giving a lively and faithful picture of the manners of the time, any neglect of which must mar the interest of his story; but even before that he placed the object of giving a correct and vivid idea of the character of the person principally concerned. And, if that aim could be more effectually attained by combining together transactions which in reality were separated by an interval of several years, he did not scruple to heighten the interest of his tale by such an expedient. Accordingly, he here places the murder of Amy Robsart in the same year with Leicester's magnificent revel at Kenilworth in Elizabeth's honour, though, in fact, the unhappy victim of Leicester's falsehood and ambition had long been in her grave; just as afterwards, in "Peveril of the Peak," he connects Lady Derby with the Popish plot, though she also had been dead many years, and was no Roman Catholic, but a member of one of the most distinguished Huguenot families in France. But, if we only allow the validity of his reasons for this departure from historical truth, it cannot be denied that he has made good use of the license; and has produced in "Kenilworth" a deeply interesting story, more interesting probably by far than if he had bound down his genius to a strict regard to dates. In its main

features "Kenilworth" is a tale of treachery and crime.
It may be compared to "Othello," both in its tragical
end, the murder of the foully slandered innocent wife;
in the motive which led to the perpetration of the crime,
jealousy; and in the vile arts employed to excite that
feeling in the breast of the too easily deluded husband.
Both Scott and Shakespeare had too correct an insight
into human nature not to recognise the important truth
that there are few, even among the worst men, who have
not some redeeming quality. And a great critic has
adduced in proof of Shakespeare's adherence to this
doctrine, that in all his plays Iago is the only character of
unalloyed wickedness; of depravity unbalanced by a
single good quality. Varney is Scott's Iago, his task
being indeed the easier, as he has a less noble disposition to work upon, inasmuch as Leicester's jealousy is
stimulated by unprincipled ambition, if indeed the latter
was not the more powerful motive of the two. And it is
the utter vileness of Leicester which, in some degree,
deprives the novel of the interest inspired by the drama.
For, without disparaging for a moment the magnificence
of the Venetian tragedy, deservedly reckoned among the
masterpieces of its author, the skill with which the whole
of Amy's story is worked up; her first exulting admiration
of her husband in his "glorious garb;" her proud comparison of his worth and greatness with Tressilian's "best
deeds in peace and war, and obscure rank;" her indignant
reproof of the latter's "base, unmannered tongue" when
he presumes to put a "question which derogates from
her honour"; so sadly followed by her subsequent trials,
her not ill-founded fears of poison, her flight to Kenil-

worth, her agonies of suspense, only terminated by her miserable death,—all these may fitly place the story by the side of the tale of the fate of Desdemona, fearing no evil till brought face to face with her doom, so suddenly announced and executed by her almost equally unhappy husband. It may be added that our pity for Amy is augmented by the repeated instances of her husband's baseness; of his plots for the assassination of Sussex; and his cowardly denial of his wife before Elizabeth. While the pathos is heightened by the introduction of scenes of comic humour, in which Wayland and Flibbertigibbet are the actors, and which are peculiarly appropriate to the moment, when all England was brought up to a pitch of unprecedented excitement by the approaching festivities.

CHAPTER IX

IN his next novel, "The Pirate," Scott may be almost said to have broken wholly new ground. The scene is laid in the Orkneys, and though, in geographical dictionaries and Acts of Parliament, these islands are classed as a part of Scotland, the manners, and even the superstitions, are so wholly different from those of the Scotch on the mainland, that the author might reasonably flatter himself that his work would have some of the attraction derived from novelty. He had conceived the idea of making them the scene of some future work when, seven or eight years before, he had touched on some of the larger islands on his way to the Hebrides. And certain documents relating to the exploits and eventual capture of a pirate captain in the early part of the last century, which had lately fallen into his hands, confirmed him in his design. None of his other works, except "The Heart of Midlothian," had so much foundation in fact ; a circumstance which seems worthy of notice, as in some sort affording a corroboration of the old adage that truth is often stranger than fiction. Cleveland, the pirate captain of the novel, is the "alias" of John Gow, a well-known pirate, who long infested those northern waters, and, in spite of the audacious lawlessness of his life, captivated the affections of a young Zetland lady of family and property, who remained faithful to his memory even after his execution. Cleveland's mistress had a less painful reason to dwell on his career and fate. And the interest of their love tale is skilfully heightened by the introduction of a second heroine, the sister of her who was too successfully wooed, the two reminding us in some degree of Isabel and Edith in "The Lord of the Isles." In a previous chapter attention has been invited to the exquisite delicacy exhibited by Scott in the drawing of his female portraits; and it is in few instances more conspicuous than in his pictures of these sisters, contrasted in outward features as well as in disposition; both highly gifted with charms of mind as well as of person; the stately dark-eyed Minna, who, in her "serious cast of beauty, her graceful ease of motion, the music of her voice, and the serene purity of her eye, seemed to indicate that she belonged naturally to some higher and better sphere;" while the "scarcely less beautiful, equally lovely, and equally innocent Brenda, with her profusion of golden locks, her innocent vivacity, her eye that seemed to look on every object with pleasure, from a natural and serene cheerfulness of disposition, attracted even more general admiration than the charms of her sister, though perhaps that which Minna did excite might be of a more intense as well as a more reverential character." In one essential point they were alike; they were warmly and equally attached to one another and to their father. Thus they presented a pair, either of whom might well prove irresistible to a sailor, whose profession afforded him but few opportunities of enjoying female society; though it was not unnatural that it was Minna to whom he was most strongly attracted. And a further contrast is afforded by the introduction of Norna, an aged dame, half-crazed with recollections of ancient griefs, and mingling with her delusions a superstitious belief in her supernatural powers, selling "fair winds" to mariners who could pay for them; and not infrequently claiming to guide the sisters (whose aunt she is, though they are ignorant of the relationship) in the path of prudence, by her insight into futurity.

The story is told in all its parts with great liveliness and power, though a rigorous critic might perhaps object that the discovery of Norna's relation to Cleveland, just at the moment when, as she conceived, she has secured his execution, is somewhat too melodramatic to be suitable to fiction of a class that aspires to a permanently high place in literature. It contains also some of the sweetest songs that ever the author's Muse inspired; and, if, as is probably the case, it was, and is, less admired than some of the others, the failure to meet with equal approval may be attributed to the difficulty of interesting readers in general in a tale relating to a petty little-known region, and to a people, who, however estimable for private virtues, and a somewhat primitive simplicity of life, have no present importance to boast of, nor traditional glories with which to appeal to the memory or imagination of more civilised readers.

In "The Fortunes of Nigel," which came out in the beginning of the following year, if Scott did not return to Scotland for his field of action, he took Scotchmen for all the more prominent personages, presenting them to us

with a variety of character not surpassed in any other
work. We have a king; a stout old earl of the old school;
his rascally heir of the newer mode; another Scotch peer,
in spite of his natural caution, the dupe, and nearly the
victim of the heir's treachery; a splenetic knight; an honest
goldsmith, whose liberal and judicious charity to this day
preserves his name in the grateful memory of his native
city; a page, as eccentric in his notion of his duty as in his
appearance, but faithfully devoted to his master's interests,
often severely straining his Presbyterian scruples, but, even
in his very lies, having no object but his master's interest
or his country's credit—of all Scott's serving-men the most
vigorously drawn and the most amusing; three of the
softer sex, one whose noble birth might have been expected to prove a sufficient preservation from the villainous
designs which were too successfully practised against her;
another, an impulsive sentimental maiden of lower birth,
to whose singular advancement the other personages,
from the king downwards, unite in contributing. And
in the portrait of James the novelist must be admitted to
have adhered to historical truth as closely as Shakespeare
himself, so fully are the king's timidity, pedantry, favouri-
tism, and propensity to mirth and practical jokes, not
always consistent either with delicacy or his royal dignity,
borne out by the testimony of all grave historians. While,
if the scenes in which we meet these noble persons give us
an insight into the high life of the period, those in Alsatia
still more surely lift the curtain from the very lowest, and
create a feeling of wonder how such a harbour for every
sort of rogue and ruffian could have been permitted so long
to set all decency and law at defiance in the very heart of

the greatest city in the world. It is no wonder that a tale
so powerfully and attractively told was, from its first
appearance, regarded as among the most brilliant of the
author's performances, or that it retains its popularity
undiminished to the present day.

"The Fortunes of Nigel" had scarcely been launched,
when it was followed by what, from one point of view,
may be called a holiday for the author, though in reality
it brought him no rest from, but only a change of work so
engrossing as for the next three months to leave him no
leisure for any other pursuits. House improving, planting, sport, and composition, were all for the time laid
aside, while his every thought was devoted to the arrangements for the reception of the first Sovereign who had
visited Scotland since the Revolution. In 1821 business
had taken him to London, where his society had again
been sought with as great eagerness as ever ; and as much
by the leaders of fashion and magnates of the land as by
men of literature and science, in whom the town was at
that time particularly rich. Entertainments of all kinds
were got up in his honour, till, as he wrote to his son,
who had lately received a commission in the 18th Hussars,
he longed to be at home, "at Abbotsford again, being
heartily tired of fine company and fine living, from dukes
and duchesses down to turbot and plovers' eggs. It is
very well," he said, "for a while, but to be kept at it
makes one feel like a poodle dog, compelled to stand for
ever on his hind legs." One sight, however, made him
amends for much of the danger to his digestion threatened
by the plovers' eggs and their accompaniments. The
coronation took place in the latter part of July. As a

mere spectacle it was sufficiently imposing; "throwing into the shade," as he described it to a Scotch newspaper, "all scenes of similar magnificence from the Field of the Cloth of Gold down to the present day"; but, even had it been less unrivalled in its sumptuousness, it would have commended itself to his sentiments of enthusiastic loyalty from the feeling of "deep veneration, without which it was impossible to behold the voluntary and solemn inter-change of vows betwixt the king and his assembled people; whilst he, on the one hand, called God Almighty to witness his resolution to maintain their laws and privileges; whilst they called, at the same moment, on the Divine Being to bear witness that they accepted him for their liege Sovereign, and pledged to him their love and duty." The king him-self "when presiding at the banquet, amid the long line of his nobles, looked 'every inch a king;' and nothing could exceed the grace with which he accepted and returned their various acts of homage rendered to him in the course of that long day."

The king's grace in what may be called private society had not been affected by his more elevated rank. He had neither found any bard to supplant the "Poet of Princes" in his estimation, nor, it may be surmised, had he forgotten the triumph he had achieved when Regent, by "check-mating" the author of "Marmion." Scott had more than one interview with him, and on one occasion found an opportunity of expressing the deep gratification it would be to Scotland, which might share with England the honour of being considered the cradle of his royal house, if he would honour that part of his dominions with a visit. His Majesty had already promised to cross over to Ire-

land that summer, where indeed he treated his hosts with
no little of their blarney, with a success that provoked
the indignation of Byron, who at this time was connecting himself so closely with the discontented party in Italy,
that he was inclined to look on all the proceedings of
royalty with more than usual disfavour[1]—all alike, from
O'Connell down to the spalpeen who paid the king's turn-
pike for him, making the air ring with their cheers on every
occasion.   And it seemed only fair that the Scotch should
have a similar opportunity of testifying their loyalty.
Good sense and good humour, fortified by the real regard
which George IV. seems to have entertained for his
petitioner, led the king to consent, and to promise a
visit to Edinburgh in 1822.   August was to be the time,
and during the preceding months the whole country was
in a fever of loyal expectation and preparation.   But, if
the people had the pleasure of the excitement, the whole
burden of the work to be done in the arrangements for
the sovereign's reception fell upon Scott.   There was of
course a committee, but, in fact, he was the committee.
One day he was called upon to settle the order in which
the clans had stood at Bannockburn against the King of
England, five hundred years before, as the precedent to be
followed in marshalling them now when they were all, (as
Wildrake was hereafter to say) "one man's bairns."   At
another time he was called in to devise a motto for a

---

[1] " Wear Fingal his trappings, O'Connell proclaim
    His accomplishments, his ! and thy country convince
    Half an age's abuse was an error of fame,
    And that Hal is ' the rascalliest sweetest young Prince.' "
                              BYRON, *The Irish Avatar.*

silver St. Andrew's cross, to be presented to His Majesty as the offering of the ladies of Scotland. It was his task to write songs for the banquets, and ballads for the street singers. And it happened that, as on the arrival of the royal yacht in Leith Roads the weather was too foul to admit of the king's landing till the next day, he was the first person to welcome his sovereign to his northern kingdom, having gone out in a boat to convey the St. Andrew's cross, which was most graciously accepted.

It was, perhaps, an indirect compliment, as a proof of the impression made on the royal memory by "Waverley" and "The Lady of the Lake," that at the levée which the king held in the old palace of Holyrood, he wore a Highlander's garb of the Stuart tartan; but it was a designed and open one when, for his visit to the Edinburgh theatre, he commanded " Rob Roy," a play in which Scott's friend Terry, the manager of one of the London theatres, had dramatised the novel.

At the end of the month, the king returned to Windsor, where he took pains to tell every one how pleased he had been with all he had seen, deservedly attributing to " our friend Scott " the credit of having made everything go off so well. Scott, as was natural, was highly flattered by Croker's report of the king's language : which was speedily followed by a more solid gratification. The last of the Stuarts was dead ; and it had occurred to Scott that it would be a not unfitting recognition of the now universal loyalty of all Scots, Highlanders as well as Lowlanders, to the dynasty, if the attainders passed against those who had suffered for their share in the '15 and the '45 were now reversed, and the titles restored. He himself drafted the memorial to be presented by the representatives of the then proscribed families. And when, with as little delay as was consistent with necessary forms, that petition was granted, by the royal recommendation ,o Parliament to pass an Act for the reversal, those whose family honours were now restored vied with each other in recognising the debt they owed to Scott for his exertions in their favour, to which they in a great measure attributed the success of their application.

The royal squadron had scarcely got clear of Leith Harbour on its return to the south before he resumed his work. He had already two novels on the stocks : " Peveril of the Peak," and " Quentin Durward," to which a third, " St. Ronan's Well," was soon added, all to be given to the public before the end of the next year. But this strain on his powers, though he does not seem to have been conscious of it, had begun to tell on his health, and in November, while " Peveril " was receiving his finishing touches, he was arrested in his work for a while by an attack which had too much of an apoplectic character not to cause some uneasiness to his friends, and even to himself. For a moment too it brought on, what of all afflictions was the most foreign to his natural temperament, a painful depression of spirits : to which we may probably attribute a fear he expressed that " 'Peveril' would smell of the apoplexy." In my own opinion it certainly does not : but we learn from Mr. Lockhart that it was subjected to criticism somewhat less favourable than usual . one objection, very generally taken, being that the part attributed to Fenella was so unnatural as to be incredible; another, that to spread a tale over so long a period as

twenty years was scarcely consistent with the unwritten
laws which ought to govern all fiction. There were even
some who thought that too many characters of greater
or less prominence were brought upon the scene. And,
finally, it was complained that the plot was unskilfully
framed. The first objection was in reality easy to be
refuted, though the refutation was never given till the
tale was republished in the collected edition of the entire
body of novels. For the pretended dumbness and deaf-
ness of Fenella only differed in the greater length of time
the imposture was kept up from a fraud actually practised
on Scott's own grandfather, one of whose servants kept up
for three or four years the pretence of labouring under
the same deprivation, till the commission of a petty theft
under her eyes threw her off her guard, and she screamed
out three or four words of angry reproof, much as Edith,
in the "Lord of the Isles," recovers her voice to bring back
the wavering Islesmen to a sense of their duty. The length
of time which elapses between the first and last scenes may
be justified by the example of Shakespeare in more than
one of his plays ; though, if such protraction of time be a
faulty violation of the rules of art, it must certainly be less
allowable in a drama, which is represented to the eyes of
the audience in two or three hours, than in a novel whose
perusal occupies many sittings. It had a precedent too
in " Guy Mannering," where a still longer period had
been allowed to elapse without any such objection being
raised in any quarter. It seemed as if the unparalleled
excellence of Scott's works had made his readers more
critical and exacting. That the winding up of the
tale by the marriage of Julian and Alice is foreseen

from the beginning, if a fault, is one shared by so many similar works that it ceases to be such. From the first entrance of the characters it is seen that Waverley is to marry Rose ; that Bertram is to become the husband of Julia ; and Frank Osbaldeston of Die Vernon ; and, again, to fortify our position by the example of Shakespeare, that Benedict is to break his vow of living a bachelor in favour of Beatrice, and that the loves of Orlando and Rosalind, though conceived at "first sight," are to find the fit recompense for their fidelity in their union.

If, however, we admit the correctness of the judgement that finds some defects in the plot, the confession would willingly have been made by the author himself. For the plot was never the chief object in his eyes ; the object of his chief study was rather the portrayal of character, if the personages were real, and the consistency of character if they were the creatures of imagination, and in both these respects no deficiency can be found in " Peveril." The loyal old knight, Sir Geoffrey ; the magnanimous Lady Derby ; the clever but infamous Christian ; the profligate, witty, but weak Buckingham ; the fanatic Bridgenorth—all seem faultless alike in conception and in execution. And, if any imperfection can be detected, it is rather in the picture of the king, presented as a good-humoured amiable voluptuary, entitled even to some credit for contriving the acquittal of the Peverils, when, in fact, his whole conduct with respect to the Popish plot stamps him with undying infamy as one of the most heartless of tyrants.

Whether the number of characters in either a novel or a drama be excessive, must depend on the genius of the artist. If they are so numerous that he is unable to manage them, but fails to keep them distinct from each other, or (still worse) makes them inconsistent with themselves, such an overestimate of his powers is undoubtedly a fault. But, on the other hand, if the personages are amply diversified, and the character of each maintained in harmonious keeping throughout the piece, any cavil at their number seems captious, and we should rather praise the author's skill than complain that he has contrived such an opportunity for its display.

Vigour and vivacity were so inseparable from Scott's nature that it is almost superfluous to point out the various scenes in this novel in which they are conspicuously exerted: but in their way it would be hard to surpass Sir Geoffrey's escort of Lady Derby to Port Royal, with its humorous sequel in the expedient with which he proposes to heal Bridgenorth's injured honour, which, in Sir Jasper's view, "lies a bleeding" ever since he was pulled out of his saddle at Hartley Nick; or the rescue of Julian from the clutches of Bridgenorth; or, in a different kind, the graceful picture of the Court, as Charles strolls through the rooms in easy familiarity, "exchanging now a glance with a Court beauty, now a jest with a Court wit, now beating time to the music, and anon losing or winning a few pieces of gold in the chance of the game to which he stood nearest,"—every person of every rank, king and flute-player, noble and gaoler, gallant knight and perjured witness, proud countess and coquettish waiting-woman, being drawn with equal fidelity and spirit, as if the author revelled in the creation of difficulties that he might display his genius in surmounting them.

But if the criticisms on " Peveril " were less favourable
than those which had greeted most of his other works,
he did not see in that circumstance any such reason
for discouragement as should induce him to lay aside
his pen : it only seemed a hint to try a new field.   As
he wrote to Ballantyne :

> " The mouse who only trusts to one poor hole
> Can never be a mouse of any soul. "

And accordingly he crossed the Channel, and in
"Quentin Durward" broke wholly new ground, laying
the scene of action in a foreign country, taking foreign
princes and nobles for his chief characters, and, it may
therefore be said, inviting the verdict of foreign critics
equally with the judgement of his own countrymen.
His aim was so high as to render failure more
conspicuous, if failure there had been, and there was
apparently more risk of failure in this undertaking, since
he could have no personal knowledge of the manners
and feelings of Frenchmen in the present age, much
less in one so far removed as that of Louis XI.   He
was not unaware of the difficulties of the subject he had
chosen ; it has been pointed out before that, in treating
of characters prominent in real history, his chief object
was to give a correct idea of their character, and the
very difficulty of so portraying Louis seemed an additional reason for making the attempt, so great would be
the credit of succeeding.   If he had been a dramatist,
"the character of Louis, the sagacious, superstitious,
jocular, and perfidious tyrant, would be for a historical

chronicle containing *his life and death*, one of the most powerful ever brought on the stage." And, feeling thus that he had a true insight into it, he resolved to try whether he could not delineate it with equal effect in a novel. It may be suspected that the introduction of Charles the Bold was an after-thought, since, in making provision for the work, it was Plessis-lès-Tours, not Dijon, Péronne, or any Burgundian city or fortress, for information about which he was anxious. But among the authorities which he consulted for further lights on the king's character were the " Memoirs " of De Comines : and, as in them he found a full account of Louis's visit to Péronne, he naturally saw how great and effective an interest the contrast between the crafty and calculating suzerain and his arrogant and fiery vassal would add to his work ; and he felt within himself a proud consciousness of power to do his subject justice. The greater the difficulty, the greater would be the glory of success. The verdict of the French was given without hesitation or ambiguity. A short time before, he had received a singular proof that he had at least one reader and admirer in the country, in a letter requesting the honour of a present of a set of the novels, and expressing a hope that the writer might be allowed to requite it with a gift of champagne. But now all Paris, still the leader of French opinion, became his admirer. As Lockhart describes the reception of the new novel there, "the sensation which it created was extremely similar to that which attended the original ' Waverley ' in Edinburgh, and ' Ivanhoe ' afterwards in London." In Germany the feeling produced was nowise different ;

"Germany had been fully awake to his merits years
before ; but the public there also felt their sympathies
appealed to with hitherto unmatched strength and
effect."

And now that the enthusiasm created by its first appearance has subsided, and given room for calmer criticism,
it must be admitted that the admiration thus excited by
"Quentin Durward" was not undeserved. Scott could not,
indeed, on this occasion exercise what Byron had described
to the Regent as among his especial gifts, his power of
making " princes fascinating " : since it would be hard to
find any who have possessed fewer attractive qualities
than those he was here portraying. But no historian, not
De Comines himself, has set the two men more vividly
before us. We have Louis, crafty, cruel, unscrupulous,
and shameless, ever moving straight to the end he
proposed to himself, bearing any amount of contradic-
tion if, by apparent yielding, he could attain that end ;
so devoid of all sense of honour as to accept with
something more than acquiescence the Lady Isabelle's
indignant comment that, if indeed he had invited her
aunt and herself into France, it would have been hard
to reconcile his treatment of them there with the character of a gentleman ; and equally indifferent to the
charges of downright falsehood which Charles's minister
does not conceal from him are in the Duke's power
to substantiate ; at the same time a slave to superstition
so abject, as to allow himself to be baffled in his projects
of revenge by the cunning threats of his astrologer,
though the Italian's own condition as a prisoner seemed
to prove him either incompetent or corrupt; yet combining

with these odious or contemptible qualities a coolness
and presence of mind amid the most imminent dangers,
to which it is impossible to refuse some degree of
respect ; and by which he eventually baffles Charles's
purposes of angry revenge as completely as Galeotti had
defeated his own.

On the opposite side we have Charles, the Achilles of
the day,

" Impiger, iracundus, inexorabilis, acer,"

haughty, passionate, and implacable ; claiming to be
regarded as "the mirror of knighthood," the very glory of
chivalry ; yet so destitute of every feeling of a true
gentilhomme as to launch the foulest menaces against
a lady, if she dared for a moment to claim a right to
a voice in the disposal of her own hand ; vain of his
wealth, and parading his magnificence with a sumptuous
splendour and pomp, as yet unseen in any court of
Christendom ; aiming at transmuting his ducal coronet
into a kingly crown ; while, at the same time, by his
treatment of Louis, he is, as it were, giving a lesson to
all Europe, that even kings enjoy no immunity from insult
and even personal violence. Apparently his character
had made a deep impression on Scott, since in a later
novel, we shall see that he again reproduces him with
even greater fulness.

The admiration these portraits excited may have been
in some degree enhanced in this country by the circumstance that Louis and Charles were less familiarly
known to us than Richard, or Mary, or Elizabeth ; so
that there was greater novelty in their " presentment,"

which was felt to be hardly a "counterfeit." But it did not need this additional attraction; for it must be acknowledged that none of our native princes had been delineated with more powerful and lifelike truth than these, not less strangely contrasted in their character than in their ultimate fortunes : Louis accomplishing all his objects, and leaving to his heirs an authority more absolute and more secure than had been possessed by the greatest of his predecessors; and Charles, as will be seen in "Anne of Geierstein," perishing ignobly in a warfare madly provoked by his own arrogant violence, and a victim to the basest treachery.

It was perhaps as another variety of "refreshment for the machine" that, after this grand work, Scott surprised his admirers by one of a wholly different class, a novel of society. It may be that, to employ the not very new simile of the elephant, who can beat down the gate of a castle or pick up a pin, he desired to show that he for whom princes and battles in the stricken field were not too great, could shine equally in dealing with a lady's tea-table. As a novel of society "St. Ronan's Well" cannot be denied to stand high, perhaps the very highest in its class; for, till we come down to our own generation, and to Thackeray's incomparable " Pendennis " and the " Newcomes," it would be difficult to find any in which the scenes of gossip, jealousy, and scandal, that make up no little of the wearisome routine of life at a watering-place, are enlivened with humour such as he gave the world in the testy, domineering, meddlesome, benevolent old Nabob, and that pattern of despotic landladies, Meg Dodds. It is no slight testimony to the supe-

riority in this point of "St. Ronan's Well" over its
fellows of the same class, that, sixty years after its first
appearance, it is still from time to time republished. But
novels of society have never been reckoned works of a
high order; and this will never be numbered among his
works of the first class. It is, however, worthy of remark
that he himself rated such works very highly; and, with
his habitual modesty, seems to have regarded the ability
of other authors in this line as superior to his own.
Miss Austen's novels "describing the movements, feelings, and characters of ordinary life" are extolled by
him in his private journal in the warmest terms. He
contrasts them with his own work as something of a
higher class, or at least of one in which it is more
difficult to attain perfection. "The Big Bowwow
strain," he says, "I can do myself like any man going;
but the exquisite touch which renders ordinary common-
place things and characters interesting from the truth
of the sentiments is denied to me." And it may be that
"St. Ronan's Well" was an experiment whether such a
power was beyond his reach or not; and that his never
repeating it was a practical confession that he was not
altogether satisfied with his performance. Few, however, will concur with him in this depreciation of his
powers; and it is worth remarking that the great French
novelist, Balzac, pronounced "St. Ronan's Well" "the
most finished" of all his productions. By "the Big
Bowwow strain" Scott evidently means those tales in
which "fierce wars" and the deeds of princes "moral-
ised his song;" many, however, of his works deal with
no such fiery deeds or dignified personages, but are as

completely occupied with the feelings and characters
of ordinary life as those of Miss Austen or the other
ladies, Miss Edgeworth and Miss Ferrier, whom
he proceeds to eulogise; yet few will place "Guy
Mannering," "The Antiquary," or "The Heart of
Midlothian," below the very best of their performances.

"Redgauntlet," which followed "St. Ronan's Well"
in the summer of 1824, was generally regarded as hardly
equal to the other historical or semi-historical novels.
Not that many of the scenes were not drawn with all
his accustomed animation, or that the leading characters
were not painted with admirable life and consistency.
But it suffered by its inevitable comparison with
"Waverley." There Charles Edward had been presented to us, not only full of youthful spirit and enterprise, but for a time triumphant in victory, and equally
inspiring when holding his court in the palace of his
ancestors at Holyrood. The contrast between these
achievements, and his visit in disguise to Fairladies,
with his prudent flight at the warning of a single king's
officer was too humiliating for the mightiest genius to
overcome, and "Redgauntlet" was therefore commonly
placed in the second rank. In Lockhart's opinion,
however, it is in one respect fuller than many others of
interest to Scott's admirers, since "it contains, perhaps, more of the author's personal experiences than any
other of the novels, or even than all the rest put together"—Saunders Fairford being recognised by those
who remembered him as no unfaithful portrait of Scott's
own father; while Alan's experiences in the Law Courts,

and perhaps some of Darsie's ramblings, whether as sportsman or a listener to Wandering Willie's anecdotes, were in their general character drawn from the personal recollections of his own early manhood.

CHAPTER X.

SCOTT had now been for many years in the enjoyment of an income of £10,000 a year from his
works alone, besides the emoluments of his office. The
modest cottage at Abbotsford had grown into a castle,
the hundred-acre farm into a domain. His position as a
man of wealth appeared secure, and not less so to himself
than to the rest of the world; and it begot claims on
his hospitality which were too congenial to his disposition
not to be gladly listened to. Besides his inborn fondness
for society, it was natural that he should feel a pride in
showing his friends a home which was so wholly the
work of his own hands. On his first entrance into
possession, the prospect had been bleak and uninviting,
having, as he had described it in some of his letters,
nothing to recommend it but the river; but the plantations, which had been his earliest care, were already
taking off the appearance of newness, while as coverts
they were giving shelter to the game; and he could
begin to calculate the time when they would have
arrived at the dignity of groves; and, since timber
in that day commanded a high price, would furnish
profitable work for the woodman. But in these

improvements the idea of profit was second to that of beauty. He had a painter's as well as a poet's eye for scenery. Indeed, he compared a planter to a painter, for "the exquisite delight" afforded by such employment. "The planter," he said, "is like a painter laying on his colours : at every moment he sees his effects coming out. There is no art or occupation comparable to this; it is full of past, present, and future enjoyment." But no sort of natural beauty was overlooked by him. He was not the man to whom "the primrose on the river's brim" was merely a yellow primrose : not only the wood, but the verdant meadow, the brown heath, the rifted rock, had all their beauty recognised by his poetic taste ; and perhaps above all he placed water : in the babbling spring, such as the Diamond of the Desert, in lake, such as Loch Katrine, and still more in river. The "rapid Anio" was not more dear to Horace, than the "Bonnie Tweed" and its feeders, Teviot and Yarrow, were to him ; and he surpassed Horace in the constancy of his partialities. If Horace loved Tibur when he was at Rome, on the other hand when at Tibur he sighed for the city; but never when at Abbotsford did Scott wish himself in Castle Street. Nor was he more diligent in the improvement of the surroundings of his home than in the embellishment of the house itself, in which his antiquarian tastes found full scope for their indulgence. Except his wife's drawing-room, the decorations of which chivalry warned him to leave to its mistress, every room was a museum. He was a member of the Roxburgh Club in London, and the founder of the Ballantyne Club in Edinburgh, having the

same objects as its London brother. He even enlivened
its suppers with a song dedicated to the praises of old
books and old wines, as Mr. Oldbuck had extolled them
some years before; and Mr. Oldbuck himself never
took greater pride in the acquisition of an old book, an
ancient carving, or any genuine relic of old times. Over
one mantelpiece hung the sword of the great Montrose,
on another lay the pistols of Charles Edward; and, as
his zeal for the preservation of Melrose or Roslin for-
bade his appropriating the slightest fragment of their
architecture, he contented himself with "casts in plaster
of the foliage, the flowers, and grotesque monsters, and
sometimes the beautiful heads of nuns and confessors,"
on which, from his earliest infancy, he had loved to gaze.
Sport was not forgotten : many a noble head of "a stag
of ten," who had bounded gracefully "down the glen,"
adorned the hall; and two noble staghounds stood
sentries over the whole collection. These, indeed, were
at least as characteristic of his tastes as his plantations or
his relics : without them we could not fancy the place to
have been Scott's. All true poets have loved dogs.
Homer immortalised Argus. Duke Theseus, in the
pride with which he extolled his hounds of "the true
Spartan breed," was, we may be sure, expressing the
feelings of Shakespeare himself. One of the tenderest
effusions of Byron's muse is dedicated to the praise of
his "friend" Boatswain. But neither the ancient nor
the modern bard equalled Scott in their appreciation of
those qualities which qualify dogs so especially to be the
companions of man, nor had any regarded the whole race
with such fondness as that with which he has, in verse or

prose, celebrated the fleet Lufra and the faithful Bevis, Elphin, in "Old Mortality,"—the Argus of his old master,—and the rough little Wasp. One of the marks by which Mr. Adolphus, in his letters to Mr. Heber, identified the author of "Waverley" with the poet of "The Lady of the Lake," was the persistence with which, wherever it was possible for a dog to contribute in any way to the effect of a scene, the very dog that was required was always to be found in his proper place and attitude.

In any other hands the house itself might well have been accounted one of the shows and boasts of the country. But it was not the antiquarian treasures it contained that strangers (often coming from distant lands) most desired to see, but the owner himself, for he was as eminently endowed with the genial qualities which make the possessor attractive, as with those grand gifts of genius which made his acquaintance sought as an honour. And, on one ground or the other, the ever-open door was called on to receive an unparalleled variety of guests. Princes led the way : the widowed husband of Princess Charlotte, and Prince Gustavus of Sweden who, since his father's dethronement, had been studying, or "what princes call studying, at Edinburgh." Then came nobles and squires beyond all power of counting, and, more magnificent than "Baron or Squire or Knight of the Shire," Mrs. Coutts, formerly an actress, soon to be a Duchess, attended by the little Duke who was to make her such, and one of her physicians ; for the health of the owner of so many millions could not be entrusted to the care of a single doctor. But she forebore to dazzle the country folks with her undimmed magnificence ; and, though she drove about Edinburgh with seven carriages and four, she contented herself with three in her descent upon Abbotsford ; and even the occupants of those, including as they did two bedchamber women, two ladies' maids, and other dependents, severely taxed the ingenuity of Lady Scott to arrange suitable accommodation for them.

There were also more congenial visitors : Sir Humphry Davy, Wordsworth, Miss Edgeworth, Moore, and Captain Basil Hall. In fact, the more eminent a man was for ability of any kind, the more eager was he to pay his tribute of admiration to, and to acknowledge the pre-eminence of, Scott. And the two last-mentioned have left journals or memoranda of their visits, which are of special value as showing what manner of man Scott was in his domestic life, and his daily intercourse with friends and acquaintances. Miss Edgeworth remarks that " Dean Swift said that he had written his books that people might learn to treat him as a great lord, but that Sir Walter wrote his that he might be able to treat people as a great lord ought to do." And so, in fact, he did treat his visitors, not with any assumption of lordly superiority, but with that courteous hospitality which puts every one at his ease, and regards all guests, whatever may be their rank or want of rank, so long as they are guests, as on a footing of equality. There was no ostentation or parade of himself or his belongings. The mornings were spent in showing his visitors whatever was most noteworthy, or what he thought most likely to interest

them in the neighbourhood, their walks being occasionally interrupted as some anecdote or appropriate tale
occurred to his recollection, which, whether in verse or
prose, "came like poetry from his lips." Captain Hall
had the good fortune to be at Abbotsford at Christmas.
To his mind the maintenance of the primitive fashions
of that festive season in the " Hogmanay Guisards," and
the largesses of cakes and silver pennies to the boys and
girls who bore their part in them, were not different
from what might have been expected from Scott's attachment to old customs. But, in what he witnessed on
Sunday morning, the host showed that his old-fashioned
notions extended to more serious things. He was setting
a noble example of the compatibility of the highest genius
with the deepest reverence, for—

" As his guests rose from breakfast," he said :
" Ladies and gentlemen, I shall read prayers at eleven,
when I expect you all to attend. He did not," the jour-
nalist continues, "treat the subject as if ashamed of it,
which some do. He did not say, 'Those who please may
come, and any one who likes may stay away,' as I have
often heard. He read the Church of England service,
and did it with singular beauty and impressiveness, varying
his voice according to the subject : and, as the first lesson
was from a very poetical part of Isaiah, he kindled up,
and read it with a great deal of animation, without, however, interfering with the solemnity of the occasion."

With his permanent neighbours, " whether high or
low, he had great influence, engendered and maintained

by a constant, quiet interchange of good offices," and to
Captain Hall it was especially "interesting to see the
consideration all ranks showed for him, treating him with
respect at once, and with kindness and familiarity." One
feature in his conduct with which Captain Hall was especially struck throughout was the delight he took in the
stories told by others, and the total absence of all desire on
his part to engross the attention of the company. Mme.
de Staël, after her first meeting with Coleridge, described
him as very good at the monologue, but with no taste at
all for the dialogue. Scott was the very reverse of this;
it never seemed to occur to him that his conversation
was better worth listening to than that of others. He
was more anxious to draw out the wit or shrewdness of
his guests than to parade his own ; and, if anything could
add to the attraction of his genius, it was the utter absence of all pretension or consciousness of it on his part.

Some of the visitors wondered how a man, who seemed
so completely to devote his whole time to his friends,
could find leisure for the production of works so numerous
and so excellent ; and, to satisfy his own mind, Captain
Hall entered into an arithmetical calculation on the subject. There is something comical in the way he arrived
at the conclusion to which he came. He counted the
number of letters (864) in each page of " Kenilworth,"
and (777) in each page of his own journal. Of this
journal he in ten days had written one hundred and
twenty such pages, which in bulk would be about equal
to one hundred and eight pages of " Kenilworth." Thirty
days, therefore, would be enough to allow for each
volume of a novel ; and as it was generally known "that

Sir Walter composed his works just as fast as he could write," he was convinced that there was no reason, as far as the time necessary for composition was required, to refuse agreement with the general opinion which assigned the authorship of the novels to his host.

Of all Scott's visitors few met with a more sincere welcome than Moore ; and there can hardly be a stronger proof of the catholicity, as some critics would call it, of his tastes, and of his eager recognition of every sort of ability, than that he should have appreciated, with apparently equal sincerity of approval, works and men so widely different as the " Excursion " and its author on the one hand, and, on the other, the Irish melodies of the minstrel of Ireland, and (Tory though he was) the witty political satires which expressed far more of Moore's genuine character than the sentimental effusions with which he enlivened the fashionable coteries of the fine ladies of London. Moore also, as has been already intimated, preserved some records of his visit ; and the incident to which he attached the greatest importance, as having afforded him at once the highest gratification and the greatest surprise, was that "he mentioned the novels, without any reserve, as his own." To employ a modern phrase, the authorship had long been "an open secret." Captain Hall, as we have just seen, had taken the trouble of making calculations which would have been thrown away if he had had any doubt on the subject. Years before, Byron, among the new books which he instructed Murray from time to time to send him during his absence from England, placed in the front rank any books "by, or reasonably presumed to be by, Walter Scott." And in 1821 an eminent London barrister, Mr. Adolphus, had published a volume of letters or essays, in which, by a comparison of the, as yet, unowned novels with the poems, he accumulated proofs sufficient to ensure a verdict at the Old Bailey, that works so kindred in spirit were not, could not be, the work of two individuals, but that the avowed author of the " Lay," and the anonymous author of " Waverley," were one and the same person.

As we have seen, it had long ago been remarked by a very shrewd critic of such matters, especially as denoting the wide difference of disposition between Scott and Jeffrey, that no one was more uniformly indulgent in his judgement of other authors than Scott.   On the other hand, few have been more severe on their own works than he.   And he began to suspect that, as he expressed it, his " vein of fiction was nearly worked out," and " to think seriously of turning his hand to history."   As he expressed his opinion to Constable, " historical writing had not been adapted to the demands of the increased circles among which literature had already found its way." And he contemplated providing those whose taste led them to the study of history, with a work of a higher class, as he regarded it, than those on which his fame was as yet founded.   Byron had for a time, as he himself said, been reckoned

" The grand Napoleon of the realms of rhyme."

Constable was aspiring to be the Napoleon of the realms of *print*, and Scott, mentioning his misgivings as to his ability to continue his *novels* with effect, asked him what he should think "of taking the field with a Life of the other Napoleon." It was his first hint of a work which he had evidently long had in his mind, perhaps ever since his visit to Waterloo and Paris ten years before. And its promulgation at this moment was probably owing to an unfavourable opinion pronounced by James Ballantyne on "The Betrothed," the first of a pair of novels, "Tales of the Crusaders" as they were entitled, which were passing through the printer's hands ; but the second of which, " The Talisman," when that too was delivered, was, in the same critic's view, so brilliant, that if he had had a little more patience, his disapproval of " The Betrothed" would probably have been kept to himself. It may be admitted that " The Betrothed " is hardly entitled to rank among the author's tales of the first class, though it would have made a high reputation for any other novelist. But all the world agreed with the printer that "The Talisman" was one of the author's masterpieces, and that too, though, as Richard I. was the chief character, it had to face a comparison with the magnificent "Ivanhoe," of which the Lion-hearted monarch had also, in the general opinion, been the hero. And it was followed by others which showed that the author's modest estimate of his genius, as a vein which had been worked out, was unduly disparaging.

For, to say nothing for the moment of the first series of "The Chronicles of the Canongate,"—"Woodstock," "Anne of Geierstein," and "The Fair Maid of Perth," which filled the whole of the second series, showed that his vein of original composition was still far from being worked out. Few things in his son-in-law's candid and generally admirable biography seem to me stranger than that Mr. Lockhart should have been so daunted by the criticism of Mr. Senior, criticism which, after all, was only partly unfavourable, as to deny to the first-mentioned, " Woodstock," a place in the very front rank of the novels. In one point only Mr. Senior's criticism appears well founded. " The Cromwell and Charles II. are inaccurate as portraits " (he admits that, " as imaginary characters they are admirable ") ; " Charles is perhaps somewhat too stiff, and Cromwell too sentimental ; " nor, though on widely different grounds, is it strange that some dissatisfaction with both these portraits should be felt by those who think that the portrait of a historical character should so far be true to history as at least not to gloss over the most odious vices and crimes. Too well known are the massacres of Drog-heda and Wexford, where, in spite of all Lord Macaulay's rhetorical artifices, it is certain not only that the entire garrisons of both towns (and these, it must be remembered, English soldiers, defending their posts in obedience to every rule of military discipline) were ruthlessly massacred, but that of the peaceful citizens scarcely one escaped the swords of Cromwell's butchers, carrying out his express orders. All the world has adopted the eloquent denunciation of Schiller in branding Tilly and Pappenheim, the destroyers of Madgeburg and its citizens, with well-deserved execration. No one has attempted to defend the slaughter, without trial, of Lord Derby, Lord Capel, the Duke of Hamilton, and scores of other noble and gentle victims, whose sole crime was resistance to the arms of the tyrant who had slaughtered their and his own sovereign ; and it is a severe trial to the admirers of the great novelist, and to those who value historical truth, to read in " Woodstock" that Cromwell was not "habitually bloodthirsty."

And as, perhaps to show his impartiality, he attributes to Charles II. something of a highbred generosity in his conduct towards Alice Lee and her lover, we must equally reprobate the attempt to place in a favourable light, for even the most brief moment, the most infamous of all modern sovereigns, who sent to the scaffold scores of innocent persons for participation in the Popish plot, a crime of which he not only knew them to be innocent, but which he also knew never to have had any existence. The great Roman satirist, in what may be called his manual for poets, lays down as one important rule that they should

" Follow report, or feign coherent things." [1]

But both principles are violated in any work of fiction that would represent the murderer of his sovereign and chief adherents in any light but that of the most ruthless shedder of innocent blood that disgraces our annals ; or the heartless prince, who jested as he signed death warrants, in no worse light than that of a thoughtless voluptuary.

It must, then, be admitted that to treat such criminals with indulgence is to put too severe a strain on the privileges of fictitious narrative ; but, if ever such a fault,— for such all our admiration for the author ought not to

[1] Roscommon's translation of Horace's line,
"Aut famam sequere, aut sibi convenientia finge."
HOR., *A. P.* 119.

prevent us from considering it,—could be atoned for by
the vigour with which the whole tale is told, and the
leading characters, widely different as they are, are portrayed, surely its pardon will be secured by the pictures
of the noble old Cavalier, Sir Henry Lee; of the loyal
"plotter," Dr. Rochecliffe; of Colonel Everard, steering
his course as well as his sense of a divided duty will
permit, and amusingly contrasted with his worthy
" clerk," the " roaring boy of Brentford," whose un-
shaken loyalty makes even his debauched effrontery
almost respectable; and, on the other side, of the profligate hypocrite " Trusty Joe ; " of the self-seeking
infidel Bletson, not the less in favour with the powers
that be for his infidelity; of the half-crazy Harrison;
of Cromwell himself, not always hardened against re-
morse for his past crimes, but not for a moment restrained by it from a resolution to commit more, and to
slay the son as he had slain the father, if such removal
could make easier the path to the throne which he so
long and so eagerly coveted, but happily coveted in
vain ; and, to crown all, by one of the most exquisite
of all the author's female portraits, the lovely, high-
minded Alice Lee. Even the critical Mr. Senior, while he
pronounces " Woodstock a picture full of false costume,
and incorrect design," admits it to be " splendidly grouped
and coloured "; and, after all, the latter qualities are of
the greatest weight in gaining the admiration of the reader.
In fact, Mr. Senior admits that the "inaccuracies" in the
characters of Charles and Cromwell, for it is to them we
must suppose him to allude, " never struck him till his
office " (as a reviewer) " forced him to pervert the work

from its proper end, and to read for the purpose of criticism, instead of enjoyment."

Scott's last novels of importance were "The Fair Maid of Perth," published in 1828 as "The second series of the Chronicles of the Canongate," and "Anne of Geierstein," published in May, 1829. Lockhart, while admitting that "The Fair Maid of Perth" has undoubtedly several scenes equal to what the best of Scott's performances can show, "acquiesces in what he regards as the general verdict, which places it only in the second rank of the novels." But his additional avowal, that "it is on the whole a work of brilliant variety, and most lively interest," will probably induce many critics to give it a higher place. When, however, he seems (for he abstains from any express assertion) to rank "Anne of Geierstein" only on a par with it, he allows himself, not unconsciously, nor unconfessedly, to be swayed by the national prejudice that the mere question whether the scenery and character described in a novel are, or are not, Scotch, is the standard by which to judge of their comparative excellence.

In his preface, when "Anne of Geierstein" appeared in the collected editions, Scott admits that, since its original publication, Sir Francis Palgrave had thrown a new and somewhat different light on the proceedings of the Vehmgericht from that which he himself had followed Goethe in adopting. But, in a work of fiction, the author is clearly justified in accepting any generally received tradition. And no one can deny the power with which the trial of the elder Philipson is recounted. But, if the character and proceedings of that mysterious tribunal had been described with accuracy as strict as the most scrupulous antiquarian or historian could require, it would not be by the merit of any single scene that such a work should be judged. A surer test to guide the judgement of the critic would be the admirable truth and discrimination with which are presented to our view the light-hearted King René, with his indomitable daughter, and Charles of Burgundy, reproduced with even greater effect than in "Quentin Durward." Nor may we pass over the vigour and consistency of the portraits of the purely imaginary personages, the honest, simplicity-loving, and at the same time fearless Landamman, the darkly designing priest of St. Paul's, and, above all, of her who has given the title to the tale, now, as a peasant-maiden, treading with unhesitating fearlessness the awful precipices of the Alps, and anon ruling her baronial hall, and awing her "impatient vassals" into submissive propriety, with as calm and self-possessed a dignity, as if she had never known such an occupation as the management of a mountain dairy, never aspired to any richer ornament than a "necklace of jet, if her uncle's fleeces bore any price at the next market."

These portraits alone would justify the most rigorous critic in ranking the tale they embellish among the master-pieces of modern fiction. But he might appeal also to a battle-piece of a spirit-stirring grandeur unsurpassed in prose, whether by Scott himself in "Waverley" or "Old Mortality," or by Napier, when he recounts the prowess of Norman Ramsay, bursting at the head of his batteries through the French ranks at Fuentes d'Onor, or of Wellington chasing King Joseph and Jourdain from point

to point of the glorious field of Vittoria. If a Swiss free-
man still recalls the name of Granson with national pride,
surely all future generations of novelists may boast with
kindred fervour of the genius of that master, who, sitting
at his peaceful desk, and boasting of no weapon but a
rapier unhacked and glinting back the sun's rays only at
a yeomanry review, could yet paint all the

" Pride, pomp, and circumstance of glorious war"

with as sympathetic a fire as if he too had borne a part in
such exploits, and were drawing on the proud recollection
of deeds of derring-do in which he himself had borne no
inglorious share. Even had the picture been less brilliant,
it could hardly have failed to obtain a warm welcome from
those the great deeds of whose forefathers it commemo-
rated. They were excited by it to an admiration as warm
as the critics of Paris had been by " Quentin Durward,"
and more than one token of their gratitude for the honour
thus done to their nation enriched the museum of
Abbotsford by memories from the fields of Granson and
Morat, in the shape of two-handed swords and halberds,
such as that with which Sigismund Biedermann beat
down the Burgundian swords, and stove in many a
helmet, on the field which for ever extinguished Margaret's hopes of vengeance on her Yorkist enemies.

But full justice to Scott's genius will not be done if
no notice be taken of the distractions of the most painful
character amid which these works were composed. The
seizure of an apoplectic character which had alarmed
his friends in 1823, had been followed by others,
more pronounced in their symptoms. His wife, his affec-

tionate partner for nearly thirty years, had long been a
sufferer from asthma, and that had been the parent of
dropsy, which soon proved to be incurable, and which,
in the May of 1826, carried her off, while the last
sheets of "Woodstock" were taxing his attention for
the revision of the proofs. These causes of anxiety
and bitter grief were, however, only known to his immediate friends. But the whole nation was excited to one
unanimous feeling of sorrow and sympathy by the intelligence that the ruin of Constable, and another firm of
publishers, which happened in the same year, involved
him in their fall; that his arrangements of long-stand-
ing with them had the effect of making him a partner
in one of the firms, and that he had to bear his
share of its losses. It was a blow which would have
crushed to the ground any man but one of such a
sturdy manly spirit. But it was encountered by him
with a noble courage which, in the eyes of the moralist,
does him more honour than even his brightest efforts
of genius. He was not without consolation and encouragement. Lord Dudley's exclamation on hearing
it said that he was ruined only gave expression
to the general feeling—"Walter Scott ruined! the
author of 'Waverley' ruined! Only let every one to
whom he has given months of delight give him sixpence,
and he will rise to-morrow richer than Rothschild."
And there were many who, would he have permitted it,
would not have confined their friendship and sympathy
to words. Friends, and even banking firms, pressed
offers of assistance on him. One admirer, whose name
he never knew, solicited leave to place £30,000 to his

credit. Mr. Pole, who had taugnt his daughters the harp, sent to offer him £500 or £600, " probably his all," as Scott records this truly munificent offer. He had reason to say, as he did, that "there was much good in the world after all. But he would involve no friend, either rich or poor; his own right hand should do it." He did not yet know, he could not, indeed, possibly have imagined, the vastness of the burden which the mismanagement of others had laid upon him. His arrangements with John Ballantyne had apparently been dictated solely by his desire to aid an old schoolfellow for whom he had conceived a great regard, and with no view to profit. Indeed, it does not appear that he had ever received a single farthing from the partnership. And, if Lockhart's description of Ballantyne was correct, it was, from the very first, one from which the best that could be expected was, that some day, like the stork in the fable, Scott might draw his head out of the wolf's mouth without destruction. For "no more reckless, thought- less, and improvident adventurer (than Ballantyne) ever rushed into business." And he had mixed up the firm in transactions with others as rash as himself; with Constable and Hurst and Robinson. Of how gigantic a character these speculations were is shown by the immensity of their liabilities. Constable be- came a bankrupt for a quarter of a million; Hurst and Robinson for a still larger sum. And their fall involved the firm of Ballantyne and Scott. An examination of Ballantyne's books showed a balance against it of nearly £120,000, to meet which Ballantyne himself had scarcely a farthing. Morally Scott was blameless for such a state of affairs, or only so far blameworthy as having trusted too implicitly to his partner's over-sanguine statements But legally he was equally responsible with him; and, even if he had not been so, his sense of commercial integrity, and of gentleman-like honour, made him acknowledge his liability for the whole debt, enormous as it was, and resolve to give himself up to the effort to clear it off by his own exertions : " If he lived, and retained his health, no man should lose a penny by him." And he prepared, without a sigh, to sacrifice all the objects which had been his pleasure and his pride. As he records his own prospects—" he had walked his last on the domains he had planted, sat the last time in the halls he had built." But this pain was spared him. The creditors of the bankrupt firms recognised his innocence of the mismanagement which had caused their losses, and not less the unflinching honesty which gave up not only what had been earned, but all he might hereafter be able to earn, till their demands should be satisfied to the last penny.

To earn money now that it was to be devoted to satisfy the creditors of the firm, he worked harder even than when he had looked forward to founding a family and enriching his descendants. His project of becoming the biographer of Napoleon has been mentioned before ; and that was now one of the anchors to which he trusted, not mistakenly, as the event proved, to ride out the storm. For a moment he put the task aside to embark in a political controversy. A Tory himself, he had many personal friends in the Tory ministry ; but he was a Scotchman before

he was a Tory, and he resented, with all the warmth
of that *perfervidum genus*, the restrictions which the panic
of 1825, which had overthrown many a firm of high re-
pute in England, induced the Government to impose on
the Scotch banking system. The biographer of Swift
remembered how the populace of Dublin long idolised
the author of the " Drapier's Letters." In a similar spirit
he now took up the cudgels on behalf of the bankers
of Edinburgh and Glasgow, and, in a series of letters by
Malachi Malagrowther, upheld their knowledge of the
best way of conducting their own business in preference
to that attempted to be forced on them by the financiers
of Downing Street. He could not quite deal with the
subject as Swift had dealt with his. Swift's clients had
been the whole Irish people : as he put it, from the rich
squire who would need an almost countless train of wag-
gons to carry home his half-year's rents, down to the
beggar who must take his leave of a pot of beer for the
rest of his life, since the utmost benevolence of a passer-
by would give him a coin which, in spite of its nominal
value, would only be received for a twelfth part of a penny.
A controversy which turned on an issue of bank notes did
not admit of such demagogic exaggerations, nor perhaps
would such in any case have been suited to the less impulsive Scotchmen. But Scott had more solid ground for his
arguments, which were so weighty as to defeat the ministerial projects, and, (though he never imputed, as indeed
he had no reason to impute, to the Government, any corrupt motive, such as had deservedly barbed the point of
Swift's diatribes) to produce a momentary coolness towards
him on the part of some of the ministers ; especially of

Lord Melville, whose influence in the Cabinet on all the affairs of Scotland was naturally predominant.

These letters, however, were only one of his refreshments, perhaps in that light the more efficacious from the personal interest which he took in the subject; and, so inveterate was his feeling that such diversions from any work of importance were aids to it rather than interruptions, that not a year passed in which essays on various subjects, and articles in reviews, did not proceed from his pen. As a literary man, he considered all scholars as his brothers, and none ever applied to him for such contributions in vain; while, meantime, the works to which he chiefly trusted for the discharge of his obligations as a trader, were carried on with steady perseverance.

It is unnecessary to say more of his novels; for the fourth series of the " Chronicles of the Canongate," " Castle Dangerous," and " Count Robert of Paris," bear such evident marks of broken health, that they have no claim to be taken into account in any record or estimate of his works and genius, though " Castle Dangerous " contains more than one scene which shows that, like Rob Roy at Aberfoil, "his foot is on its native heath," and that he is again the Walter Scott of " Waverley " and " The Abbot."

CHAPTER XI.

BUT it is as a historian that we must regard him for the remainder of his life, his chief work now being the "Life of Napoleon," which, as we have seen, he had proposed to undertake before he had any suspicion of the troubles impending over his head. From the first moment of his conceiving the plan, he had busied himself, and made all his friends busy themselves, in the collection of materials. But he soon perceived that to make the work correspond to his estimate of what it should be, and worthy of his fame, he must go himself to headquarters, to Paris, where alone he could obtain access to official documents which were indispensable, and where he might also meet many of those who had had personal intercourse with the great emperor, and be willing, and even pleased, to contribute the information and anecdotes which they possessed, some hoping to augment, others perhaps to cloud the fame of a hero who, both for good and evil, had left so imperishable a mark on the history of his adopted country.

In October, 1826, he set out on his journey, accompanied by his unmarried daughter, Anne ; taking London

11

on his way, that he might avail himself of access to
documents relating to Napoleon's residence at St. Helena,
which had been preserved in the Foreign Office, of which
his friend Canning was the head. Had he not at this
time been "seized," as he terms it in his journal, "with
a zeal for work," he might not have made much progress
in his researches, so numerous were the invitations which
crowded on him from every quarter, from the king whose
royal command required him to devote a day to visiting
him at Windsor, down to Terry the actor, whose home
above the Adelphi Theatre in the Strand was "like a
squirrel's cage." He records with pleasure the renewal
of his intercourse with all his old friends, and, though his
journal is silent on the subject, we cannot doubt that
his spirits were refreshed by the manifestations of their
regard, as unrestrained and cordial as ever, if indeed
it was not heightened by the deep and respectful
sympathy which his misfortunes, and his gallant beha-
viour under them, excited and deserved. But he could
not spare the great city more than ten days, so impatient was he to get to Paris, where, of course, far more
was to be learnt of Napoleon in his days of power ; the
records of our own Foreign Office being confined to
the period of his captivity. Here again he was welcomed
by an almost equal variety of admirers, from our own
ambassador, Lord Granville, and Count Pozzo di Borgo, a
Corsican by birth, like Napoleon himself, but now the
Czar's representative, down to the Dames de la Halle, a
body of ladies whose position and privileges were recognised, if not in royal edicts, at all events by well-established
custom. In a former age they had claimed their right to

make Marie Antoinette[1] an offering of fruit and flowers.
And now they approached the great Englishman with a
similar offering: "a bouquet like a maypole, and a speech
full of honey and oil, which cost him ten francs."

One of Napoleon's marshals, the gallant Marshal Macdonald, was of Scotch descent, and he was as com-
municative on the subject which had the chief interest
for Scott as Pozzo di Borgo had been, having also had the
opportunity of knowing much more from the campaigns
which he had made under Napoleon's orders. Scott could
not make a much longer stay in Paris than he had made in
London, but he was well pleased with his visit. It was
with a natural pride that he learnt, by undeniable evidence,
that his works had met "with an extensive and favourable
reception in a foreign land, where there was so much,
à priori, to oppose their progress;" and he flattered himself also that "for his work he had done a good deal;
above all, he had been confirmed strongly in the im-
pressions he had formed of the character of Napoleon,
and might attempt to draw him with a firmer hand."
And, on his return to London, he obtained an addition

---

[1] On the occasion of the Dauphin and Dauphinesse (Marie
Antoinette) making their first State visit to Paris after their marriage,
" a banqueting table was arranged for six hundred guests, and these
guests were not the nobles of the nation, nor the clergy, nor the
most renowned warriors, nor the municipal officers, but the fish-
women of the market. A custom, so old that its origin cannot be
traced, had established the right of these dames to bear an especial
part in such festivities. In the course of the morning they had
made their future queen free of their market, with an offering of
fruit and flowers" (The author's "Life of Marie Antoinette,"
chap. vii.).

to his materials of scarcely less value than the personal recollections of Pozzo di Borgo and Macdonald ; for the Duke of Wellington gave him "a bundle of remarks on Bonaparte's Russian campaign, which he had written in his carriage during his late mission to St. Petersburg,"[1] and invited him to correspond with him if he required any information which he might be able to supply. Again he found his society universally courted. He was even requested to call on the Commander-in-Chief, the Duke of York, though the poor prince had not two months' more life before him. Again he was feasted by Cabinet Ministers, and had requests for his opinion of more than one candidate for Scotch appointments. But again, too, he soon began "to tire of these gaieties. The late hours and constant feasting disagreed with him, and he wished for a sheep's head and toddy against all the French cooking and champagne in the world."

His excursion had barely lasted seven weeks: before the end of November he was back at Edinburgh, working hard at the materials he had brought with him, and never flinching for a moment, though he was now the frequent victim of severe rheumatism, caught, in all probability, from the damp sheets of some French inn. His anxious relatives too soon saw that this new complaint was making inroads on his constitution, not only from the severity of the pain, but because it increased his lameness, and debarred him from much of the exercise which is perhaps more necessary to the literary man than

[1] In 1826 he had been sent as ambassador-extraordinary to congratulate the new Emperor (Nicholas) on his accession to the Russian throne.

to those whose lot is differently cast, and which was more
necessary to himself than in former days, since in his
eagerness to finish the " Life " he had greatly changed his
habits, and devoted to his desk the hours which, in more
prosperous times, had been happily allotted to social enjoyment with his family and friends. He was conscious
that he was overdoing it. In the spring of the next year,
he received some " curious papers from Sweden," probably
from Bernadotte himself; and, in recording their arrival,
he adds that " he has wrought himself blind, between
writing and collating, and, except about three or four
hours for food and exercise, he has not till to-day *devauted*[1]
from his task."

By such steady work the " Life " was completed in an
astonishingly short time, when its bulk is taken into consideration. When he first contemplated it, he estimated
its size at four volumes. It had grown into nine, though
they were not all devoted to Napoleon himself, the first
two being a sort of Introduction, in an account of the
French Revolution, a knowledge of the general character
and leading incidents and horrors of which he not unnaturally regarded as essential to a correct comprehension
of the career and character of the extraordinary man, who,
though himself wholly unconnected with them, made
them the steps by which he himself should re-establish the
throne and place himself on it. In this Scott imitated his
countryman Robertson, who, in a former generation, had
prefaced his " Life of Charles V." by an elaborate description of the state of Europe at the commencement of the

---

[1] I suppose a local or obsolete word, which Lockhart thinks
necessary to explain in a note as meaning " ceased."

century in which that monarch reigned. At Midsummer, 1827, the " Life " was published ; two years after he had first broached the idea to Constable, though, according to Lockhart's estimate, if the time occupied by his journey and the other works which he executed within those two years be deducted, the work had really occupied hardly more than twelve months. It cannot be too bold to assert that no work of such magnitude was ever completed in so brief a space of time, and it may fairly be added, of such excellence also. It had a prodigious sale, partly due to the grandeur of the subject, partly to the greatness of the writer's own reputation. In the lives of Dryden and Swift he had proved that the skill of a biographer was among his talents, and, since it is the characteristic of true genius to rise with the greatness of the subject, it was natural that the highest expectation should be raised when the greatest writer of his age undertook a memoir of the most extraordinary man whom that or any preceding age had produced. He was not so unreasonable as to expect to please every one with his portrait of a man who, if he had been unduly admired by some even of our own country-men, had been regarded with an equal extravagance of hatred by others. While the book was going through the press, he intimated his sense that " he should displease 'ultras,' such as Croker, on the subject of Boney ; who was certainly a great man, though far from a good man, and still further, from a good king." But, if that feeling was entertained in any quarter, it does not appear to have been expressed. Goethe, who had himself conversed with Napoleon, could " conceive nothing more delightful than leisurely and calmly to sit down and listen to such a

man, the most celebrated narrator of the century, while
clearly, truly, and with all the skill of a great artist he recalled to him (Goethe) the incidents on which through life
he had meditated, and the influence of which is still daily
in operation." And the only exception to the general praise
was that some critics, hypercritics they may fairly be called,
objected to the lavish imagery of the writer's historical
style. Lockhart apologises for it as a part of his nature,
which he could not throw off. "He could not, whatever
character he might wish to assume, cease to be one of
the greatest of poets. Metaphorical illustrations, which
men born with prose in their souls hunt for painfully,
and find only to murder, were to him the natural and
necessary offspring and playthings of an ever-teeming
fancy." But, if it did not wear too much the appearance
of effrontery to dispute the dictum of a former editor of
The Quarterly Review, we would make bold to deny that
any apology is needed. Byron reckons among the undying glories of Rome, "Livy's pictured page," and
Lockhart's admission that the style of the whole work
is perfectly unaffected and natural, does of itself disarm
the charge of the greater part of its force. If, as is
generally allowed, poetry be the highest class of composition, most surely a certain infusion of the poetical element must give a grace to prose, provided it do
not exceed the bounds of good taste by immoderate
indulgence. It is when its introduction is manifestly
laboured, when its metaphors and similes are far-fetched
and out of place, that it becomes offensive. Rhetorical
artifices are bad, because everything artificial is bad ; but
comparisons and richness of embellishment, whose object

manifestly is not to impress the reader with an idea of the brilliancy of the writer, but to bring the scene or person described more vividly before his mind's eye, are not only legitimate, but graceful and appropriate ornaments. No one has ever condemned Burke's glowing picture of Marie Antoinette, " glittering like the morning star, full of life and splendour and joy ; " nor Macaulay's tale of the relief of Derry, when " all night the bells of the rescued city made answer to the Irish guns with a peal of joyous defiance," though breathing not a little of the spirit which sang in noble verse—

> " How well Horatius kept the bridge
> In the brave days of old." [1]

That the " Life " can no longer be appealed to as the standard work on the subject, is undoubtedly true, and is inevitable. Such a flood of fresh light has been thrown in the present generation both on the Revolution in its earlier stages, and on the career and character of Napoleon himself, by recent publications,[2] that no work can now be considered as completely satisfactory which was composed in ignorance of the revelations which they contain. But no one has denied that what may be termed the external

---

[1] " Lays of Ancient Rome," i. 70.

[2] The correspondence of Marie Antoinette in the collections of M. Feuillet de Conches and M. Arneth; "The Histoire de la Terreur" of M. Mortimer-Ternaux ; the " Origines de la France Contemporaine," by M. Taine ; " The Life of Napoleon," by Lanfrey ; and the far more valuable one (down to 1814) by the Comte de Ségur ; with the voluminous, though carefully-weeded, correspondence of the Emperor himself, are sufficient by their mere titles to show how imperfect any history of Napoleon must be which was composed before the publication of those works.

features of the Revolution, and its eventual master, are portrayed in this "Life" with very general correctness, as they undoubtedly are with picturesque vigour. And the impartiality with which Napoleon himself is presented, must seem the more admirable, if it be recollected with what a personal hatred he was in his lifetime regarded by the vast majority of Englishmen, a feeling in which Scott himself shared to its fullest extent.

One of his objects the book fulfilled in a degree probably beyond his expectations : it produced, before the end of the year, no less a sum than £18,000, a sum which, added to the profits of the novels already mentioned, diminished the debt to Ballantyne's creditors by little less than £40,000. And so sensible were the creditors of the unparalleled greatness of his efforts to save them from eventual loss, and of the sterling integrity which made over to them all the fruits of his labours, that, by a resolution which did as great honour to themselves as to him, they recorded their sense of his exertions, not by a barren expression of thanks, but by a testimonial of the most acceptable character, a present of Abbotsford with all its contents, the furniture, plate, and paintings, the library with its concomitants of relics and curiosities of every description, as an heirloom to keep alive, in future generations of his race, the memory of their gifted ancestor. Such an offering was, as they described it, "the best means they had of expressing their very high sense of his most honourable conduct, and in grateful acknowledgment for the unparalleled and most successful exertions he had made, and continued to make, for them." And, as such, it was deeply valued.

For a moment there seemed a chance of the "Life" bringing with it one consequence of a less pleasing nature. A General Gourgaud, one of Napoleon's suite at St. Helena, took offence at some statements contained in it, founded on documents in our own Colonial Office, which implied that the communications on the subject of Napoleon's treatment, which the general made to our Government, were greatly at variance with the representations which he subsequently made to his friends in Paris. The General's displeasure ultimately vented itself in a furious letter to some of the London newspapers. But at first Scott thought the language which he held on the subject indicated an intention of inviting him to decide the question on (as it was then the fashion to style it) the field of honour. Scott came of too warlike a race to cry "craven" to any such invitation, but prepared, to use the language of Byron, "to hold out his iron ;" and, that he might not be taken by surprise, provided himself with a second. To a friend, who probably thought that a scholar, with whatever brilliancy he might sing of battles, in the actual encounter would not be on fair terms with one whose trade was conflict and bloodshed, and who, indeed, had the reputation of a practised and skilful duellist, Scott explained, that "if he were capable in a moment of weakness of doing anything short of what his honour demanded, he should die the death of a poisoned rat in a hole, out of mere sense of his own degradation."

The success of the "Life" acted as an inducement to further labours in the path of history. Within six months of the publication of the "Life" he sent both the first series of his "Tales of a Grandfather," the tales being a history of Scotland, intended for children (indeed, the grandson, Lockhart's eldest son, John Hugh, for whose instruction they were professedly composed, was not yet seven years old), but not written in the childish style that some purveyors of infantine literature had recently employed. "He was persuaded that both children and the lower class of readers hate books which are written down to their capacity, and love those that are composed for their elders and betters. He would therefore make, if possible, a book that a child should understand, yet a man should feel some temptation to peruse, should he chance to take it up."

How completely he had carried out his idea, was shown by the prodigious sale of the Tales, which exceeded that of any of his novels since "Ivanhoe," and which seemed such a proof that his hold on the public taste was undiminished, that more than one London publisher sought to enlist his services by the most munificent offers. The proprietor of an annual, named "The Keepsake," offered him £800 a year as the editor. Another firm sought to tempt him to edit a journal by a yearly salary of £1,500 or £2,000. But he could not condescend to be a purveyor to "the toyshops of literature." And, apart from any considerations of loss of dignity, any such permanent engagement must have interfered with a project that he and Cadell, one of his publishers, had formed, of publishing all his poems and novels in a vast uniform series, at a cheaper rate than they had hitherto been sold; though they were to be enriched, as no previous edition had been, with separate prefaces and notes to each poem

and novel. At the same time he continued his historical
labours; a second series of the "Tales of a Grandfather"
came out in 1828; a third in 1829; a fourth, on the
" History of France," in 1830; and in 1829 he also
furnished Dr. Lardner's " Cyclopædia " with what Lockhart calls a compendium of Scotch History, in two
volumes, as a companion to Moore's " History of Ireland."

But the furtherance of Cadell's scheme was the object
which now began to engross all his intention. His
expectations of success were so high that in every
mention of it in his journals, he calls it the *opus
magnum ;* but his anticipations fell far short of the
reality. Each poem was to fill one volume; each novel,
as a rule, two; though one, " Peveril," ran to three; and
some, and those not the worst, such as " The Legend
of Montrose," and " The Talisman," did not extend
beyond one. At first the publisher, Cadell, thought an
edition of 7,000 likely to meet the demand. Before the
prospectus had been out a week, he found that 10,000
or 12,000 would be required. And, when the first
volume was published in May, 1829, 35,000 were sold
before the end of the year; and Scott might reasonably
calculate that, before the entire series was completed, his
share of the profit would have nearly, if not entirely,
wiped off all the outstanding claims of Ballantyne's creditors and his own.

He had need of encouragement; for he could not
conceal from himself that his health was rapidly breaking.
The very next month after the first appearance of the
new edition of " Waverley," his physicians found them-

selves called on to contend with ruptures of small blood-
vessels, and attacks of nervousness very foreign to his
disposition, but too evidently premonitory symptoms of
something more formidable; and which, in the first months
of the next year, were verified by an unmistakable seizure
of paralysis. For the moment it yielded to care and
skill; but it is the nature of such attacks to recur; and,
indeed, this had left behind it more than one reminder
of which he was conscious. He seemed to himself "to
speak with some impediment;" his lameness was incon-
veniently increased; "even his handwriting seemed to
stammer." Before the end of the year, the attack was
repeated, though but slightly; but the spring of 1831
brought on a third, combining paralysis and apoplexy,
which confined him to his bed for some days, and which
for several hours filled his whole family with fears that he
would never rise from it.

He did quit it, however, and his next entry in his
journal shows how resolutely he made head against
nervousness. "They have cut me off from animal food,
and from fermented liquors of every kind, and, thank
God, I can fast with any one. I walked out, and found the
day delightful; the woods too looking charming, just
bursting forth to the tune of the birds. I have been
whistling on my wits like so many children, I cannot
miss any of them." But here he was flattering himself;
when a week or two afterwards Lockhart reached Abbotsford, he found his whole appearance fearfully altered.
He required to be lifted on his pony. What probably
affected him more was that he ceased to be able to
write; and the last portion of " Count Robert of Paris,"

for he would not obey the doctor's entreaties to lay his work aside, was dictated to an amanuensis.

Unfortunately at this time political excitement tended to increase his distemper. In the winter of 1830 the Wellington Ministry had been overthrown ; the Duke had been succeeded by Earl Grey ; and the first session of 1831 saw the introduction of the Reform Bill, the sweeping boldness of which astounded all who were not in the confidence of the new Ministry, and, indeed, some who held office in it. Those who remember that time need never be reminded how fierce and universal an excitement drove all the kingdom, Reformers and Anti-Reformers alike, for a time out of their propriety ; and, ill and weak as he was, few were more deeply moved than Scott himself. The middle and lower classes in Scotland were always inclined to Radicalism ; and little inclined to allow fair play to any one who failed to sympathise with them. Public meetings were held in every town and county, and in Selkirkshire Scott conceived that his office of sheriff made it a moral duty to raise his voice in denunciation of the Ministerial measure. To the dismay of his medical advisers, he resolved to speak, and to warn his countrymen against the danger to a nation so wholly different from the French people of following " the French Model." Though his words were few, and carefully inoffensive, to the lasting disgrace of the Jedburgh population, his opposition effaced all their former pride in his genius and patriotism ; he was hooted from the hustings, but, whatever they forgot, he, amid all his natural feelings of indignation, could not forget that he was a gentleman, but, bowing as he retired, took his farewell

in the words of the doomed gladiators of Rome, which
implied at the same time too true a consciousness that
his own end was near at hand, *Moriturus vos saluto.* At
the election which followed on the rejection of the first
Bill, the conduct of the mob was still more disgraceful.
At Selkirk they pelted his carriage with stones ; and
at Jedburgh, where he went to vote for his kinsman of
Harden, he even heard cries of *"burke Sir Walter,"* as
he quitted the town. And it is difficult to doubt that the
violence thus exhibited towards himself, combined with
his forebodings as to the effect of the Ministerial policy
on the future prosperity and honour of the nation, had
an unfavourable effect on a constitution so broken as his
evidently was.

When all hope of permanent amendment from
medicine has been given up, physicians have still one
more resource which is not unfrequently beneficial,
change of climate ; and they now earnestly pressed on
him the absolute necessity of escaping from the rigours
of a Scotch winter by a journey to the milder regions of
the South. Resolute as had been his opposition to the
measures of the Ministers, one of them at least did not
allow the hostility of the politician to diminish his personal regard for the man. One of the last acts of the
Wellington Ministry had been to offer him the compliment of a seat at the Privy Council, an honour never
before conferred on any one who had no other claim
but literary pre-eminence. But, though sensible of, and
grateful for the proposal, he felt that "when one is old
and poor he should avoid taking rank," and, with expressions of gratitude for the compliment, avowed

himself fully satisfied with the distinction of which he had been the subject in a happier time. But now, when Sir James Graham, the First Lord of the Admiralty in the Whig Cabinet, on hearing that he was recom· mended a voyage to the Mediterranean, offered to place a frigate at his disposal for the voyage, that was a kind- ness calculated to be of such real service, by enabling him to avoid the fatigue of an overland journey, no trifling consideration at a time when as yet railways were not, that it was thankfully accepted; and at the end of September he left Abbotsford. He passed a week or two with Lockhart in London, where meetings with some of his old friends cheered him up so much that, though conscious of increasing weakness, and of what was sadder to him than bodily pain, "a heartless muddiness of mind," he did not relinquish the expectation of benefit from his voyage; and expressed to one of his friends, who had called to bid him farewell, the hope of "having a ride together again some day."

"Merrily, merrily, went the bark," when, in the last week of October, the *Barham* set sail with her precious freight; and, after the first day or two of sea-sickness had passed away, those who were not aware that the London physicians had discovered disease of the brain to be at the root of his maladies, might have cherished a belief in the efficacy of the sea air and change of scene, so keenly did he seem to enjoy the various sights which met his view as he sat on the frigate's deck. He even felt strong enough to land on a strange volcanic island, which, a few months before, had appeared above the surface of the sea, and received the name of Graham's island, though the visit could not save it, a few days afterwards, from disappearing as suddenly as it had risen : he even wrote home to one of his Scotch friends a lively description of it for the information of the Royal Society of Edinburgh, of which at one time he had been President, and an account of his own display of "his old talents of horsemanship," as "mounted on the shoulders of an able and willing seaman, he rode nearly to the top of the island."

Malta was the *Barham's* first destination. His arrival had been expected with all the interest that curiosity and admiration could inspire. Every preparation that could tend to his comfort had been made by the governor. And, for a moment, the novelty of the different scenes that met his eye seemed to have a beneficial effect on his spirits He even attended a ball which was given in his honour, certainly as singular a compliment to a man in his state of health as could well be imagined ; and he himself gave one or two dinner parties at his hotel, at which one of the guests has recorded in his journal that he seemed to have recovered much of his old animation, and talked freely, with "the same felicitous introduction of traditionary stories and happy quotations," which had always been characteristic of his conversation. From Malta the *Barham* conveyed him to Naples, and there he was even presented at Court, and went to the Opera. For a moment he felt a renewal of his former spirit, and of his taste for national ballads ; buried himself in the collection of specimens of Neapolitan and Sicilian minstrelsy ; and went so far as to plan a new novel, to bear the name of "The Siege of Malta." It was no little encouragement to him in these projects to learn that "Old Mortality" had been translated into Italian. At another time, as he told one of his friends, he contemplated turning to poetry again, to see whether in his "old age he was not capable of equalling the rhymes of his youthful days." "He had relinquished it because Byron had beaten him out of the field in the description of the strong passions, and deepseated knowledge, of the human heart." But he feared no other rival; and now, in the Mediterranean, the old tradition of the dragon at Rhodes, and its destruction by De Gazan struck him as an attractive subject for a new poem, of which he began to sketch the outline. He was fortunate in his weather, and after three months' stay in that genial climate, he felt so much invigorated that "it seemed likely that he might get better, though he did not think he should ever ride or walk again, but must be confined to vehicular exercise."

But it is evident that he had misgivings as to the improvement which he tried to see; and, as he had never met him, it is strange that he was so much impressed with the news of the death of Goethe, which took place in March. Before the intelligence reached Naples he had been anxious to return home; and it renewed his impatience to do so. "Alas! for Goethe," were his words, "but he at least died at home." "Let us to Abbotsford." And in the middle of April he set out from Naples, stopping a few days at Rome, where the agreeable society which he met again revived his spirits for a moment; but his heart was on the Tweed, and in the second week of May he left Rome, taking the line of the Tyrol. But the weather was often severe, and the cold and the fatigue told with fatal effect : as was sadly seen when, at Nimeguen, on the 9th of June, he was struck down by a fit in which apoplexy and paralysis were combined. He began to fear that he should not be spared to reach home, and, in spite of his weakness, pressed eagerly on his journey. He reached London, but the effort had been too much for him, and more than three weeks elapsed before he could leave it, and then it was but too evident that he was only going home to die.

But even in that thought he found comfort. And in the inmost depths of his heart he felt the emotions which, in his earliest poem, he had attributed to the last Minstrel : "the filial bond that knitted him to the land of his sires," the longing to "feel the breeze down Ettrick's breast," "although it chilled his withered check ; " and, except that he was not, and never could be "forgotten," there was prophecy in the Minstrel's prayer that he might—

> " Still lay his head by Teviot stone,
> Though there, forgotten and alone,
> The Bard might draw his parting groan."

Few tales are more pathetic than the description how, as he caught sight of his own towers, weak as he was, he sprang up in the carriage with a cry of delight ; how, as he skirted the woods which he had planted, his excitement became so eager and violent that his companions, his daughters and Lockhart, could hardly keep him in the carriage ; and how, when he had been lifted into his dining-room and his dogs came round him, fawning on him and licking his well-remembered hands, "he alternately sobbed and smiled over them until sleep oppressed him."

It was the 11th of July : the next day " something like a ray of hope broke on " him, and on those about him, though it could only be that of a temporary respite. He was happy, he told them, to be at home ; he felt better than he had done " since he left it, and might perhaps disappoint the doctors after all." He was wheeled in a Bath chair round his garden ; and, when he had been taken back into the house, and his son-in-law, who tended him with a dutiful affection, read to him a chapter from the Gospels, he expressed himself as greatly cheered by having been able to " follow " the reader " distinctly," " he felt as if he were yet to be himself again." But the delusion, for such it was, if it imposed on himself, could not deceive those who tended and loved him ; day by day, his strength visibly declined. After a few more such days he was confined to his room, and often to his bed. But there was still so much of the original vigour left in his constitution, that he lingered long, though apparently without pain, and it was not till the 21st of September that the long struggle was terminated, and he finally passed away in the presence of all his children.

The family vault was in Dryburgh Abbey : there his ancestors for many generations had been laid ; there, six years before, he had followed his own wife to the grave, and there on the 26th of September, 1832, he himself was buried.

That his death was regarded as a national loss, was attested by the unprecedented honour paid him by nearly every newspaper, which in England as well as in Scotland, assumed the mourning border which they would have worn on announcing the death of a Prince. How bitter was the grief of those who had had the honour and happiness of his acquaintance, was proved by the " deep sob " which, as Lockhart records it, " burst from a thousand lips " as the coffin was taken from the hearse, and " borne on the shoulders of his afflicted serving-men " to his last resting-place.

CHAPTER XII.

IN endeavouring to form a correct and adequate idea of the position to which Scott is entitled in the world of literature, it must, in the first place, be remembered that he is almost the only writer in any language for whom a place in the front rank of both poets and prose writers can be claimed. Dryden was indeed a consummate master of prose style, but the critical prefaces to which he confined his efforts, admirable as they are, cannot be considered as of sufficient originality or importance to entitle him to such a distinction. Goldsmith's prose, whether in "The Vicar of Wakefield," in "The Citizen of the World," or, as far as mere style is concerned, in history, can scarcely be surpassed; but his poems, exquisite cabinet pictures though they be, are on too small a scale to allow us to class him among our great poets. Byron, alluding, it may be supposed, to Voltaire's poetry, especially of the dramatic kind, as well as to his prose, has, in a well-known couplet,[1] placed him on a level with Scott, and even with Shakespeare; and there is probably little doubt that patriotic vanity leads

---

[1] "Had there not been one Shakespeare, one Voltaire,
Of one or both of whom he seems the heir."

many of his countrymen to endorse this estimate; but it is certainly one that has never found general acceptance in this country. Even their own countryman, Schlegel, while expressing his admiration of the genius of Goethe and Schiller, confines it to their poetry; while, if the dramas of Machiavelli be excepted, we know of no Italian who has attempted to shine in both classes of composition.

But Scott had established his reputation as a poet of lofty genius before he won what, in the opinion of the general public, is even a higher rank as the greatest of novelists And it will be better, as more natural, to consider first the qualities of genius displayed in his poems, and to proceed from them to the examination of the powers displayed in his prose fictions.

It may be admitted at the outset that, in richness of poetical imagination, he cannot be placed on a level with his great contemporary, Byron, nor with Shelley; that he presents us with no such wealth of gorgeous imagery, nor, as he himself, we have seen, confessed, with such powerful delineation of strong passion as holds the attention captive in " The Giaour," and " The Bride of Abydos." But he has qualities of his own, not less indispensable as ingredients in poems of the the highest class, nor less essential as characteristics of loftiest poetical genius. In particular he has an animation and sustained energy of action unequalled in the description of battles since the days of Homer, and not confined to " the rapture of the strife," but equally powerful in the ride of Deloraine to Melrose, the mission of the Fiery Cross, and in the resolution with which Arthur puts aside all inferior temptations, and with hand " on Caliburn's resistless brand," presses on his way to the presence of the castle's Queen, the half-immortal Gwendolen. Somewhat akin to these gifts is a grand power in the portrayal of character in man, and, (a far rarer gift,) in woman also. And if we may regard these as the figures in the picture, they are set in frames of exquisite beauty, moulded by an eye of unsurpassed feeling for the beauties of nature, and a skill in painting them with the richest variety, and the most picturesque distinctness. To these must be added a fertility of invention unrivalled by any writer of any kind in our language since Shakespeare. The number of poems and novels, taken together, is nearer forty than thirty. In all these is not one plot, and scarcely one incident, resembling another ; while the personages whose fortunes are chiefly concerned, or by whose actions the catastrophe is brought about, form a gallery of portraits displaying a wealth of conception, and a mastery of execution, to which, except in the works of our great dramatist, we shall look in vain for a parallel. In the poems the comparative smallness of their number, and their limitation to one class of subjects,

" To Knighthood's dauntless deed, and Beauty's matchless eye "—

forbid us to expect that variety of character which is more naturally looked for in the novels, which present a greater variety of objects and ranks. Yet, even when confined to brave knights and ladies fair, genius such as Scott's could embellish his pictures by the nicest discrimination of character. In one poem we have a gallant Prince, whose son is the hero of another ; but, except in

contempt of danger, no two can be more different than
the reckless warrior, defying the might of England on
Flodden Field, and the courteous "Commons' King"

> "bending low
> To his white jennet's saddle-bow,
> Doffing his cap to city dame,
> Who smiled and blush'd for pride and shame."

All knights were bound by the same vows and obligations ; yet how wide is the difference between the
betrayer of Constance, the ruiner of his rival by base
forgery, and the noble De Argentine, than whom "knight
more true in thought and deed ne'er spurr'd a steed."
While, to turn to the softer sex, the saying attributed by
Pope to his friend, that " most women have no characters
at all," has never been more conclusively and trium-
phantly refuted than by the portraits of the stern Lady of
Branksome, yielding to Fate alone what she would grant
to no human affection or influence, and of Constance,
undaunted even in the hour of supremest agony, when
contrasted with the heroines of gentler mood,—with the
duteous Ellen, the self-sacrificing Isabel, the hardly tried
Clare and Edith, and, we may even add, the witching
Lady Heron.

If we pass on to the novels, " they are all one reckon-
ings, save the phrase is a little variations." For it can
hardly be doubted that no small or unimportant part of
their fascination is due to the presence in them also of
the poetical element, of qualities identical in character,
though different in degree and manifestation, with those
that charm us in the poems. We find the same anima-

tion of action, the same truth and vigour in the delineation
of character, the same vividness in the description of
scenery, the same lofty tone of purity and honour, while
to all these varied excellences is added a rich humour,
for the indulgence of which the poems did not afford
equal scope, but which is so prominent a feature in many
of the novels that it was evidently as much a part of
Scott's intellect as any of its higher attributes.

Byron when, as we have seen, he described Scott as
especially " the poet of Princes," could not have anticipated that humbler prose could ever rival the pictures
of the victorious Bruce, or the chivalrous James. And
that man must have been very confident in his strength,
who undertook to portray in prose princes so widely
different as the Lion-hearted Richard, and the most un-
warlike René, king of the Troubadours and of few other
subjects; the rash and reckless Charles of Burgundy, and
the crafty unscrupulous Louis; the graceful gallant
Chevalier, leading his followers to triumph at Preston,
and his pedantic ancestor with his unkingly tremors and
practical jokes ; Mary, the Queen of all Hearts ; and
the haughty, politic Elizabeth, in whom strength and
weakness were so strangely blended, and yet whose very
weakness contributed to the maintenance and strengthen-
ing of her authority.

But it was in his personages of inferior dignity that
his inventive originality, and the richness of his humour,
were more abundantly displayed.   Our limited space
forbids us to dwell on them as fully as our inclination
would prompt.   It must suffice to say that they are
drawn from every rank and class of society, and that

there are scarcely any two between whom the slightest likeness can be traced. Even where there is one point of resemblance, the difference in every other only serves to show the discriminating power of the artist in a stronger light. Except in loyalty to their sovereign, or to him whom they recognise as such, who can be more different than Sir Henry Lee, the Baron, and Redgauntlet ? or, in the gentler sex, than Lady Derby, Lady Margaret Bellenden, Catherine Seyton, Alice Lee, and Die Vernon? Again, the Highland chieftains, Fergus and Rob Roy; the Nabobs, Colonel Mannering and Touchwood ; the villains, Varney, Christian, Rashleigh Osbaldeston, and Glossin—all present the greatest diversity of character and conduct. Nay, the one quality of humour itself we find displayed with the most fertile variety. We have it delicate in the Baron; in Oldbuck; in that prince of advocates, Paulus Pleydell; in the elder Osbaldeston, with his disdain of verse-making, and his faithful clerk, Owen, in similarly commercial spirit, reducing " the golden rule of moral conduct to the arithmetical form of the Rule of Three : let A do to B as he would have B do to him, the product will give the rule of conduct required." We have it again, in its most laughter-provoking breadth, in the Baillie ; in the Dominie ; in that model of military adventurers, the follower of the immortal Gustavus, and Laird of Drumthwacket, Major Dugald Dalgetty ; and in the servants, Richie, and Caleb Balderstone, with their lying excuses and exaggerations, designed for the upholding of their master's credit ; and Andrew Fairservice, whose maxim that service is no inheritance leads him to prefer his own interests to his master's reputation in a way that

brings him in no slight danger of a halter. We have it
also in entire scenes : in the old bedesman's demolition
of the antiquary's pride in the identification of the Kaim
of Kimprunes with the Prætorium of Julius Agricola ;
in Rob Roy's invasion of Justice Inglewood's dining and
justice-room—an episode of richest comedy, to be hereafter referred to more particularly when we deal with
Scott's humour as a whole ; and in others too numerous to recapitulate, but which will readily occur to the
memory of every reader. All alike attest the rich fertility
of the author's invention, and his masterly skill in carrying out his conceptions.

It must be added that the whole series of the novels,
as of the poems, is invested with a peculiar and all-per-
vading grace, with a genial cheerfulness of spirit, and an
uniformly high manly tone of feeling, whether chivalrous,
patriotic, or sentimental, which make them all the
healthiest study for the young, as they are likewise the
most welcome and attractive of relaxations to those of
riper age and more mature judgement.

Even Jeffrey, the least sympathetic of critics, was
compelled to acknowledge the Homeric vigour of
"the tale of Flodden Field." That of Bannockburn,
if inferior to it (which, indeed, has sometimes been
denied), certainly yields to no other picture of warlike
deeds since Hector forced his way through the gates
of the camp of the Greeks, and threatened their fleet
with destruction, and Achilles in his turn pursued
Hector round the walls of Troy. It would generally
be thought more difficult to infuse such spirit and fire
into a prose description ; but with Scott, as with all

whose powers are of the very highest class, the very
greatness of a difficulty begets an increased ability to
surmount it. The description of the destruction of
Edward's cavalry at Bannockburn might be thought to
defy all rivalry—

> " Rushing, ten thousand horsemen came,
> With spears in rest, and hearts on flame,
>   That panted for the shock !
> With waving crests, and banners spread,
> And trumpet clang and clamour dread ;
> The wide plain thunder'd to their tread
>   As far as Stirling rock !
> Down, down, in headlong overthrow,
> Horsemen and horse, the foremost go
>   Wild floundering on the field !
> The first are in destruction's gorge,
> Their followers wildly o'er them urge,—
>   The knightly helm and shield,
> The mail, the acton, and the spear,
> Strong hands, high hearts, are useless here.
> Loud from the mass confused the cry
> Of dying warriors swells on high,
> And steeds that shriek in agony :
> They came like mountain torrent red,
> That thunders o'er its rocky bed ;
> They broke like that same torrent's wave,
> When, swallowed by some darksome cave,
> Billows on billows burst and boil,
> Maintaining still the stern turmoil ;
> And to their wild and tortured groan
> Each adds new terrors of his own."

But spirit-stirring as this is, it may not unequally be
matched with the overthrow of Charles of Burgundy at
Granson, as told by Sigismund Biederman, whose prosaic

nature was roused into eloquence by the thought of the unprecedented triumph, and of the share he himself had borne in it.

"Oh, good Arthur, you would have given ten years of life but to have seen the sight! There were thousands of horse, all in complete array, glancing against the sun; and hundreds of knights with crowns of gold and silver on their helmets. . . . Suddenly the cannon were silent, and the earth shook with another and continued growl and battering, like thunder under ground. It was the men-at-arms rushing to charge us. But our leaders knew their trade, and had seen such a sight before! It was 'Halt! halt! Kneel down in the front, stoop in the second rank; close shoulder to shoulder like brethren; lean all spears forward, and receive them like an iron wall!' On they rushed, and there was a rending of lances that would have served the Unterwalden old women with splinters of firewood for a twelvemonth. Down went armed horse—down went accoutred knight—down went banner and bannerman—down went peaked boot and crowned helmet; and of those who fell not a man escaped with life. So they drew off in confusion, and were getting in order to charge again, when the noble Duke Ferrand and his horsemen dashed at them in their own way, and we moved onward to support them. Thus on we pressed; and the foot hardly waited for us, seeing their cavalry so handled. . . . Hundreds were slain unresisting, and the whole army was in complete flight."

The various masterpieces of description of scenery in the poems are so stamped on the memory of all readers, that we abstain from doing more than referring to them. Prose writers in general seem to have abandoned the idea of making such pictures effective; but Scott, whether in prose or verse, was equally at home with inanimate as with living subjects; equally, also with the pleasing and the terrible. Delicately varied was the beauty of Flora's sylvan boudoir, to which "the path ascended rapidly from the edge of the brook, and the glen widened into a sylvan amphitheatre, waving with birch, young oaks, and hazels, with here and there a scattered yew tree. The rocks now receded, but still showed their grey and shaggy crests rising among the copsewood. Still higher rose eminences and peaks, some bare, some clothed with wood, some round and purple with heath, and others splintered into rocks and crags. At a short turning the path, which had for some furlongs lost sight of the brook, suddenly placed Waverley in front of a romantic waterfall. It was not so remarkable for great height or quantity of waters as for the beautiful accompaniments which made the spot interesting. After a broken cataract of about twenty feet, the stream was received in a large natural basin, filled to the brim with water, which, when the bubbles of the fall subsided, was so exquisitely clear that, though it was of great depth, the eye could discern each pebble at the bottom. Eddying round this reservoir, the brook found its way over a broken part of the ledge, and formed a second fall, which seemed to seek out the very abyss; then wheeling out from among the smooth dark rocks which it had polished for ages, it

wandered murmuring down the glen, forming the stream
up which Waverley had just ascended."

A fearful contrast to a spot so formed by nature, as
might be fancied, for a lady's bower, are the passes, if
they may be so called, of the Alps. And that along
which the Philipsons were proceeding, after they left
Lucerne, was unexpectedly found to have been made im-
passable by an earthslip, which had carried the road
itself away, and hurled it down into a stream several
hundred feet below. "The immediate cause of this
phenomenon might have been an earthquake, not un-
frequent in that country. The bank of earth, now a
confused mass of ruins inverted in its fall, showed some
trees growing in a horizontal position, and others, which,
having pitched on their heads in their descent, were at
once inverted and shattered to pieces, and lay a sport to
the streams of the river, which they had heretofore
covered with gloomy shadow. The gaunt precipice
which remained behind, like the skeleton of some huge
monster divested of its flesh, formed the wall of a fearful
abyss, resembling the face of a newly-wrought quarry,
more dismal of aspect from the rawness of its recent
formation, and from its being as yet uncovered with any
of the vegetation with which nature speedily mantles
over the bare surface even of her sternest crags and
precipices."

Surely, even if there had been no "Lay," no "Lady of
the Lake," no "Lord of the Isles," such word-painting of
such subjects would have entitled the author, like Mr.
Oldbuck, "to pretend to some poetical genius," and may
well bear out the opinion that, among the attractions of

the novels, one, and that not the least, is the large infusion into them of the poetical element.

But something higher than the very richest descriptive poetry is needed to warrant the author's claim to the pre-eminence which is here assigned to him. In the poems we have already seen that that want is richly supplied by the consummate and varied excellence of his female portraits, to which we have endeavoured to do justice in a former chapter. We may venture to say that that excellence is at least equally conspicuous in the novels. Exquisite as are the pictures of Ellen Douglas, of Edith of Lorn, of Isabel Bruce, and the other heroines of the poems, they are fully equalled, to say the very least, by the high-minded Flora ; the equally loyal and unselfish but more fortunate Catherine Seyton ; the bewitching Die Vernon, Edith Bellenden, Anne of Geierstein, and Alice Lee, perhaps the most fascinating of all—the whole, whether in prose or verse, whether matrons or maids, forming a gallery of portraits of which it is suf-ficient to say that the perfection of the execution is worthy of the high purity of the conception. Even women in a lower sphere of life are delineated with a care and delicacy that betoken Scott's wide and keen sympathy with every kind of excellence ; with the unswerving truthfulness, the unsparing sisterly affection of Jeanie Deans, the almost saintly purity of Catherine Glover ; while, even the grim Martha Trapbois is in-vested with interest, if we might not even say with some degree of attractiveness, by her strong shrewd sense, her scrupulous honesty, and her filial reverence for her father's memory.

In a former chapter humour has been mentioned as
more conspicuous, because more appropriate, in the
novels than in the poems. Humour, that is, as distinguished from wit, which, if the difference between them
be rightly understood, was not the kind of pleasantry in
which Scott, though far from deficient in it, was most apt
to indulge. But, of the two, humour seems the higher
quality. Wit is verbal, conversant with language; combining terseness and keenness of expression with nicety
of observation; humour has, comparatively speaking,
little to do with language, and is of different kinds,
varying with the class of composition in which it
is found. In one of his "Imaginary Conversations,"
Landor remarks, " It is no uncommon thing to hear
'such an one has humour rather than wit;' here
the expression can only mean *pleasantry;* for whoever
has humour has wit, although it does not follow that
whoever has wit has humour. Humour is wit apper-
taining to character; and indulges in breadth of drollery
rather than in play or brilliancy of po.nt. Wit vibrates
and spirts; humour springs up exuberantly, as from a
fountain, and runs on. . . . The French have little
humour, because they have little character. They excel
all nations in wit, because of their levity and sharpness."
The critic's view of humour, that it "appertains to
character," it is surely not too much to say, is more
fully and richly illustrated by Scott than by any other
writer in the language since Shakespeare. And here
again it may be remarked that of the various personages who may throughout be regarded as strikingly ex-
emplifying this quality, no two resemble one another in

the very minutest point. To begin with the beginning,
with "Waverley," as the first of the novels, the Baron, for
delicacy of drawing, was perhaps never surpassed in
any subsequent tale. Sir Roger de Coverley is often
extolled as the masterpiece of Addison. As a highbred gentleman the Baron is fully his equal, the pecu-
liarities of neither derogating in the least from their
character as such; while he is superior to him as a man
of action, and also as guiding his conduct not by what
others think of, or expect from him, but by what is due
to his own dignity, and the honour of his family, and
his ancestral privileges. The Antiquary is conceived in
a very different, though nowise inferior, vein of humour;
and he is the more interesting, inasmuch as we can hardly
doubt that the author was in some points, perhaps,
not unconsciously, painting himself. Time and space
would fail us to do justice to the immortal Baillie, whether
embarrassed by his kinsman's unexpected presence in the
Tolbooth, singeing "Garschattachin's plaid with redhot
coulter, or divested of hat and periwig, and hanging in the
air by the middle like bawdrons, or a cloak flung over a
cloak-pin." The Baillie was apparently one of the author's
own chief favourites; but still higher praise will probably
be thought due to the conception of the *ci-devant* officer
of the great Gustavus, the immortal Dalgetty; equally
diverting in the narrative of his experiences in the armies
of Germany, Spain, and Holland; in his dealings with his
new friends and allies at Darlinvarach; in the lectures
on the fortification of Ardenvohr which he bestows on
Sir Duncan; and, above all, in his detection of the
treacherous Argyll, and his substitution of the Mar-

quis for himself in his own dungeon at Inverary. Even "St. Ronan's Well," though a mere novel of society, and as such not claiming to stand on the same level with works of a higher class, is enlivened with more than one richly humorous delineation, and of most varied character; such as the sentimental Lady Penelope; that model of landladies, Meg Dods, insisting on her right to "a *corpus delicti*, a *habeas corpus*, or any other *corpus* that she liked, so long as she was ready to lick and lay down the ready siller;" the ladies being matched by Mr. Cargill, the most absent of learned divines, and the equally original occupant of Mrs. Dods' blue room, the "Nabob."

In these instances the humour pervades the whole conception of the character. Elsewhere we find some single scene or incident equally provocative of amusement, as in the meeting at Justice Inglewood's, already mentioned, where "the frightened craven, Morris, was scared out of his seven senses by seeing the real man while he was charging the innocent stranger, and the gowk of a clerk, and the drunken carle of a justice"— a scene which Rob Roy could not recollect without a laughter that stifled his pity for Morris's end by "the ill-fared accident at the Loch." Still more irresistible is the delight of King James when he makes "jingling Geordie stare as if he took his native prince for a warlock," by producing the long-lost carcanet of rubies, the discovery of which the worthy goldsmith had just pronounced to be impossible.

Again, if we would find a parallel to these humorous pictures, we have but one author in our language to whom we can look, viz., to him who drew Falstaff and Fluellen; Touchstone with his "lie seven times removed," and the corresponding number of retorts, quips, replies, reproofs, and counter-checks, and the conclusion consequent on them all, the praise of "If" as the only peacemaker; Mrs. Quickly with her encouragement to the fat knight on his death-bed; Bottom roaring like any sucking-dove; Slender sighing, but sighing in vain, for sweet but mischievous Anne Page; Benedict converted from his resolution to die a bachelor; and Rosalind tricking Phœbe and Silvius into their mutual happiness.

Such was Scott as an author. It remains to speak of him as a man. In the preceding chapters we have obtained some insight into his tastes and habits. The duties of his legal office confined him for a part of the year to Edinburgh, "his own romantic town." But all his time, when his own master, was given to Abbotsford. And it is chiefly there that we must look if we would know what manner of man he was. We must think of him, not so much in his pursuits as a sportsman, nor in the judicious energy he displayed in the improvement of his estate, which, in the comparatively short period of a single generation, his judgement converted from a bleak plain, with no attraction for the eye but the neighbourhood of the river, into a fertile domain, studded with picturesque, and at the same time profitable, plantations. A more genuine test of character is afforded by a man's intercourse with the outer world; that is, with others; first with his own relations, and secondly with his friends and acquaintances, more or less intimate, at home or abroad. And it is therefore with a survey of Scott as the head of a family, and as a member of general society, that we may fitly conclude the present sketch.

Moore has pleaded, as an excuse for the least excusable part of the conduct of Byron, that a faithful discharge of domestic and family duties is inconsistent with "the poetical temperament." How little Scott stood in need of such an argument in his behalf, is shown by his letters to his wife and children, including his daughter-in-law, which Lockhart has given with a judicious liberality. I will only venture to quote some passages from one to his younger son Charles, then at a private tutor's in Wales, as a specimen of the manner in which he earnestly inculcates good advice as to the prosecution of his studies, while at the same time he mingles with graver subjects a mention of other pursuits in which he is far from desiring the youth not to indulge in moderation : "I am glad to hear you are attending closely to your studies to make up for lost time. Sport is a good thing both for health and pastime ; but you must never allow it to interfere with serious study. You have, my dear boy, your own future to make with better assistance than I had when the world first opened on me. And I assure you that had I not given some attention to learning (I have often regretted that from want of opportunity, indifferent health, and some indolence, I didn't do all I might have done), my own situation, and the advantages I may be able to procure for you, would have been very much bounded. Consider therefore study as the principal object. Many men have read and written their way to independence

and fame, but no man ever gained it by exclusive attention to exercises or pleasures of any sort. . . . Our
Abbotsford hunt went off very well. We killed seven hares,
I think, and our dogs behaved very well. A large
party dined, and we sat down about twenty-five at table.
Every gentleman present sang a song *tant bien que mal*,
excepting Walter, Lockhart, and I myself"—(these last
sentences are more like the gossip of a friend on terms
of equality, introduced as a pleasing variety to the grave
counsels, and presently he proceeds) . . " Read, my
dear, read that which is useful. Man only differs from
birds and beasts because he has the means of availing
himself of the knowledge acquired by his predecessors.
The swallow builds the same nest which its father and
mother built, and the sparrow does not improve by the
experience of its parents. The son of the learned pig, if
it had one, would be a mere brute, fit only to make
bacon of. It is not so with the human race. Our
ancestors lodged in caves and wigwams, where we construct
palaces for the rich, and comfortable dwellings for the
poor. And why is this, but because our eye is enabled
to look back upon the past, to improve upon our ancestors' improvements, and to avoid their errors. This can
only be done by studying history, and comparing it with
passing events. God has given you a strong memory,
and the power of understanding that which you give your
mind to with attention : but all the advantages to be
derived from these qualities must depend on your own
determination to avail yourself of them, and improve
them to the uttermost. That you should do so will be
the greatest satisfaction I can receive in my advanced

life, and when my thoughts might be entirely turned on the success of my children." He felt that the authority of a parent is strengthened when the guidance that youth requires comes as the advice of a friend, rather than as the command of a taskmaster.

To others, of every rank, he was the most engaging of companions; often, in cases of necessity, the most judicious and active of friends. And to none did he appear to greater advantage than to his guests. Of such, in the latter days of his prosperity, he had a constant stream ; and to them he was the cordial host, whose courteous manner and zeal for their amusement showed that the exercise of hospitality was a genuine pleasure. To his poorer neighbours, and especially to his own dependents, his uniform kindness and playful peculiarity endeared him, so that one and all regarded him as a friend even more than as a master. And this feeling was, if possible, strengthened by their affection for his admirable wife, the Lady Bountiful of the district, to whom all who were sick, or needy, or in any kind of distress, never applied in vain for consolation or for assistance.

Above all, we would point to his relations with his brother authors. No man was ever more free from all jealousy towards those who might be considered rivals. And his was not a mere passive good nature, but a cordial, genial friendship. There was no sort of ability which he failed to appreciate. Wordsworth and Moore, widely different as they were, were greeted with equal warmth ; as also were Southey the rigid Tory, and Hallam the champion of the Whigs. Foreigners fared equally well. He corresponded with Goethe, and Washington

Irving, the latter of whom sent home to America a glowing account of the happy days he spent on the banks of the Tweed. Byron never returned to Scotland after the days of his childhood, but that there was no one to whom the doors of Abbotsford would have been more gladly opened may be seen in his correspondence, and in the zeal with which Scott more than once stood up in the defence of his works and of himself in the *Quarterly:* though a man of less generosity of soul might have felt, if not envy, at least some soreness at the recollection of the degree in which the popularity of his own Scotch poems had been overshadowed by the preference of the public for the Eastern tales of his younger rival. It may easily be supposed that many whom he did not himself seek out, sought him, and to those who hoped to rise by their literary talents, but to whom nature, or it might be fortune, had been less propitious, his ear was never closed. His sympathy with their aspirations and hopes was shown in warmth of encouragement, when encouragement seemed judicious; in other cases by advice, and not unfrequently by gifts from his purse.

Mr. Lockhart has given a great number of his letters to correspondents of all classes : and he did well, since no stronger or more trustworthy evidence of a man's real disposition can be produced than his unstudied and confidential correspondence; and it is not too much to say that the whole body of Scott's letters does not contain one unfriendly or ill-natured sentence. The impression which they cannot fail to leave is that there never was a man whom one would have been more glad to know. And it must strengthen our respect for the brilliancy of his genius, when we see that he on whom all intellectual endowments, fancy, humour, invention, were so prodigally bestowed, was also one of the most lovable of mankind.

THE END

INDEX.

BIBLIOGRAPHY.

BY

JOHN P. ANDERSON

(British Museum).

I. PROSE WORKS.
II. POETICAL WORKS.
III. POETICAL AND DRAMATIC WORKS.
IV. SELECTIONS.
V. MISCELLANEOUS.
VI. SUPPOSITITIOUS WORKS.

VII. APPENDIX—
Biography, Criticism, etc.
Plays, etc., founded on Scott's Works.
Songs, etc., set to Music.
Magazine Articles.
VIII. CHRONOLOGICAL LIST OF WORKS.

I. PROSE WORKS.

The Miscellaneous Prose Works of Sir Walter Scott. 6 vols. Edinburgh, 1827, 8vo.
The Prose Works of Sir W. S. [With supplementary volume containing notes, . . . by the author; glossary, etc.] 9 vols. Paris, 1827-34, 8vo.
——New edition, with notes historical and illustrative. 8 vols. Paris [1840], 4to.
The Miscellaneous Prose Works of Sir W. S. [Index. With illustrations.] 30 vols. London, 1834-71, 8vo.
——Another edition. 3 vols. Edinburgh, 1841-47, 8vo.

Novels and Tales (Waverley, Guy Mannering, Antiquary, Rob Roy, Black Dwarf, Old Mortality, Heart of Midlothian, Bride of Lammermoor, Legend of Montrose) of the author of Waverley. 16 vols. Edinburgh, 1821, 8vo.
——Another edition. 12 vols. Edinburgh, 1823, 12mo.
Historical Romances (Ivanhoe, Monastery, Abbot, Kenilworth), of the author of Waverley. 8 vols. Edinburgh, 1822, 8vo.
——Another edition. 6 vols. Edinburgh, 1824, 12mo.
Novels and Romances (Pirate, Fortunes of Nigel, Peveril of the Peak, Quentin Durward) of the

author of Waverley. 9 vols. Edinburgh, 1824, 8vo.

Novels and Romances. Another edition. 7 vols. Edinburgh, 1825, 12mo.

Tales and Romances of the author of Waverley. (Introductions and notes and illustrations to the novels, tales, and romances of the author of Waverley.) 20 vols. Edinburgh, 1827-33, 8vo.

Tales and Romances of the author of Waverley. (Introductions and notes and illustrations, 3 vols.) 16 vols. Edinburgh, 1828-33, 12mo.

Novels, Tales and Romances. By Sir W. S. Abridged and illustrated by S. Percy. Vol. 1. London [1828], 8vo.
No more published.

Waverley Novels. [Parker's second edition.] 43 vols. Boston [U.S.], 1829, 8vo.

Waverley Novels. Author's Favourite Edition. [With illustrations.] 48 vols. Edinburgh, 1830-34, 8vo.
This edition is stereotyped, and is illustrated by 96 steel plates.

Waverley Novels. [Cabinet Edition.] 25 vols. Edinburgh, 1841-43, 8vo.
Stereotyped, and illustrated by 25 woodcut vignette titles, portrait, and fac-simile.

Waverley Novels. [Abbotsford Edition.] 12 vols. Edinburgh, 1842-47, 8vo.
Contains 120 steel and nearly 2000 wood engravings from Wilkie, Landseer, Allan, Stanfield, Roberts, etc.

Novels. [People's Edition.] With introductions and notes. 5 vols. Edinburgh, 1846, 8vo.
Stereotyped, and each volume has a woodcut title-page after Harvey, and vol. i. a portrait of Scott on steel, and a fac simile.

Waverley Novels. [Library Edition.] 25 vols. Edinburgh, 1852-53, 8vo.

Waverley Novels. [Railway Edition.] 25 vols. Edinburgh, 1854-60, 8vo.

Waverley Novels. [Illustrated Roxburghe Edition.] 48 vols. Edinburgh, 1859-61.

Waverley Novels. [Shilling Edition.] 25 vols. Edinburgh, 1862-64, 12mo.

Waverley Novels. [Sixpenny Edition.] 25 vols. Edinburgh, 1866-68, 8vo.

Waverley Novels. Centenary Edition. 25 vols. Edinburgh, 1870-71, 8vo.

Waverley Novels. Pocket Edition. Edinburgh, 1873, etc., 16mo.

The Handy Volume "Waverley" [Novels]. 25 vols. London, 1877, 16mo.

Edition de luxe of the Waverley Novels. Illustrated with original engravings by A. Marie, F. Lix, M. Riou, and H. Scott. London [1882, etc.], 8vo.

The Waverley Novels. 13 vols. London [1883-84], 8vo.

————

The Black Dwarf, and A Legend of Montrose. Edinburgh, 1856, 8vo.

——Another edition. With steel plates from designs by G. Cruikshank and other artists. London, 1875, 8vo.

Sir W. S.'s Novels. The Heart of Midlothian, The Antiquary, Quentin Durward, Peveril of the Peak, St. Ronan's Well. London [1868], 8vo.

Two Stories : The Monastery and The Abbot. From the original of Sir W. S. For children.

2 parts. Privately printed. Clapham, 1869, 16mo.

The Betrothed, and the Highland Widow. With designs by F. W. Topham and C. Fielding. New edition, etc. London, 1876, 8vo.

The Black Dwarf, Chronicles of the Canongate, and other tales. With illustrations. London, 1879, 8vo.

The Surgeon's Daughter, Castle Dangerous, and glossary. With plates. London, 1876, 8vo.

——Another edition. London, 1879, 8vo.

The Abbot. By the author of Waverley. 3 vols. Edinburgh, 1820, 12mo.

Other editions: London [1868], 8vo; London, 1875, 8vo, with steel plates from designs by G. Cruikshank; London, 1878, 8vo, with illustrations.

Anne of Geierstein; or, The Maiden of the Mist. By the author of "Waverley," etc. 3 vols. Edinburgh, 1829, 8vo.

Other editions: London, 1876, 8vo; London, 1879, 8vo, with illustrations.

The Antiquary. By the author of "Waverley" and "Guy Mannering." 3 vols. Edinburgh, 1816, 12mo.

Other editions:—Berlin, 1822, 8vo; Edinburgh, 1854, 8vo; London, 1875, 8vo, with plates from designs by G. Cruikshank, etc.; London, 1878, 8vo, with illustrations; London, [1880], 8vo; London [1883], 8vo.

The Betrothed. *See* "Tales of the Crusaders."

The Black Dwarf. *See* "Tales of My Landlord," series i.

The Bride of Lammermoor. *See* "Tales of My Landlord," series iii.

Castle Dangerous. *See* "Tales of My Landlord," series iv.

Chronicles of the Canongate. [First series. The Highland Widow; The Two Drovers; The Surgeon's Daughter.] 2 vols. Edinburgh, 1827, 8vo.

The introduction is subscribed Walter Scott, and in it the authorship of the Waverley Novels is formally avowed.

Chronicles of the Canongate. Second series. [Saint Valentine's Day; or, The Fair Maid of Perth.] 3 vols. Edinburgh, 1828, 8vo.

——St. Valentine's Day; or, The Fair Maid of Perth. By the author of "Waverley," etc., forming the second series of Chronicles of the Canongate. Second edition. 3 vols. Edinburgh, 1828, 16mo.

A duplicate, with new title-pages of the first edition, which was published under the title of "Chronicles of the Canongate."

——The Fair Maid of Perth. With plates from designs by G. Cruikshank and other artists. New edition, with the author's notes. London, 1876, 8vo.

——Another edition, with illustrations. London, 1878, 8vo.

Count Robert of Paris. *See* "Tales of My Landlord," series iv.

The Fortunes of Nigel. By the author of "Waverley," etc. 3 vols. Edinburgh, 1822, 8vo.

——The Fortunes of Nigel. With steel plates from designs by G. Cruikshank. New edition, with the author's notes. London, 1875, 8vo.

——Another edition, with illustrations. London, 1878, 8vo.

Guy Mannering; or, the Astrologer. By the author of "Waverley." 3 vols. Edinburgh, 1815, 12mo.

Other editions : — Edinburgh,
1854, 8vo ; London [1875], 8vo ; London, 1878, 8vo, with illustrations.
The Heart of Midlothian. See
"Tales of My Landlord," series ii.
Other editions : — Edinburgh,
1856. 8vo ; London, 1875, 8vo, with
steel plates from designs by G.
Cruikshank and other artists; London, 1878, 8vo, with illustrations;
London [1884] 8vo ; London [1884],
8vo (Cassell's Red Library).
The Highland Widow. See
"Chronicles of the Canongate,"
series i.
Ivanhoe : a romance. By the
author of "Waverley." [The
preface signed Laurence Templeton.] 3 vols. Edinburgh,
1820, 8vo.
——Second edition. 3 vols. Edinburgh, 1820, 8vo.
A duplicate of the first edition,
with the words "second edition"
added on the title-page.
Other editions :—Edinburgh, 1858,
8vo ; London, 1875, 8vo, with designs by G. Cruikshank and other
artists ; London, 1877, 8vo, with
illustrations ; London, 1878, 8vo,
with illustrations ; London [1880],
8vo, London [1882], 8vo ; London
[1883], 8vo, edited by A. Mackay.
——Ivanhoe. Condensed by R.
Johnson. New York, 1876, 8vo.
——Phonographic edition, etc.
(Nankivell's Phonographic Library). 3 pts. London, 1885,
16mo.
Kenilworth : a romance. By
the author of "Waverley." 3
vols. Edinburgh, 1821, 8vo.
Other editions : — London, 1875,
8vo, with steel plates from designs
by G. Cruikshank and other artists ;
London, 1877, 8vo, with illustrations ; London [1880], 8vo ; London
[1883], 8vo.
Legend of Montrose. See "Tales
of My Landlord," series iii.
The Monastery : a romance. By
The author of "Waverley."
3 vols. Edinburgh, 1820, 12mo.

Other editions : — London, 1876,
8vo, with designs by G. Cruikshank
and other artists ; London, 1878,
8vo, with illustrations.
Old Mortality. See "Tales of My
Landlord," series i.
Other editions :—Edinburgh, 1855,
8vo ; London [1874], 8vo ; London,
1875, 8vo, with designs by G. Cruikshank and other artists ; London,
1878, 8vo, with illustrations ; London [1884], 8vo, Cassell's Red
Library.
——The Story of Old Mortality,
for Children, by S. O. C. Edinburgh, 1872, 16mo.
Peveril of the Peak. By the
author of "Waverley." 4 vols.
Edinburgh, 1822, 8vo.
Other editions :—London, [1867],
8vo ; London [1875], 8vo, with steel
plates from designs by G. Cruikshank ; London, 1879, 8vo, with
illustrations.
The Pirate. By the author of
"Waverley." 3 vols. Edinburgh, 1822, 12mo.
Other editions :—Paris, 1822, 8vo,
3 vols.; London, 1875, 8vo, with
steel plates from designs by G.
Cruikshank ; London, 1879, 8vo,
with illustrations.
Quentin Durward. By the author
of "Waverley," etc. 3 vols.
Edinburgh, 1823, 8vo.
Other editions :—London [1868],
8vo ; London, 1875, 8vo, with steel
plates from designs by G. Cruikshank ; London, 1878, 8vo, with
illustrations.
Redgauntlet ; a tale of the
eighteenth century. By the
author of "Waverley." 3 vols.
Edinburgh, 1824, 8vo.
Other editions :—London, 1876,
8vo, with designs by G. Cruikshank
and other artists ; London, 1878,
8vo, with illustrations.
Rob Roy. By the author of
"Waverley." 3 vols. Edinburgh, 1818, 12mo.
Other editions :—Edinburgh, 1855,
8vo ; London, 1875, 8vo, with steel

plates from designs by G. Cruikshank; London, 1878, 8vo, with
illustrations; Manchester, 1887,
8vo.

St. Ronan's Well. By the author
of "Waverley," etc. 3 vols.
Edinburgh, 1824, 8vo.
  Other editions:—London [1868],
  8vo; London, 1875, 8vo, with designs
  by G. Cruikshank and F. W.
  Topham; London, 1879, 8vo, with
  illustrations.

The Surgeon's Daughter. *See*
"Chronicles of the Canongate,"
series i.

Tales of a Grandfather, being
Stories taken from Scottish
History. Humbly inscribed to
Hugh Littlejohn, Esq. 3 vols.
Edinburgh, 1828, 12mo.
——Second Series. 3 vols.
Edinburgh, 1829, 12mo.
——Third Series. 3 vols. Edin-
burgh, 1830, 12mo.
——[Fourth Series.] Tales of
a Grandfather, being Stories
taken from the History of
France. Inscribed to Master
John Hugh Lockhart. 3 vols.
Edinburgh, 1831, 12mo.

Tales of My Landlord [first
series]. Collected and arranged
by Jedediah Cleishbotham [*i.e.*,
Sir Walter Scott]. (The Black
Dwarf, Old Mortality.) 4 vols.
Edinburgh, 1816, 12mo.
——Second edition. 4 vols.
Edinburgh, 1817, 12mo.
——Third edition. 4 vols. Edin-
burgh, 1817, 12mo.
——Fifth edition. 4 vols. Edin-
burgh, 1819, 12mo.
——Second Series. (The Heart of
Midlothian.) 4 vols. Edin-
burgh, 1818, 12mo.
——Third Series. (The Bride of
Lammermoor and The Legend of
Montrose.) 4 vols. Edinburgh,
1819, 12mo.

Tales of My Landlord. Fourth
and last Series. (Count
Robert of Paris and Castle
Dangerous.) 4 vols. London,
1832, 12mo.

Tales of the Crusaders. By the
author of "Waverley." 4 vols.
Edinburgh, 1825, 8vo.
  Vols. i., ii.—The Betrothed.
  Vols. iii , iv.—The Talisman.

The Talisman. *See* "Tales of
the Crusaders."
  Other editions:—London, 1876,
  8vo, with designs by G. Cruikshank
  and F. W.Topham; London, 1878,8vo,
  with illustrations; London [1885],
  8vo, *Cassell's Red Library.*

The Two Drovers. *See* "Chronicles
of the Canongate," series i.

Waverley; or, 'Tis Sixty Years
Since. 3 vols. Edinburgh,
1814, 12mo.
——Fifth edition. 3 vols. Edinburgh, 1815, 12mo.
——Sixth edition. 3 vols. Edinburgh, 1816, 12mo.
  Other editions:—Edinburgh,1854,
  8vo; London [1875], 8vo; London,
  1877, 8vo, with illustrations; London [1880], 8vo; London [1882], 8vo.

Woodstock; or, the Cavalier: a
tale of the year sixteen hundred
and fifty-one, by the author of
"Waverley." 3 vols. Edinburgh,
1826, 8vo.
  The proof sheets of this work,
  with the author's autograph corrections and additions, eighteen
  letters to James Ballantyne written
  during the progress of the work,
  and Ballantyne's criticisms, are in
  the Library of the British Museum.
  Other editions:—London, 1876,
  8vo, with designs by G. Cruikshank
  and other artists; London, 1879,
  8vo, with illustrations.

II. POETICAL WORKS.

The Poetical Works of Walter
Scott [with the notes of the
author]. 12 vols. Edinburgh,
1820, 12mo.

The Poetical Works of Walter Scott. Another edition [with portrait]. 7 vols. Paris, 1821, 8vo.
——Another edition. Paris, 1827, 8vo.
——Another edition. 11 vols. Edinburgh, 1830, 12mo.
——Another edition, complete in one volume. (Memoir, etc.) Paris, 1831, 8vo.
——Another edition. [Edited by J. G. L.—*i.e.*, John Gibson Lockhart. With an appendix.] 12 vols. Edinburgh, 1833-34, 8vo.
Contains 24 illustrations on steel from Turner's drawings, designed expressly for the edition, and two fac-similes.
——Another edition. With all his introductions and notes; also various readings, and the editor's notes. [Edited by J. G. L.—*i.e.*, Lockhart]. Edinburgh, 1848, 8vo.
With an engraved title-page, bearing date 1847.
——Another edition. With a life of the author. London, 1850, 12mo.
——Another edition. With a memoir of the author. Illustrated by engravings. Edinburgh, 1852, 8vo.
——Another edition, with life. Edinburgh [1855], 8vo.
——The Poetical Works of Sir W. S. With eight illustrations by Corbould. (*Routledge's British Poets.*) London, 1857, 8vo.
——Another edition. With a memoir of the author. 9 vols. Boston [U.S.], 1857, 8vo.
——Another edition. With memoir and critical dissertation by G. Gilfillan. 3 vols. Edinburgh, 1857, 8vo.
——Another edition. With a

memoir of the author. Edinburgh, 1857, 8vo.
——Another edition. With all his introductions, notes, various readings, and notes by J. G. Lockhart. Illustrated by numerous engravings after J. M. W. Turner, R. Foster, and J. Gilbert. Edinburgh, 1857, 8vo.
——Another edition. With illustrations by K. Halswelle. (The life of Sir W. Scott, by A. Leighton.) Edinburgh, 1861, 8vo.
——Another edition. With memoir of the author. London, 1862, 8vo.
——Another edition, illustrated. With memoir of the author. London, 1864, 8vo.
——The Complete Poetical Works of Robert Burns and Sir Walter Scott, illustrated with fine steel portraits, etc. New edition. London, 1866, 8vo.
Re-issued in 1872 in *Blackwood's Universal Library of Standard Authors.*
——The Globe Edition. With a biographical and critical memoir by F. T. Palgrave. London, 1866, 8vo.
——Another edition. (*Routledge's Cabinet Edition of the Poets.*) London [1868], 16mo.
——Another edition. Illustrated by F. Gilbert. London, 1868, 8vo.
——The Globe Edition. With a biographical and critical memoir by F. T. Palgrave. London, 1869, 8vo.
——Another edition. Edited, with a critical memoir, by W. M. Rossetti. Illustrated by T. Seccombe. London, 1870, 8vo.

The Poetical Works of W. S.
——Another edition. With memoir and critical dissertation. (*Cassell's Library Edition of the British Poets.*) 3 vols. London, [1870-71], 8vo.
——Another edition. With notes, and life of the author. With illustrations. London [1872], 8vo.
——Another edition. [With an introduction by the late W. Spalding. Illustrated.] Edinburgh, 1872, 8vo.
——Another edition. [*Handy Volume Edition.*] 7 vols. London, 1876, 16mo.
——Another edition. With memoir of the author. London, 1877, 8vo.
——Another edition. London [1878], 8vo.
——Another edition. (*Miniature Library of the Poets.*) 2 vols. London, 1880, 16mo.
——Another edition. (*Excelsior Series.*) London [1880], 8vo.
——Another edition. With life, etc. (*The Landscape Series of Poets.*) Edinburgh [1881], 8vo.
- ——Another edition. Edited, with a critical memoir, by W. M. Rossetti. Illustrated. London [1882], 8vo.
——Another edition. With illustrations. London, 1882, 8vo.
——Another edition. With prefatory notice, biographical and critical, by W. Sharp. (*The Canterbury Poets.*) 2 vols. London, 1885-6, 16mo.
——Poems. (*Cassell's Miniature Library of the Poets.*) 2 vols. London [1886], 16mo.
——Poetical Works. Edited by William Minto. 2 vols. Edinburgh, 1888 [1887], 8vo.

——————

Ballads, Songs, and Poems. London, 1868, 8vo.
The Bridal of Triermain and Harold the Dauntless. Two Poems. Fourth edition. Edinburgh, 1819, 8vo.
——Another edition. London, 1868, 8vo.
Glenfinlas and other ballads, etc. With the Vision of Don Roderick: a poem. Illustrated with engravings from the designs of R. Westall, etc. London, 1812, 8vo.
The Lay of the Last Minstrel and the Lady of the Lake, with introductions and notes by F. T. Palgrave, etc. (*Globe Readings*, etc.) London, 1883, 8vo.
The Lord of the Isles, Marmion, and the Lay of the Last Minstrel. Glasgow [1885], 32mo.
Marmion and the Lord of the Isles, with introductions and notes by F. T. Palgrave, etc. (*Globe Readings.*) London, 1883, 8vo.
Miscellaneous Poems. Edinburgh, 1820, 8vo.
The Select Poetical Works of Sir W. S., comprising The Lay of the Last Minstrel, Marmion, The Lady of the Lake, ballads, lyrical pieces, etc. Glasgow, 1838, 8vo.
The Select Poetical Works of Sir W. S. Lay of the Last Minstrel, Marmion, Lady of the Lake, and Rokeby. [With the notes of the author.] London, 1849, 8vo.
The Vision of Don Roderick, The Field of Waterloo, and other poems. [With notes.] Edinburgh, 1815, 8vo.

The Vision of Don Roderick, Waterloo, etc. London, 1868, 8vo.

The Waverley Song Book; or, songs and ballads of Sir W. S. Glasgow [1871], 8vo.

Ballads and Lyrical Pieces. Edinburgh, 1806, 8vo.
"Advertisement"—These ballads have been already published in different collections, some in *The Minstrelsy of the Scottish Border*, others in *The Tales of Wonder*, and some in both these miscellanies. They are now first collected into one volume. The songs have been written at different times for the musical collections of Mr. George Thomson and Mr. White.

——Second edition. Edinburgh, 1806, 8vo.

——Fourth edition. [With illustrations by Westall.] Edinburgh, 1812, 8vo.

The Bridal of Triermain ; or, the Vale of St. John. In three cantos. Edinburgh, 1813, 8vo.

——Second edition. Edinburgh, 1813, 8vo.

——Another edition. Philadelphia, 1813, 12mo.

——Fifth edition. Edinburgh, 1817, 12mo.

The Eve of Saint John. A Border ballad. Kelso, 1800, 4to.

The Field of Waterloo. A poem. Edinburgh, 1815, 8vo.

——Second edition. Edinburgh, 1815, 8vo.

——Third edition. Edinburgh, 1815, 8vo.

——Another edition. Boston [U.S.], 1815, 8vo.

Harold the Dauntless ; a poem in six cantos. By the author of "The Bridal of Triermain." Edinburgh, 1817, 8vo.

The Lady of the Lake; a poem. (Notes.) Edinburgh, 1810, 4to.

——Second edition. [Illustrated with engravings from the designs of R. Westall.] Edinburgh, 1810, 8vo.
There is a second title-page bearing the date 1811.

——Another edition. [Illustrated with engravings from paintings by R. Cook. London, 1810, 4to.
With an engraved title-page also, date 1811.

——Fourth edition. (Notes.) Edinburgh, 1810, 8vo.

——Sixth edition. (Notes.) Edinburgh, 1810, 8vo.

——Eighth edition. [With engravings from the designs of R, Westall.] Edinburgh, 1810, 8vo.
There is also an engraved title page bearing the date 1811.

——Ninth edition. (Notes.) Edinburgh, 1811, 8vo.

——Eleventh edition. [With notes.] Edinburgh, 1816, 8vo.

——Another edition. Edinburgh. 1821, 8vo.

——Another edition. Edinburgh, 1825, 8vo.

——Another edition. Edinburgh, 1836, 8vo.

——Another edition, illustrated. London, 1838, 12mo.

——Another edition. Edinburgh, 1844, 24mo.

——Another edition, illustrated. London, 1845, 8vo.

——Another edition. Königsberg, 1850, 16mo.

——Another edition. Edinburgh, 1851, 18mo.

——Another edition, with all his introductions, various readings, and the editor's notes. Illustrated by numerous engravings on wood from drawings by B. Foster and J. Gilbert. Edinburgh, 1853, 8vo.

——(*Universal Library—Poetry*, vol. i.) London, 1853, 8vo.

——Another edition. Illustrated. London, 1859, 8vo.

——Another edition. Dublin, 1862 [1861], 16mo.

——Another edition. [Illustrated with photographs.] London, 1863, 4to.

——Another edition. London, 1863, 16mo.

——Another edition. With notes. London, 1868, 8vo.

——Another edition. [With photographs by G. W. Wilson, and illustrations by B. Foster, Sir J. Gilbert, etc.] Edinburgh, [1869], 8vo.

——Another edition. With notes and analytical and explanatory index. Edinburgh, 1871, 8vo.

——Another edition. With life and notes. London, 1872, 16mo.

——Another edition. Glasgow [1883], 32mo.

——Another edition. Edited, with notes, by W. J. Rolfe. With illustrations. Boston [U. S.], 1885, 8vo.

——(*Cassell's National Library*, vol. xiii.) London, 1886, 8vo.

——With map and notes. (*Collins's English Classics.*) London [1886], 8vo.

——(*Routledge's Pocket Library.*) London, 1887, 16mo.

——The Lady of the Lake. [Canto the first and fifth.] 2 parts. London [1869], 8vo.

——First Canto. (*Annotated Poems of English Authors*, ed.

Stevens and Morris.) London, 1877, 8vo.

——Scott's Lady of the Lake. 307 lines from Canto First. With life and notes. London, 1885, 8vo.

The Lay of the Last Minstrel, a poem. London, 1805, 4to.

——Third edition. Edinburgh, 1806, 8vo.

——Fifth edition. London, 1806, 8vo.

——Sixth edition. [With notes.] London, 1807, 8vo.

——Eighth edition. With ballads and lyrical pieces. (Illustrated with engravings from the designs of R. Westall.) London, 1808, 4to.
With engraved title-page also, dated 1809.

——Tenth edition. London, 1809, 8vo.

——Eleventh edition. London, 1810, 8vo.

——Twelfth edition. London, 1811, 8vo.

——Fifteenth edition. [With notes.] London, 1816, 8vo.

——Another edition. Edinburgh, 1825, 12mo.

——Another edition. Edinburgh, 1836, 8vo.

——Another edition, illustrated. London, 1838, 12mo.

——Another edition. Edinburgh, 1844, 24mo.

——(*Universal Library—Poetry*, vol. i.) London, 1853, 8vo.

——Another edition, with all his introductions, and the editor's notes. Illustrated by engravings from drawings by B. Foster and J. Gilbert. Edinburgh, 1854, 8vo.

The Lay of the Last Minstrel.
——Another edition. With notes.
London, 1868, 8vo.
——Another edition. With photographic illustrations by R. Sedgfield. London, 1872 [1871], 4to.
——Another edition. With notes and a chronological summary of his life, and index. Edinburgh, 1872, 8vo.
——The Lay of the Last Minstrel in six cantos. Edited by Súrésh Chandra Dév, with notes, etc. Calcutta, 1880, 8vo.
——Another edition; introduction and canto i., with notes. Edited by W. T. Jeffcott and G. J. Tossell. London [1882], 8vo.
——Lay of the Last Minstrel, introduction and canto i. Edited by W. Minto (*Clarendon Press Series*). Cambridge, 1882, 8vo.
——Another edition. Cambridge, 1886, 8vo.
——Another edition. With life and notes. London, 1885, 8vo.
——Another edition. Illustrated. London, 1887 [1886], 8vo.
The Lord of the Isles, a poem in six cantos, illustrated with engravings from R. Westall. London, 1815, 4to.
——Fifth edition. Edinburgh, 1815, 8vo.
——Another edition. With all his introductions, and the editor's notes. Illustrated by numerous engravings from drawings by B. Foster and J. Gilbert. Edinburgh, 1857, 8vo.
——Another edition. With notes. London, 1868, 8vo.
——Another edition. [With photographic illustrations by W. R. Sedgfield and S. Thompson.] London, 1871, 4to.

The Lord of the Isles.
——Another edition. With notes and analytical and explanatory index. Edinburgh, 1871, 8vo.
Marmion: a tale of Flodden Field. [Illustrated with engravings from the designs of R. Westall; with notes to each canto.] London, 1808. 4to.
With engraved title-page, dated 1809.
——Second edition. Edinburgh, 1808, 8vo.
——Fifth edition. [Illustrated with engravings, etc.] London, 1810, 8vo.
There is also an engraved title-page.
——Seventh edition. [With engravings from the designs of R. Westall.] Edinburgh, 1811, 8vo.
An engraved title-page, and the plates bear the date 1809.
——Eighth edition. Edinburgh, 1811, 8vo.
——Ninth edition. Edinburgh, 1815, 8vo.
——Twelfth edition. Edinburgh, 1825, 8vo.
——Another edition. Edinburgh, 1836, 8vo.
——Another edition, illustrated. London, 1838, 12mo.
——Another edition. Edinburgh, 1844, 24mo.
——Another edition, illustrated. London, 1845, 8vo.
——Another edition, with all his introductions, and the editor's notes. Illustrated by engravings on wood from drawings by Birket Foster and J. Gilbert. Edinburgh, 1855 [1854], 8vo.
——Another edition. [With photographic illustrations by T. Annan.] London, 1866, 4to.

Marmion.

——Another edition. With notes. London, 1868, 8vo.

——Another edition, with introduction, notes, map, and glossary, by E. C. Morris. London, 1869, 8vo.

——Another edition, with notes, and analytical and explanatory index. Edinburgh, 1873, 8vo.

—— ——Christmas in the Olden Time. (From Marmion, canto v.) Illustrated. London [1887], 8vo.

Rokeby, a Poem. Edinburgh, 1813, 4to.

——Second edition. Edinburgh, 1813, 8vo.

——Third edition. Edinburgh, 1813, 8vo.

——Fourth edition. [Illustrated with engravings from T. Stothard.] Edinburgh, 1813, 8vo. There is also an engraved title-page.

——Fifth edition. Edinburgh, 1813, 8vo.

——Sixth edition. [With notes.] Edinburgh, 1815, 8vo.

——Another edition. London, 1841, 24mo. With a second engraved title-page.

——Another edition. With notes. London, 1868, 8vo.

The Vision of Don Roderick : a Poem. Edinburgh, 1811, 4to.

——Second edition, 1811, 8vo.

III. POETICAL AND DRAMATIC WORKS.

The Poetical Works of Sir W. S. 11 vols. Edinburgh, 1821-30, 8vo.
Stated with title-pages of vol. i.-x. to be in 10 vols. To these vol. xi. was added, bearing date 1830, and containing the author's dramatic pieces and sketches.

The Complete Poetical and Dramatic Works of Sir W. S. With an introductory memoir by W. B. Scott. With illustrations. London [1877], 8vo.

The Complete Poetical and Dramatic Works of Sir W. S. With an introductory memoir by W. B. Scott. London, 1883, 8vo.

———

The Doom of Devorgoil : a melodrama. Auchindrane ; or, the Ayrshire Tragedy. Edinburgh, 1830, 8vo.

Halidon Hill : a dramatic sketch from Scottish history [in two acts, and in verse]. Edinburgh, 1822, 8vo.

IV. SELECTIONS.

Caledonia described by Scott, Burns, and Ramsay. [Selections from their poetical works.] With illustrations by J. Macwhirter, etc. London, 1878, 4to.

Characters of Eminent Persons, humorous and poetical pieces. Edinburgh, 1855, 8vo. Vol. vii. of a series, entitled "The Abbotsford Miscellany."

Diamonds from the Waverley Mines ; or, maxims, observations, and reflections, selected from the novels of Sir W. S. By J. Cauvin. London, 1872, 8vo.

The Genius and Wisdom of Sir W. S., comprising aphorisms selected from his various writings. With a memoir. London, 1839, 12mo.

Historical, legendary, and romantic Tales from the works of Sir Walter Scott. Selected by W. T. Dobson. With illustrations, etc. London, 1886 [1885], 8vo

Legends of the North and Border Minstrelsy, selected chiefly from the works of Sir W. S. With illustrations. [Edited by R. Teutou.] London, 1835, 8vo.

Narratives and Descriptive Pieces. [Selections from Sir W. S.'s works.] Edinburgh, 1855, 8vo.
This forms vol. vi. of a series, entitled "The Abbotsford Miscellany."

Readings for the Young, from the works of Sir W. S. 3 vols. Edinburgh, 1848, 8vo.

Readings from Sir W. S. The Talisman, Ivanhoe, Anne of Geierstein, and Marmion. With notes, etc. London [1884], 8vo.

Romantic Narratives. Edinburgh, 1855, 8vo.
Vol. iv. of a series, entitled "The Abbotsford Miscellany."

Royal Characters from the works of Sir W. S., historical and romantic. Selected and arranged by W. T. Dobson. With illustrations. London, 1881, 8vo.

The Scott Birthday Book. Edited by C. H. Dicken. [Short extracts from the works of S. in prose and verse for every day in the year.] London, 1879, 16mo.

Scottish Scenes and Characters. Edinburgh, 1855, 8vo.
Vol. v. of a series, entitled "The Abbotsford Miscellany."

A selection from the works of Sir W. S. Edited by Mortimer Collins. (*Moxon's Miniature Poets.*) London, 1866, 8vo.

A Selection [of pieces in verse] from the works of Sir W. S. Edited by Mortimer Collins. (*Moxon's Miniature Poets.*) London, 1885, 8vo.

Tales of Chivalry and Romance. Edinburgh, 1855, 8vo.
Vol. iii. of a series, entitled "The Abbotsford Miscellany."

The Waverley Poetical Birthday Book, with selections from the poems of Sir W. S. London, [1882], 16mo.

Waverley Poetry: being the poems scattered through the Waverley Novels, attributed to anonymous sources, but presumed to be written by Sir W. S. Boston [U.S.], 1851, 12mo.

The Waverley Sketch Book; or, a collection of the most striking pictures and interesting events in the Waverley Novels. Arranged by C. Olliffe. Paris, 1840, 8vo.

V. MISCELLANEOUS.

The Miscellaneous Works of Sir W. S., Bart., containing introductory remarks on popular poetry; and new introductions to Lay of the Last Minstrel; Marmion; Lady of the Lake; Rokeby; and Lord of the Isles; also the tragedy of Macduff's Cross; Doom of Devorgoil; and the Ayrshire Tragedy. Edinburgh, 1836, 8vo.

Introductions and notes and illustrations to the novels, tales, and romances of the author of Waverley. 3 vols. Edinburgh, 1833, 8vo.

An account of the death and funeral procession of Frederick, Duke of York, etc. To which is subjoined Sir W. Scott's character of his Royal Highness. [With woodcuts by J. Bewick]. By John Sykes. Newcastle, 1827, 4to.

Auld Robin Gray; a Ballad. By the Rt. Honourable Lady Anne Barnard, born Lady Anne Lindsay, of Balcarras. [Edited by Sir W. S.] Edinburgh, 1825, 4to.

Presented as a contribution to the Bannatyne Club by Sir W. Scott.

A Bannatyne Garland, quhairin the President speaketh (Finis, quoth the Knight of Abbotsford [*i.e.* Sir W. S.]. *L.L.* [Edinburgh, 1823], 8vo.

The Bannatyne Miscellany; containing original papers and tracts relating to the history and literature of Scotland. [Edited by Sir W. S., D. Laing, and T. Thomson.] 3 vols. Edinburgh, 1827-55, 4to.

Beauties of Sterne, with some account of his writings by Sir W. S. Amsterdam, 1836, 12mo.

The Border Antiquities of England and Scotland; comprising specimens of architecture and sculpture, and other vestiges of former ages, accompanied by descriptions. Together with illustrations of remarkable incidents in Border History and Tradition, and original poetry. 2 vols. London, 1814-17, 4to.

The Chase, and William and Helen : two ballads from the German of G. A. Bürger [by Sir W. S.]. Edinburgh, 1796, 4to.

Chronological Notes of Scottish affairs from 1680 till 1701 ; being chiefly taken from the diary of Lord Fountainhall. [Edited by Sir W. S.]. Edinburgh, 1822, 4to.

A Collection of Scarce and Valuable Tracts. Selected from an infinite number in print and manuscript, in the Royal, Cotton, Sion, and other public, as well as private, libraries ; particularly that of the late

Lord Somers. The second edition, revised, augmented, and arranged by W. S. 13 vols. London, 1809-15, 4to.

The Image of Irelande, with a Discouerie of Woodkarne. By John Derricke. With the notes of Sir W. S, etc. Edinburgh, 1883, 4to.

A reprint of the notes to Derrick's work in "Lord Somers's Tracts," edited by Sir Walter Scott.

Criminal Trials, illustrative of the tale entitled, "The Heart of Midlothian," etc. Edinburgh, 1818, 12mo.

Description of the Regalia of Scotland. Edinburgh, 1819, 16mo.

Numerous editions. This account of the Regalia of Scotland forms part of "The Provincial Antiquities," 1819.

English Minstrelsy. Being a selection of fugitive poetry from the best English authors, with some original pieces hitherto unpublished. [Edited by Sir W. S.] 2 vols. Edinburgh, 1810, 8vo.

The Ettricke Garland : being two excellent new songs [the first by Sir W. S. and the second by James Hogg] on the lifting of the banner of the House of Buccleuch at the football match on Carterhaugh, etc. Edinburgh, 1815, 8vo.

The copy in the British Museum Library is preceded by a MS. letter of Sir W. Scott, and followed by two cuttings from newspapers, the first containing an account of the death of his piper, and the second an inedited letter.

Goetz of Berlichingen, with the Iron Hand : a Tragedy translated from the German of Goethe, by W. S. London, 1799, 8vo.

The History of Scotland. (*Lardner's Cabinet Cyclopædia.*) 2 vols. London, 1830, 8vo.

Illustrations of Northern Antiquities from the earlier Teutonic and Scandinavian romances; being an abstract of the book of Heroes, and Nibelungen Lay; with translations of metrical tales from the old German, Danish, Swedish, and Icelandic languages; with notes, dissertations, etc. (Abstract of the Eyrbiggia-Saga: being the early annals of that district of Iceland lying around the promontory called Sudefells, by W. S.) [*i.e.*, Walter Scott]. Edinburgh, 1814, 4to.

Kinmont Willie: a Border Ballad, with an historical introduction, by Sir W. S. (*Carlisle Tracts,* No. vi.) Carlisle, 1841, 8vo.

Laneham's Letter describing the magnificent pageants presented before Queen Elizabeth at Kenilworth Castle in 1575, referred to in the romance of Kenilworth [by Sir W. S.]. London, 1821, 8vo.

Lays of the Lindsays, being Poems by the Ladies of the House of Balcarras. [Edited by Sir W. S.] Edinburgh, 1824, 4to.

This volume was originally designed by Sir Walter Scott as a contribution to the Bannatyne Club, but after it was printed the volume was suppressed.

Letters of Sir W. S., addressed to the Rev. R. Polwhele, D. Gilbert, Esq., Francis Douce, Esq. London, 1823, 12mo.

Letters on Demonology and Witchcraft, addressed to J. G. Lockhart, Esq. London, 1830, 12mo.

Forming part of the "Family Library." Other editions, New York, 1845, 12mo; London [1876], 8vo, illustrated; London, 1884, 8vo, with introduction by H. Morley.

The Letting of Humour's Blood into the Head Vaine, etc. By S. Rowlands. [Being epigrams and satires. Edited, with advertisement and notes, by Sir W. S.] Edinburgh, 1814, 8vo.

A reprint of the edition of 1611. Without pagination. The same work as "Humours Ordinarie." Reprinted in 1815 in 4to.

The Life of Edward, Lord Herbert of Cherbury, written by himself, with a prefatory memoir [by Sir W. S. ?] (*Universal Library. Biography,* vol. i.) London, 1853, 8vo.

The Life of Napoleon Buonaparte, Emperor of the French. With a preliminary view of the French Revolution. By the Author of "Waverley." 9 vols. Edinburgh, 1827, 8vo.

——[Cancels in the first edition of the Life of Napoleon, by the Author of "Waverley." With MS. corrections and notes.] [Edinburgh, 1827] 8vo.

This is in the Library of the British Museum.

A Memoir of the life and writings of the late W. Taylor, of Norwich. Containing his correspondence with R. Southey, and original letters from Sir W. S., etc. By J. W. Robberds. 2 vols. London, 1843, 8vo.

Memoirs of Capt. George Carleton, including anecdotes of the war in Spain, under the Earl of Peterborough, written by himself. [Edited by Sir W. S.] Edinburgh, 1808, 8vo.

There were 25 copies printed on large paper.

Memoirs of Robert Carey, and Fragmenta Regalia: being a history of Queen Elizabeth's favourites, by Sir R. Naunton. With explanatory annotations [by Sir W. S.]. Edinburgh, 1808, 8vo.

Memoirs of the Duke of Sully, etc. A new edition, revised and corrected ; with additional notes, and an historical introduction attributed to Sir W. S. 4 vols. London, 1856, 8vo.

Memoirs of the Insurrection in 1715. By John, Master of Sinclair. With notes by Sir W. S. (*Abbotsford Club.*) Edinburgh, 1858, 4to.

Memoirs of the Marchioness de la Rochejaquelin. Translated from the French. (*Constable's Miscellany*, vol. v.) Edinburgh, 1827, 12mo.

Memoirs of the Reign of King Charles I. By Sir Philip Warwick. [Edited by Sir W. S.] Edinburgh, 1813, 8vo.

Memorials of Coleorton, being letters from Coleridge, Wordsworth and his sister, Southey, and Sir Walter Scott, to Sir George and Lady Beaumont, of Coleorton, Leicestershire, 1803 to 1834. Edited by William Knight. 2 vols. Edinburgh, 1887, 8vo.

Memorials of George Bannatyne, 1545-1608. [Edited by Sir W. S. With a memoir of Bannatyne by the editor, etc.] Edinburgh, 1829, 4to.
Part of the "Bannatyne Club."

Memorials of the Haliburtons. [Edited by Sir W. S.] Edinburgh, 1820, 4to.
Thirty copies only printed for private circulation. The preliminary notice is dated Abbotsford, March 1820. An additional thirty copies were reprinted in 1824, on paper slightly larger than the former.

Memorie of the Somervilles ; being a history of the baronial house of Somerville. [Edited by Sir W. S.] 2 vols. Edinburgh, 1815, 8vo.

Military Memoirs of the Great Civil War, being the military memoirs of J. Gwynne ; and an account of the Earl of Glencairn's expedition, as General of his Majesty's forces, in the Highlands of Scotland in 1653 and 1654, by a person who was eye and ear-witness to every transaction [*i.e.*, John Graham of Duchrie ?]. With an appendix. [Edited by Sir W. S.] Edinburgh, 1822, 4to.

Minstrelsy of the Scottish Border ; consisting of historical and romantic ballads, collected in the southern counties of Scotland ; with a few of modern date [by Sir W. S. and others], founded upon local tradition. [Compiled and edited, with an introduction, by Sir W. S.] 3 vols. Kelso, 1802, 8vo.
——Second edition. 3 vols. Edinburgh, 1803, 8vo.
——Third edition. 3 vols. Edinburgh, 1806, 8vo.
——Fourth edition. 3 vols. Edinburgh, 1810, 8vo.
——Fifth edition. 3 vols. Edinburgh, 1812, 8vo.
——Fifth Edition. 3 vols. Edinburgh, 1821, 8vo.
——Reprint of the original edition. London, 1869, 8vo.
——Reprint of the original edition. London [1883], 8vo.
Part of "The People's Standard Library."

Northern Memoirs, calculated for the meridian of Scotland. To which is added the contemplative and practical angler.

Writ in the year 1658. By Richard Franck. A new edition, with preface and notes. [By Sir W. S.] Edinburgh, 1821, 8vo. [The Novelists' Library.—Edited, with prefatory memoirs, by Sir W. S.] 10 vols. London, 1821-24, 8vo.

——Lives of the Novelists. 2 vols. Paris, 1825, 12mo.

The Novels and Miscellaneous Works of Daniel de Foe. With prefaces and notes, including those attributed to Sir W. S. (*Bohn's British Classics.*) 6 vols. London, 1854-56, 8vo.

Original Memoirs written during the great Civil War; being the life of Sir H. Slingsby, and memoirs of Capt. Hodgson. With notes, etc. [Edited by Sir W. S.] Edinburgh, 1806, 8vo.

Papers relative to the Regalia of Scotland. [Edited by Sir W. S.] Edinburgh, 1829, 4to.
> Presented to the members of the Bannatyne Club by William Bell, Esq.

Paul's Letters to his Kinsfolk. Edinburgh, 1816, 8vo.
> There is a copy in the Library of the British Museum with MS. corrections by the author.

——France and Belgium. Originally published in "Paul's Letters to his Kinsfolk." 2 parts. Edinburgh, 1855, 8vo.
> This work forms vol. i. and ii. of a series, entitled "The Abbotsford Miscellany."

A Penni worth of Witte: Florice and Blauncheflour, and other pieces of ancient English poetry, selected from the Auchinleck Manuscript. [With an account of the Auchinleck Manuscript by Sir W. S.] Edinburgh, 1857, 4to.
> Printed for the Abbotsford Club.

The Poetical Works of Anna Seward, with extracts from her literary correspondence. Edited [with a biographical preface] by W. S. 3 vols. Edinburgh, 1810, 8vo.

The Poetry contained in the Novels, Tales, and Romances of the author of Waverley. Edinburgh, 1822, 8vo.

Proceedings in the Court-martial held upon John, Master of Sinclair, Captain-Lieutenant in Preston's regiment, for the murder of Ensign Schaw of the same regiment, and Captain Schaw, of the Royals, 17th October 1708, with correspondence respecting that transaction. [Edited by Sir W. S.] Edinburgh, 1828, 4to.
> Part of the "Roxburghe Club."

Provincial Antiquities and Picturesque Scenery of Scotland, with descriptive illustrations by Sir W. S. 2 vols. London, 1826, 4to.
> Published in 10 parts between 1819 and 1826.

Queenhoo-Hall; a Romance, and Ancient Times, a Drama. By the late Joseph Strutt, author of Rural Sports and Pastimes of the People of England. [Edited by Sir W. S.] 4 vols. Edinburgh, 1808, 12mo.

Religious Discourses. By a Layman. London, 1828, 8vo.

The Sale-Room. [By Sir W. S. and others.] No. 1-28. Edinburgh, 1817, 4to.
> This periodical existed from January 4 to July 12, 1817.

Secret History of the Court of James the First, etc. With notes and introductory remarks. 2 vols. [Edited by Sir W. S.] Edinburgh, 1811, 8vo.

Sir Tristrem: a Metrical Romance of the Thirteenth Century, by Thomas of Ercildoune, called the Rhymer. Edited from the Auchinleck MS. by W. S. Edinburgh, 1804, 8vo.
——Second edition. Edinburgh, 1806, 8vo.
———Third edition. Edinburgh, 1811, 8vo.
——Fourth edition. Edinburgh, 1819, 8vo.
A short account of successful exertions in behalf of the fatherless and widows after the war in 1814; containing letters from Mr. Wilberforce, Sir W. Scott, Marshal Blucher, etc. By Rudolph Ackermann. Oxford, 1871, 16mo.
Sketch of the Life and Character of the late Lord Kinnedder. [Edited by Sir W. S.] Edinburgh, 1822, 4to.
Only a few copies printed for private distribution.
The state papers and letters of Sir Ralph Sadler. Edited by A. Clifford. To which is added a memoir of the life of Sir R. Sadler, with historical notes by Walter Scott. 2 vols. Edinburgh, 1809, 4to.
Thoughts on the proposed change of currency, and other late alterations, as they affect, or are intended to affect, the kingdom of Scotland, etc. (Three Letters to the Editor of the *Edinburgh Weekly Journal* from Malachi Malagrowther, Esq.—*i.e.*, Sir W. Scott.) 3 parts. Edinburgh, 1826, 8vo.
——A Letter from Malachi Malagrowther, Esq., to the Editor of the *Edinburgh Weekly Journal*, on the proposed change of currency and other

late alterations, as they affect, or are intended to affect, the kingdom of Scotland. Second edition. Edinburgh, 1826, 8vo.
——A Second Letter to the Editor of the *Edinburgh Weekly Journal* on the proposed change of currency, etc. Edinburgh, 1826, 8vo.
Trial of Duncan Terig, *alias* Clerk, and Alexander Bane Macdonald, for the murder of Arthur Davis, Sergeant in General Guise's Regiment of Foot. June, A.D., 1754. [Edited by Sir W. S.] Edinburgh, 1831, 4to
Presented to the members of the Bannatyne Club by Sir W. Scott.
Trivial Poems and Triolets. Written in obedience to Mrs. Tomkin's Commands. By Patrick Carey. [Edited, with notes, by Sir W. S.] London, 1820, 4to.
Two Bannatyne Garlands from Abbotsford. 8vo.
About 40 copies only were printed and presented by the Secretary to those members of the Bannatyne Club who dined together on the 25th Anniversary of the Club. One of these ballads, "The Reever's Penance," was written by Robert Surtees of Mainsforth, Durham, the other by Sir Walter Scott.
The Visionary. Nos. 1, 2, 3 [being political satires first published in the *Edinburgh Weekly Journal*, each signed Somnambulus]. Edinburgh, 1819, 12mo.
——Reform and Ruin! a dream. [Signed Somnambulus.] Sunderland, [1820], 8vo.
Reprinted from No. 2 of "The Visionary."
The Works of John Dryden, now first collected. Illustrated with notes, historical, critical, and

explanatory, and a life of the author, by Walter Scott. 18 vols. London, 1808, 8vo.

——Second edition. 18 vols. Edinburgh, 1821, 8vo.

——Another edition. Revised and corrected by G. Saintsbury. Edinburgh, 1882, etc., 8vo.

——The Life of John Dryden. London, 1808, 4to.

Only 50 copies printed. This biography forms the first volume of "The Works of John Dryden," 1808.

The Works of Jonathan Swift, containing additional letters, tracts, and poems, not hitherto published; with notes and a life of the author by Walter Scott. 19 vols. Edinburgh, 1814, 8vo.

There is in the library of the British Museum, pp. 261-459, 1-280 of vols. xi. and xii. of an edition of Swift's works used by Sir Walter Scott for his edition of Swift, with copious MS. notes by him.

——Second edition. 19 vols. Edinburgh, 1824, 8vo.

VI. SUPPOSITITIOUS WORKS.

Autobiography of Sir W. S. Philadelphia, 1831, 12mo.

Die Erstürmung von Selama, oder die Rache. Eine schottische Sage von W. S. 3 Thle. Quedlinburg, 1825, 8vo,

Moredun. Narration de l'année 1210. Roman posthume et inédit de Sir W. S. Précédé d' une Introduction par E. de Saint Maurice Cabany. (Moredun: a tale of the Twelve Hundred and Ten.) 3 vols. Paris, 1855, 8vo.

The text of the novel, which is in English, was printed at Edinburgh, and the French Introduction at Paris.

The Bridal of Caölchairn ; and Miscellaneous Poems. By W. S. [i.e., John Hay Allan]. Fifth edition. London, 1822, 8vo.

Allan Cameron, en Roman, efterladt af Sir W. S. [i.e., Calais], oversat af F. Schaldemose. 2 Deel. Kjöbenhavn, 1841. 16mo.

La Pythie des Higlands, roman inédit. Par Sir W. S. [i.e., Jules A. David]. 2 vols. Paris, 1844, 8vo.

Walladmor. Frei nach dem Englischen des W. S. [or rather written in German] von W. . . . s. [i.e., Georg Wilhelm Heinrich Haering]. Berlin, 1824, 8vo.

——Walladmor. "Freely translated into German from the English of Sir Walter Scott" [by W . . . s, or, rather, originally written in German by G. W. H. Haering. And now freely translated from the German into English by T. De Quincey]. 2 vols. London, 1825, 16mo.

Schloss Avalon. Frei nach dem Englischen des W. S. vom Uebersetzer des Walladmor. 3 Bde. Leipzig, 1827, 8vo.

The Lay of the Scottish Fiddle: a tale of Havre de Grace. Supposed to be written by W. S. [i.e., James Kirke Paulding]. New York, 1813, 12mo.

——Another edition. London, 1814, 12mo.

VII. APPENDIX.

BIOGRAPHY, CRITICISM, ETC.

Adams, W. H. Davenport.—Master Minds in Art, Science, and Letters. London [1886], 8vo. Sir Walter Scott, pp. 279-335.

Airy, Sir George Biddell.—On the Topography of the "Lady of the Lake." London, 1873, 8vo. Privately printed.

Aiton, William.—A history of the encounter at Drumclog, and battle at Bothwell Bridge, with an account of what is correct and what is fictitious in the "Tales of my Landlord" [i.e., in "Old Mortality"] respecting these engagements, etc. Hamilton, 1821, 8vo.

Allibone, S. A. — A Critical Dictionary of English Literature and British and American Authors. 3 vols. London, 1859-71, 3vo.
Sir W. Scott, vol ii., pp. 1064-1979.

Anderson, William.—The Scottish Nation. 3 vols. Edinburgh, 1863, 4to.
Sir Walter Scott, with portrait, vol. ii., pp. 415-421.

Bagehot, Walter. — Literary Studies. 2 vols. London, 1879, 8vo.
The Waverley Novels, vol. ii., pp. 146-183.

——Third edition. 2 vols. London, 1884, 8vo.
The Waverley Novels (1858), vol. ii., pp. 146-183.

Ballantyne, A. — Refutation of the Misstatements and Calumnies contained in Mr. Lockhart's Life of Sir Walter Scott respecting the Messrs. [James and John] Ballantyne. By the Trustees and Son of the late James Ballantyne. London, 1838, 8vo.

——Reply to Mr. Lockhart's pamphlet, entitled "The Ballantyne Humbug handled." By the authors of a "Refutation of the Misstatements and Calumnies," etc. London, 1839, 8vo.

Bartlett, Alfred D.—An historical and descriptive account of Cumnor Place, Berks. Followed by some remarks on the statements in Sir Walter Scott's Kenilworth. Oxford, 1850, 8vo.

Bates, William. — The Maclise Portrait-Gallery of "Illustrious Literary Characters," with memoirs, etc. London, 1883, 8vo.
Sir Walter Scott, pp. 31-37.

Belfast, Earl of.—Poets and Poetry of the Nineteenth Century. A course of lectures. London, 1852, 8vo.
Scott, pp. 99-131.

Billington, William.—Facts, Observations, etc., being an exposure of the misrepresentations of the author's Treatise on Planting contained in Mr. Withers's Letters to Sir W. Scott . . . with remarks on Sir W. Scott's Essay on Planting, etc. Shrewsbury, 1830, 8vo.

Biographical Magazine.—Lives of the Illustrious. (The Biographical Magazine.) London, 1854, 8vo.
Sir W. Scott, vol. v., pp. 1-17.

Brown, James H. — Scenes in Scotland, with sketches and illustrations. Glasgow, 1833, 8vo.
Sir W. Scott—Sketch of his Literary life, pp. 36-62; Last illness, death and funeral, pp. 222-239.

Browne, James. — A Free Examination of Sir Walter Scott's opinions respecting Popery and the Penal Laws, as collected from Mr. Lockhart's "Life," and from various passages in Sir Walter Scott's works, etc. Edinburgh, 1845, 8vo.

Bryant, William Cullen.—Orations and Addresses. London, 1873, 8vo.

   Scott Statue, pp. 387-393.

Bucke, C.—A Letter intended (one day) as a supplement to Lockhart's Life of Sir Walter Scott [on Sir Walter Scott's mention of the author's dispute with Kean]. London, 1838, 8vo.

Buonaparte, Louis.—Réponse à Sir Walter Scott, sur son Histoire de Napoléon, etc. Seconde edition. Paris, 1829, 8vo.

——A Reply to Sir Walter Scott's History of Napoleon: a translation from the French. London, 1829, 8vo.

C., S. O.—Stories from Waverley, or rather from the Waverley Novels, for children. From the original of Sir W. S. By S. O. C. First (-second) series. 2 vols. Edinburgh, 1870, 16mo.

——Third edition. Edinburgh, 1873, 16mo.

Canning, Albert S. G.—Philosophy of the Waverley Novels. London, 1879, 8vo.

Carlyle, Thomas.—The Collected Works of T. C. 16 vols. London, 1858, 8vo.

   Sir W. Scott. vol. v., pp. 135-184; appeared originally in the *Westminster Review*, 1838.

Case, J. F.—Réfutation de la " Vie de Napoléon " de Sir W. Scott. Par M. * * * [*i.e.*, J. F. Case.] 2 vols. Paris, 1827, 12mo.

Chambers's Miscellany.—Famous Men, being biographical sketches from Chambers's Miscellany. London [1886], 8vo.

   Life of Sir W. Scott, 31 pp.

Chambers, Robert.—Life of Sir Walter Scott. With Abbotsford notanda by R. Carruthers.

Edited by W. Chambers. London, 1871, 8vo.

——Illustrations of the Author of Waverley; being notices and anecdotes of real characters and incidents, supposed to be described in his works. Edinburgh, 1822, 8vo.

——Second Edition. Edinburgh, 1825, 8vo.

——Reprinted from the Edition of 1825. Edinburgh, 1884, 8vo.

——Lives of Illustrious and Distinguished Scotsmen, etc. 4 vols. Glasgow, 1835, 8vo.

   Sir W. Scott, vol. 4, pp. 205-213.

Channing, William Ellery.—Remarks on the Character of N. Buonaparte [by W. E. Channing] occasionied by the publication of Scott's Life of Napoleon. From the *Christian Examiner*, vol. iv., No. 5. Boston [U.S.], 1827, 8vo.

——Analysis of the character of Napoleon Bonaparte, suggested by the publication of Scott's Life of Napoleon. Boston [U.S.], 1828, 8vo.

Chorley, Henry F.—The Authors of England. A series of medallion portraits of modern literary characters, engraved from the works of British Artists, etc. London, 1838, 4to.

   Sir W. Scott, pp. 7-13.

——New edition. London, 1861, 4to.

   Sir W. Scott, pp. 7-13.

Christian, Edward. — Historical notices of Edward and William Christian, two characters in Peveril of the Peak. [By M. Wilks ?] [London, 1822] 8vo.

Churton, E.—A Lay to the Last Minstrel. Inscribed to the memory of Sir Walter Scott.

[Preceded by a critique on his writings.] London, 1874, 8vo.

Cleishbotham, Jedediah, *pseud.* —New Landlord's Tales ; or, Jedediah in the South. 2 vols. London, 1825, 12mo.

Cochrane, J. G.—Catalogue of the library at Abbotsford (*Maitland Club*). Edinburgh, 1838, 4to.

Cochrane, Robert.—The Treasury of Modern Biography, etc. London, 1878, 8vo.
Sir Walter Scott, pp. 110-120.

Cornish, Sidney W.—The Waverley Manual, or, handbook of the chief characters, incidents, and descriptions in the Waverley Novels, etc. Edinburgh, 1871, 8vo.

Courthope, William John.—The Liberal Movement in English Literature. London, 1885, 8vo.
Revival of Romance : Scott, Byron, Shelley, pp. 111-156 ; reprinted from the *National Review.*

Cunningham, Allan. — Biographical and critical history of the British Literature of the last fifty years. Paris, 1834, 8vo.
Sir W. Scott, pp. 40-50, 143-151, 216-222, 255-268, 278, 315.

Dennis, John.—Heroes of Literature. English Poets, etc. London, 1883, 8vo.
Sir Walter Scott, pp. 300-321.

Devey, J.—A comparative estimate of modern English Poets. London, 1873, 8vo.
Scott, pp. 212-225.

Dickson, N. — The Bible in Waverley ; or, Sir Walter Scott's use of the Sacred Scriptures. Edinburgh, 1884, 8vo.

Dixon, W. H.—Sir Walter Scott's Centenary. The Speech of W. H. D., at the banquet in celebration of the above event,

together with the Ode written by M. Barr. London, 1871, 8vo.

Dodds, Rev. James. — Personal Reminiscences and Biographical Sketches. Edinburgh, 1887, 8vo.
Sir Walter Scott, pp. 183-192.

Doyle, Sir Francis Hastings.— Lecture on Poetry delivered at Oxford. Second series. London, 1877, 8vo.
Walter Scott, pp. 78-140.

Dulcken, W.—Worthies of the World, etc. London [1881], 8vo.
Sir Walter Scott, pp. 401-416.

Eberty, Felix. — Walter Scott. Ein Lebensbild. Aus englischen Quellen zusammengestellt. 2 Bde. Breslau, 1860, 8vo.
——Walter Scott. Zÿn leven en werken. Met een voorrede van C. W. Opzoomer. 2 Deel. Amsterdam, 1869, 12mo.

Edinburgh Theatrical Fund.—An account of the first Edinburgh Theatrical Fund Dinner, held at Edinburgh, on Friday, 23rd February 1827 ; containing a correct and authentic report of speeches ; which include, among other interesting matter, the first public avowal, by Sir Walter Scott, of being the author of the Waverley Novels. Edinburgh, 1827, 8vo.

Elze, Karl.—Sir Walter Scott. [A biography]. *Germ.* 2 Bde. Dresden, 1864, 8vo.

Encyclopædia Britannica. Ninth edition. Edinburgh, 1886, 4to.
Scott, by Prof. W. Minto, vol. xxi.

Eunomia.—Eunomia, with brief hints to country gentlemen and others of tender capacity on the principle of the new sect of political economical philosophers termed Eunomians, with some strictures upon banks, etc., in answer to the Rt. Hon. Sir J. Sinclair, Bart., Malachi Malagrowther, etc. London, 1826, 8vo.

Everett, Edward. — The Mount Vernon Papers. New York, 1860, 8vo.
Abbotsford visited and revisited, pp. 115-123, 135-144.

F.— The Waverley Anecdotes, illustrative of the incidents, characters, and scenery described in the novels and romances of Sir W. S. [Compiled by F.] London, 1833, 8vo.
——Another edition. London [1887], 8vo.

Fitzpatrick, W. J.—Who wrote the earlier Waverley Novels ? Being an investigation into certain mysterious circumstances attending their production, and an inquiry into the literary aid which Sir W. Scott may have received from other persons. [By W. J. F.—*i. e.*, W. J. Fitzpatrick]. London, 1856, 8vo.
——Second edition, completely rewritten, etc. Who wrote the earlier Waverley Novels ? An essay showing that Sir W. Scott's relation to Waverley, Guy Mannering, and the Tales of my Landlord, was, at the most, that of an editor [and attributing the authorship to Thomas and Elizabeth Scott]. London, 1856, 8vo.

Forbes, Alexander, — Thoughts concerning Man's condition and duties in this life, etc. Fourth edition. With a biographical sketch of the author by Lord Medwyne, and a review by Sir W. Scott. Edinburgh, 1854, 12mo.

French, Gilbert J.—Parallel Passages from two tales elucidating the origin of the plot of Guy Mannering. Manchester, 1855, 8vo.
——An enquiry into the origin of the authorship of some of the earlier Waverley Novels. Bolton, 1856, 8vo.
Privately printed.

G., S. v.—Walter Scott. Ein romantisch - Kritisiren des Gemälde scines schriftstellerischen Geistes aufgestellt von S. v. G. Naumburg, 1826, 16vo.
——Another edition. Leipzig, 1833, 16mo.

G * * *, General.—[*i.e.*, Gaspard Gourgand.] — Réfutation de la Vie de Napoléon, par Sir Walter Scott. Par le Général G * * *. 2 pts. Paris, 1827, 8vo.

Gibson, John.— Reminiscences of Sir Walter Scott. Edinburgh, 1871, 8vo.

Gillillan, G.—Life of Sir W. Scott, etc. Edinburgh, 1870, 8vo.
——Second edition. Edinburgh, 1871, 8vo.

Gillies, R. P.—Recollections of Sir Walter Scott. [By R. P. Gillies.] London, 1837, 8vo.

Gleig, George Robert.—The Life of Sir Walter Scott. Reprinted, with corrections and additions, from the *Quarterly Review*, etc. Edinburgh, 1871, 8vo.

Graham, William. — Lectures, Sketches, and Poetical Pieces. Edinburgh, 1873, 8vo.
Address at the Scott Centenary dinner at Innerleithen, pp. 153-163.

Graves, H. M.—An Essay on the Genius of Shakespeare, with critical remarks on the characters of Romeo, Hamlet, Juliet, and Ophelia, together with some observations on the writings of Sir W. Scott, etc. London, 1826, 8vo.

Grey, Earl. — Earl Grey, the British Reformer—Signor Rivoillo, the Italian Musician—Sir Walter Scott, Bart., the Scottish Novelist. [A verse upon each, accompanied by a woodcut]. [Edinburgh, 1832]. s. sh., 8vo.

Hagberg, Carl August.—Cervantes et Walter Scott, parallèle littéraire soumis à la discussion publique l'avant-midi du 21 Nov. 1838. Lund, 1838, 8vo.

Hamilton, Walter.—Parodies of the Works of English and American Authors. Collected and annotated by W. H. London, 1886, 4to.
Sir Walter Scott, vol. iii, pp, 71-90.

Hannay, David.—Glimpses of the Land of Scott. Illustrated by J. Macwhirter. London, 1887, 4to.

Hazlitt, William.—The Spirit of the Age ; or, contemporary portraits. London, 1825, 8vo.
Sir Walter Scott, pp. 129-156.

——The Plain Speaker ; opinions of books, men, and things Second edition. 2 vols. London, 1851, 8vo.
Sir Walter Scott, Racine, and Shakespeare, vol. ii., pp. 257-278

Heber, Richard. — Letters to Richard Heber, Esq., containing critical remarks on the series of novels [by Sir W. S.], beginning with "Waverley," etc. London, 1821, 8vo.

Hogg, James. — The domestic manners and private life of Sir W. Scott. With a memoir of the author, notes, etc. Glasgow, 1834, 12mo.
——Another edition. Edinburgh, 1882, 8vo.

Howitt, William. — Homes and Haunts of the most eminent British Poets. Third edition. London, 1857, 8vo.
Scott, pp. 446-486.

Hunnewell, James F.—Lands of Scott. Edinburgh, 1871, 8vo.

Hutton, Richard H.—Sir Walter Scott. (*English Men of Letters*, ed. Morley.) London, 1878, 8vo.

Irving, Washington. — Abbotsford and Newstead Abbey. London, 1850, 8vo.

Jacob, Carl Georg. — Walter Scott. Für die Leser seiner Werke. Ein biographisch literarischer Versuch. Köln am Rhein, 1827, 16mo.

Jeaffreson, J. Cordy.—Novels and Novelists, from Elizabeth to Victoria. 2 vols. London, 1858, 8vo.
Walter Scott, vol. ii, pp. 31-83.

Jeffrey, Francis.— Contributions to the *Edinburgh Review*. London, 1853, 8vo.
"The Lay of the Last Minstrel," Aug. 1810, pp. 465-482 ; "Waverley," Nov. 1814, pp. 670-676 ; "Waverley Novels," March 1817, Feb. 1818, Jan. 1820, June 1822, pp. 676-703.

Jerdan, William.—Men I have known. London, 1866, 8vo.
Four epochs in the life of Scott, pp. 393-399.

Jerrold, Blanchard.—The Best of All Good Company. Part ii. A Centenary Day with Sir Walter Scott, August 15th, 1871. London, 1871, 8vo.

Keble, John.—Occasional Papers and Reviews. Oxford, 1877, 8vo.
Life of Sir Walter Scott, pp. 1-80 ; reprinted from the *British Critic*, 1838.

Landon, Letitia E. — Life and literary remains of L. E. L. by

Laman Blanchard. 2 vols. London, 1841, 8vo.
The Female Picture Gallery. Scott's Female Characters, vol. ii, pp. 81-194.

Lang, Andrew.—Letters to Dead Authors. London, 1886, 8vo.
To Sir Walter Scott, Bart., pp. 152-161.

Lectures.—The Afternoon Lectures on English Literature delivered at . . . Dublin, 1863. London, 1863, 8vo.
On the Classical and Romantic Schools of English Literature as represented by Spenser, Dryden, Pope, Scott, and Wordsworth, by William Rushton, first series, pp. 41-92.

——The Afternoon Lectures on Literature and Art delivered in Dublin, 1867 and 1868. Fifth series. Dublin, 1869, 8vo.
The Poetry of Sir Walter Scott, by Rev. J. H. Jellett, pp. 51-89.

Lee, H.—The Life of the Emperor Napoleon; with an appendix, containing an examination of Sir W. Scott's Life of Napoleon Bonaparte, etc. Vol. i. London, 1834, 8vo.

Lennox, Lord William Pitt.—Celebrities I have known, etc. Second series. 2 vols. London, 1877, 8vo.
Walter Scott, vol. ii, pp. 21-33.

Leslie, Charles R.—Autobiographical Recollections. 2 vols. London, 1860, 8vo.
References to Sir W. Scott.

Lockhart, C. S. M.—The Centenary Memorial of Sir W. Scott, Bart. [With illustrations]. London, 1871, 8vo.

Lockhart, J. G.—Memoirs of the life of Sir Walter Scott, Bart. 7 vols. Edinburgh, 1837-38, 12mo.
——Another edition. 10 vols. Edinburgh, 1839, 16mo.

Lockhart, J. G.—Another edition. Edinburgh, 1845, 8vo.
——Another edition. Edinburgh, 1850, 8vo.
——Another edition (Chandos Library). London [1881], 8vo.
——The Life of Sir W. Scott. Abridged from the larger work by J. G. L. With a prefatory letter by J. R. Hope Scott. Edinburgh, 1871, 8vo.
——Epitome of Lockhart's Life of Scott by H. J. Jenkinson. Edinburgh, 1873, 8vo.
——The Ballantyne - Humbug handled, in a letter to Sir A. Fergusson [in answer to a pamphlet, entitled "Refutation of the Misstatements and Calumnies contained in Mr. Lockhart's Life of Sir W. Scott, Bart., respecting the Messrs. Ballantyne. By the Trustees and Son of the late James Ballantyne."] Edinburgh, 1839, 8vo.

MacCrie, Thomas—Vindication of the Covenanters, in a review of the "Tales of my Landlord." Edinburgh, 1845, 8vo.

Mackay, Charles.—Forty Years' Recollections of Life, Literature, etc., from 1830 to 1870. 2 vols. London, 1877, 8vo.
Sir Walter Scott and his Monument, vol. i., pp. 175-206.
——Through the Long Day; or, Memorials of a literary life during half a century. London, 1887, 8vo.
The Scott Monument at Edinburgh, vol. i., pp. 143-148.

Mackenzie, R. Shelton.—Sir Walter Scott; the story of his life. Boston [U.S.], 1871, 8vo.

MacLeod, Donald.—Life of Sir W. Scott. New York, 1852, 12mo.

Martineau, Harriet.—Miscellanies. 2 vols. Boston [U.S.], 1836, 8vo.

Characteristics of the Genius of of Scott, vol. i., pp. 1-12; appeared originally in *Tait's Edinburgh Magazine*, 1832. Achievements of the Genius of Scott, pp. 27-56; originally appeared in same magazine, 1833.

Mason, Edward T.—Personal Traits of British Authors, etc. Edited by E. Mason. 2 vols. New York, 1885, 8vo.

Sir Walter Scott, vol. ii., pp. 5-78.

Massachusetts Historical Society. —Tribute to Walter Scott on the one hundredth anniversary of his birthday, Aug. 15, 1871. Boston [U.S.], 1872, 8vo.

Addresses by the President, the Hon. R. C. Winthrop, Ralph Waldo Emerson, and Letters from O. W. Holmes, W. C. Bryant, etc., pp. 139-156.

Masson, David.—British Novelists and their Styles, etc. Cambridge, 1859, 8vo.

Scott and his influence, pp. 155-207.

Miller, Hugh.—Essays, historical and biographical, political and social, literary and scientific. Edinburgh, 1862, 8vo.

The Abbotsford Baronetcy, pp. 487-495.

——Leading Articles on various Subjects. Edinburgh, 1870, 8vo.

The Scott Monument, pp. 111-118.

Mitchell, Donald G.—About old Story-Tellers, etc. New York, 1878, 8vo.

A Scotch Magician, pp. 166-197.

Moir, D. M.—Sketches of the poetical literature of the past half-century. Cambridge, 1851, 8vo.

Scott, pp. 116-127.

Napier, Sir W. F. P.—History of the War in the Peninsula and in the South of France. (Answers to some attacks in Robinson's Life of Picton, etc. Justificatory pieces, in reply to Colonel Gurwood, Mr. Alison, Sir W. Scott, etc.) 6 vols. London, 1828-40, 8vo.

Nayler, B. S.—A Memoir of the Life and Writings of Walter Scott, etc. Amsterdam, 1833, 12mo.

Nichols, John.—Illustrations of the Literary History of the Eighteenth Century, etc. 8 vols. London, 1817-58, 8vo.

Numerous references to Scott.

Nicoll, Henry J.—Landmarks of English Literature. London, 1883, 8vo.

Sir Walter Scott, pp. 323-340.

Notes and Queries. — General Index to Notes and Queries. Five Series. London, 1856-1880, 4to.

Numerous references to Scott.

Oliphant, Mrs. M. O.—The Literary History of England, etc. 3 vols. London, 1882, 8vo.

Walter Scott, vol. ii., pp. 94-180.

Parton, James. — Some noted Princes, Authors, and Statesmen of our Time. Edited by J. P. New York [1886], 8vo.

Sir Walter Scott's Home, by Louise Chandler Moulton, pp. 225-229.

Poets.—Evenings with the Poets, etc. London, 1860, 8vo.

Scott, pp. 276-280.

Prescott, William H.—Critical and Historical Essays. Second edition. London, 1850, 8vo.

Sir Walter Scott, pp. 120-166; originally contributed to the *North American Review*, April 1838.

Pry, Peter.—Marmion Travestied; a tale of modern times. By Peter Pry. London, 1809, 8vo.

Quiz, Jeremiah. — The Ass on Parnassus ; and from Scotland Ge ho !! comes Roderigh Vich Neddy Dhu, Ho! Jeroe !! Canto i., ii. of a poem entitled " What are Scots Collops ? " a prophetic tale, written in imitation of the Lady of the Lake. By J. Q London, 1811, 4to.

—— Marmion Feats ; A day before the Tournament.—A prophetic tale, written in imitation of the Lady of the Lake, being a sequel to the Ass on Parnassus, etc. London, 1811, 4to.

Reed, Henry.—Lectures on the British Poets. London, 1857, 8vo.

Scott, pp. 241-259.

Rice, Allen T. —Essays from the North American Review. Edited by A. T. R. New York, 1879, 8vo.

Sir Walter Scott, by W. H. Prescott (1838), pp. 3-63.

Richardson, David Lester.— Literary Chit-Chat, etc. Calcutta, 1848, 8vo.

Sir Walter Scott and Lord Byron, pp. 163-179.

Rogers, Charles.—The Centenary Garland : being pictorial illustrations of the novels of Sir W. Scott, in their order of publication, by G. Cruikshank and other artists. With descriptions, memoir, etc. [By C. Rogers.] Edinburgh, 1871, 4to.

Rogers, May.—The Waverley Dictionary : an alphabetical arrangement of all the characters in Sir Walter Scott's Waverley Novels, etc. Chicago, 1879, 8vo.

Rogers, Samuel.—Recollections of the Table-Talk of Samuel Rogers. Third edition. London, 1856, 8vo.

Numerous references to Sir Walter Scott.

Rossetti, William Michael.—Lives of Famous Poets. London [1885], 8vo.

Walter Scott, pp. 219-234.

S., W.—To His Majesty's Ship Barham, appointed to convey Sir W. Scott to Naples. [Verses signed W. S.]—[1831], 4to.

Scott, John.—Journal of a Tour to Waterloo and Paris, in company with Sir Walter Scott, in 1815. London, 1842, 12mo.

Scott, Sir Walter.—Illustrations of W. S.'s Lay of the Last Minstrel : consisting of twelve views of the rivers Borthwick, Ettrick, Yarrow, Tiviot, and Tweed. Engraved by J. Heath from designs by J. C. Schetky, with anecdotes and descriptions. London, 1808, 4to.

——The Lady of the Lake : a romance. Founded on the poem, so called, by W. S. 2 vols. London, 1810, 12mo.

——Jokeby, a burlesque on [Sir Walter Scott's] Rokeby : a poem in six cantos. By an Amateur of Fashion. Fifth edition. London, 1812, 12mo.

—— ——Sixth edition. London, 1813, 12mo.

——The Lay of the Poor Fiddler, a parody on the Lay of the Last Minstrel, with notes and illustrations. By an admirer of Walter Scott. London, 1814, 8vo.

——Illustrations of the Novels and Tales of the Author of Waverley : a series of portraits of eminent historical characters introduced in these works. Accompanied with biographical notices. Pts. 1-7. London, 1823, 8vo. No more published.

——A Discourse on the comparative merits of Scott and Byron, as writers of poetry. Delivered before a Literary Institution in 1820. [Glasgow], 1824, 8vo.

——The Fortunes of Nigel, Lord Glenvarloch, and Margaret Ramsay. An interesting narrative [founded upon Sir W. Scott's Novel]. London [1825], 8vo.

——A Summary Account of Sir W. S., the Scottish Novelist. Edinburgh [1832 !], s. sh., 8vo.

——Soirées d' Abbotsford, chroniques et nouvelles recueillies dans les salons de W. S. Paris, 1834, 8vo.

——A Parallel of Shakespeare and Scott; being the substance of three lectures. . . . 1833 and 1834. London, 1835, 8vo.

——Guide pittoresque du voyageur en Ecosse, représentant les principaux édifices et tous les lieux cités par Walter Scott. Paris, 1838, 8vo.

——Statues of Old Mortality and his pony, and of Sir W. S., at Laurel Hill Cemetery, near Philadelphia. Philadelphia, 1839, 8vo.

——Auxiliary subscription for securing the erection of the Scott Monument in Edinburgh, on the scale of 1º0 feet in height. Edinburgh, 1840, 12mo.

——The Waverley Gallery of the principal Female Characters in Sir W. S.'s romances. From original paintings by eminent artists. Engraved under the superintendence of C. Heath. London, 1841, 8vo.

——Narrative of the Life of Sir W. S., begun by himself and continued by J. G. Lockhart. 2 vols. Edinburgh, 1848, 12mo.

——Life of Sir. W. S., begun by himself and continued by J. G. Lockhart. (An abridgment embracing only what may more strictly be called narrative.) Second edition. Edinburgh, 1853, 8vo.

——Particulars and conditions of Sale of Copyrights, etc., of the Works of Sir Walter Scott, Bart., comprising his Novels, Poetry, Prose Writings, etc. London [1851], 4to.

——Beautés de W. S. Magnifiques portraits des héroines de W. S. accompagnés chacun d' un portrait littéraire per MM. A. Dumas, Carmouche, E. Souvestre, F. Soulié, Fournier, J. Janin, H. Rolle, Lafitte, etc. Paris [1852], 8vo.

——A Few Hours with Scott; being sketches in the way of supplement to the "Lord of the Isles" and "Rokeby." By one of his old readers. Edinburgh, 1856, 8vo.

——The Land of Scott; or, tourist's guide to Abbotsford, the Country of the Tweed and its tributaries, and St. Mary's Loch. [With views printed in colours.] London, 1858, 16mo.

——The Land of Scott, etc. (*Nelson's Handbooks for Tourists.*) London, 1859, 8vo.

——The Scott Exhibition, 1871. Catalogue of the Exhibition held in Edinburgh, in July and August 1871, on occasion of the Commemoration of the Centenary of the birth of Sir Walter Scott. [Preface by Sir W. Stirling Maxwell.] Edinburgh, 1872, 4to.

Senior, Nassau William.—Essays on Fiction. London, 1864, 8vo.
Sir Walter Scott, pp. 1-188.

Shairp, John Campbell.—Aspects of Poetry; being lectures delivered at Oxford. Oxford, 1881, 8vo.
The Homeric Spirit in Walter Scott, pp. 337-406.

Sime, William.—To and fro; or, views from sea and land. London, 1884, 8vo.
Scott's Influence in French Literature, pp. 172-178.

Skene, James. — A Series of Sketches of the Existing Localities alluded to in the "Waverley Novels." Etched from original drawings by J. S. Edinburgh, 1829, 8vo.

Sorell, Thomas Stephen.—Notes of the Campaign of 1808-9, in the North of Spain, in reference to some passages in Lieut.-Col. Napier's History of the War in the Peninsula, and in Sir W. Scott's Life of Napoleon Bonaparte. London, 1828, 8vo.

Sproat, Gilbert M.—Sir Walter Scott as a Poet, etc. Edinburgh, 1871, 8vo.

Stephen, Leslie.—Hours in a Library. London, 1874, 8vo.
Some words about Sir Walter Scott, pp. 213-255.

Stevens, H. I., and A.—Scott and Scotland; or, historical and romantic Illustrations of Scottish Story. With steel engravings. London [1845], 8vo.

Taylor, J.—The Caledonian Comet [i.e., Sir W. S. A satirical poem, by J. Taylor]. London, 1810, 8vo.

Tegg, William. — Anecdotes of Napoleon Buonaparte and his times. Selected from the writings of Sir W. Scott, etc. London, 1878, 16mo.

Ticknor, George.—Life, Letters, and Journals of G. T. 2 vols. London, 1876, 8vo.
Numerous references to Scott.

Tillotson, John. — The New Waverley Album. Illustrated with numerous engravings on steel, after designs by C Stanfield, D. Roberts, W. Daniell, C. Fielding, etc. The text by J. T. London [1859], 4to.

——Album of Scottish Scenery: a series of views, illustrating several places of interest mentioned in Sir W. Scott's Poems and Novels. By D. Roberts, W. Westall, J. M. W. Turner. With descriptions by J. T. London [1860], 4to.

Touchstone, Timothy, pseud.—A letter to the author of Waverley, Ivanhoe, etc., on the moral tendency of those works. London, 1820, 12mo.

Tuckerman, Bayard.—A History of English Prose Fiction, etc. New York, 1852, 8vo.
Scott, pp. 278-284.

Turner, J. M. W.—A descriptive catalogue of drawings expressly made for "Views in England and Wales," and also for Sir Walter Scott's poetical works. [London, 1833] 8vo.

Vedder, David.—Memoir of Sir W. Scott, with critical notices of his writings. Compiled from authentic sources. Dundee, 1832, 12mo.

Veitch, John.—The History and Poetry of the Scottish Border, etc. Glasgow, 1878, 8vo.
Sir Walter Scott, pp. 406-518.
——The Feeling for Nature in Scottish Poetry. 2 vols. Edinburgh, 1887, 8vo.
Sir Walter Scott, vol. ii., pp. 183-228.

Ward, Thomas Humphrey.—The English Poets, etc. Edited by T. H. W. Second edition. 4 vols. London, 1883, 8vo.
Walter Scott, by Goldwin Smith, vol. iv., pp. 186-220.

Warner Richard. — Illustrations, historical, biographical, and miscellaneous, of the Novels by the author of "Waverley." With criticisms, general and particular. 3 vols. London, 1823-24, 12mo.

Watt, James Crabb. — Great Novelists — Scott, Thackeray, Dickens, Lytton. London [1885], 8vo.
Scott, pp. 1-95.

Waverley, E. B.—[*i.e.*, John Wilson Croker.]—Two letters on Scottish affairs from Edward Bradwardine Waverley, Esq., to Malachi Malagrowther, Esq. [Sir Walter Scott: in reply to his "Thoughts on the proposed change of currency," etc]. London, 1826, 8vo.

Weir, William. — Life of Sir Walter Scott, with critical notices of his writings [begun by W. W. and completed by George Allan]. Edinburgh, 1834, 8vo.

Welsh, Alfred H.—Development of English Literature and Language. Chicago, 1882, 8vo.
Scott, vol. ii., pp. 321-330.

Whipple, Edwin P.—Essays and Reviews. 2 vols. Third edition. Boston [U.S.], 1856, 8vo.
Scott, vol. i., pp. 319-329.

White, James. — Robert Burns and Walter Scott. Two Lives. London, 1858, 8vo.

Willis, N. P.—Famous Persons and Famous Places. London, 1854, 8vo.
References to Scott.

Withers, William.—A Letter to Sir Walter Scott, Bart., respecting certain errors in his late essay on planting, etc. London, 1823, 8vo.

Wright, G. N.—Landscape-historical illustrations of Scotland and the Waverley Novels, from drawings by J. M. W. Turner, etc. Descriptions by G. N. W. 2 vols. London [1836-38], 4to.

Yonge, Charles Duke.—Three Centuries of English Literature. London, 1872, 8vo.
Scott, pp. 294-322.

Young, Charles Mayne. — A Memoir of C. M. Y., tragedian, with extracts from his son's journal. By Julian C. Young. 2 vols. London, 1871, 8vo.
Visit to Abbotsford, vol. i., pp. 137-150.

PLAYS, ETC., FOUNDED ON SCOTT'S WORKS.

The Waverley Dramas, from the novels of Sir W. S. [Guy Mannering, by D. Terry; Rob Roy, by I. Pocock; Heart of Midlothian, Kenilworth, Antiquary, Fortunes of Nigel, Peveril of the Peak, and Ivanhoe, by D. Terry?] London, 1845-1823, 12mo.
Each play has a distinct pagination. The title-page only is of the date of 1845, the plays having been published earlier, some without a date, and others with the date of 1823.

Le Chateau de Loch-Leven, Mélo-drame historique en trois actes [and in prose], imité [from The Abbot] de W. S. Par R. C. Guilbert de Pixérécourt. Paris, 1822, 8vo.

The Antiquary ; a musical play in three acts from Sir W. S. To which is prefixed a memoir of his life. By D. Terry. (*Cumberland's British Theatre*, vol. xxxi.)

The Antiquary, a musical play, in three acts [and in prose, with songs], taken from the celebrated novel of that name. By D. Terry. London, 1820, 8vo.

King Arthur and the Knights of the Round Table ; a new grand chivalric entertainment in three acts [and in verse. Adapted from the "Bridal of Triermain"]. London, 1834, 8vo.

La Fiancée de Lammermoor, pièce héroïque en trois actes [and in prose] imitée du roman de Sir W. S. par V. Ducange. Paris, 1828, 8vo.

——(*Théâtre Contemporaine Illustré*, Liv. 425). Paris, 1860, fol.

Lucia di Lammermoor. A tragic opera in three acts [and in verse. Dramatised from Sir W. Scott's "Bride of Lammermoor"], *Ital.* and *Eng.* London [1848], 12mo.

The Bride of Lammermoor, a drama in four acts [and in prose]. Adapted from Sir W. S.'s celebrated romance, by J. W. Calcraft. (*Lacy's Acting Edition of Plays*, etc., vol. xxviii.) London [1857], 12mo.

An English Version of Lucia di Lammermoor ; a grand opera in three acts. [Adapted from S. Camerano's Italian drama,

founded on Sir W. S.'s "Bride of Lammermoor"]. Music by Donizetti. (*Lacy's Acting Edition of Plays*, etc., vol. lxxviii.) London [1868], 12mo.

The Fair Maid of Perth ; or, the Battle of the Inch. A grand historical drama, in three acts. Founded on Sir W. S.'s Novel. By H. M. Milner. (*Lacy's Acting Edition of Plays*, etc., vol. lxxi). London [1866], 12mo.

Nigel ; or, The Crown Jewels : a play in five acts, founded on Sir W. Scott's romance, "The Fortunes of Nigel." London, 1823, 8vo.

The Fortunes of Nigel. A melo-dramatic romance, in three acts, by Edward Fitz-Ball. (*Cumberland's Minor Theatre*, vol. iv.) London [1828], 12mo.

Guy Mannering ; or, the Gipsey's Prophecy : a musical play in three acts [in prose, with songs, founded on Sir W. Scott's Romance of "Guy Mannering"]. Second edition. London, 1816, 8vo.

——Third edition. London, 1817, 8vo.

——Fourth edition. London, 1818, 8vo.

Guy Mannering ; or, the Gipsey's Prophecy : a drama in three acts. (*Hodgson's Juvenile Drama*). London [1822], 12mo.

La Sorcière, ou l' Orphelin Écossais : mélodrame en trois actes et en prose, tiré [from Guy Mannering] de Walter Scott, par MM. Frédéric [Dupetit-Méré] et Victor [Henri Joseph Brahain Ducange]. Paris, 1821, 8vo.

Guy Mannering. By D. Terry. (*The British Drama*, vol. i.) London, 1864, 8vo.

The Heart of Midlothian ; or, the Lily of St. Leonard's. A drama in three acts. (*Hodgson's Juvenile Drama*). London [1822], 12mo.

The Heart of Midlothian : a melodramatic romance in three acts, by Thomas Dibdin. (*Cumberland's Minor Theatre*, vol. i). London [1825], 12mo.

The Heart of Midlothian ; or, the Sisters of St. Leonard's. A drama in three acts. Adapted, with introductions, from S. Dibdin's play, by T. H. Lacy. (*Lacy's Acting Edition of Plays*, vol. lvii.) London [1863], 12mo.

Ivanhoe; or, the Knight Templar [a play in three acts, and in prose], adapted from the novel of that name. London, 1820, 8vo.

Ivanhoe; or, the Jew and his daughter. [Founded on Sir Walter Scott's romance.] London, 1820, 12mo.

Ivanhoe. A chivalric play, founded on the popular romance of Ivanhoe. By W. T. Moncrieff. London, 1820, 8vo.

The Hebrew : a drama in five acts [and in verse ; founded on Sir W. Scott's "Ivanhoe"]. By George Soane. London, 1820, 8vo.

Ivanhoe; or, the Jew of York. A drama in three acts. (*Hodgson's Juvenile Drama*.) London [1822], 12mo.

Ivanhoe ; or, the Jew's Daughter : a melodramatic romance in three acts. By Thomas Dibdin. London, 1820, 8vo.

——Another edition. (*Cumberland's Minor Theatre*, vol. ii.) London [1828], 12mo.

Ivanhoe, an extravaganza, by Henry J. Byron. (*Lacy's Acting Edition of Plays*, vol. 59.) London [1864], 12mo.

The Last Edition of Ivanhoe, an extravaganza, by the Brothers Brough. (*Webster's Acting National Drama*, vol. xvi.) London [1849], 12mo.

Ivanhoe, a historical drama, in three acts. Dramatised by Fox Cooper. (*Dick's Standard Plays*, No. 385). London [1883], 12mo.

The Maid of Judah ; or, the Knights Templars ; a serious opera in three acts, dramatised from Sir W. S.'s Ivanhoe by M. R. Lacy. (*Cumberland's British Theatre*, vol. xxv).

The Templar and the Jewess : a grand romantic opera in three acts, from Sir W. S.'s novel of Ivanhoe. *Germ.* and *Eng.* London [1842], 12mo.

Ivanhoé, opéra en trois actes, imité de l'Anglais par MM. *** [*i.e.*, E. Deschamps and A. F. L. de Wailly]. Paris, 1826, 8vo.

Der Templer und die Jüdin. Grosse romantische Oper in drei Aufzügen nach W. S's Roman " Ivanhoe," frei bearbeitet von W. A. Wohlbruck. Leipzig, 1829, 12mo.

Il Templario. Opera seria in tre atti cavato del Romanzo d'Ivanoe de W. S. da G. M. Marini. *Ital.* and *Fr.* Parigi, 1868, 8vo.

Les Normands. Grand opéra en cinq actes. [Founded on Sir W. S.'s " Ivanhoe."] Paroles et musique de A. Castegnier. Trouville [1886], 12mo.

Le Château de Kenilworth, mélodrame en trois actes, tiré du

roman de Sir W. S. par MM. Boirie et H. Lemaire. Paris, 1822, 8vo.

Kenilworth. A drama in two acts. By T. Dibdin. (*Cumberland's British Theatre*, vol. xxxix.)

Kenilworth, a comic operatic extravaganza, in one act, by Andrew Halliday and Frederick Lawrance. (*Lacy's Acting Edition of Plays*, vol. xxxviii.) London [1859], 12mo.

Kenilworth. A drama in two acts, by T. Dibdin and A. Bunn. (*Lacy's Acting Edition of Plays*, etc., vol. xcviii.) London, [1874], 12mo.

Oxberry's edition. Kenilworth, a melodrama. By W. Oxberry. (*English Drama*, vol. xix.) London, 1824, 8vo.

Schauspiele von J. R. Lenz. Nach W. Scott's Kenilworth und Ivanhoe, by J. R. L. 2 pts. Mainz, 1826, 8vo.

The Earl of Leicester : a Tragedy. [Founded on Sir W. Scott's novel of Kenilworth.] By Samuel Heath. London, 1843, 8vo.

Leicester, drama in vyf bedryven. Naer W. S. door F. Roelants. Brussel, 1852, 8vo.

The Lady of the Lake ; a melodramatic romance in three acts [and in verse], taken from the popular poem of that title. By E. J. Eyre. London, 1811, 8vo.

The Lady of the Lake. A drama in three acts [and in verse], founded on the popular poem written by W. S., Esq., etc. Dublin [1811], 12mo.

——Another edition. Dublin, 1811, 12mo.

The Knight of Snowdoun : a musical drama in three acts [founded on the " Lady of the Lake "]. By Thomas Morton. London, 1811, 8vo.

La Donna del Lago ; melodramma in musica [in two acts, and in verse. Founded on Sir W. S.'s " Lady of the Lake," by A. L. Tottola]. Firenze, 1825, 12mo.

—— Another edition. Roma, 1827, 12mo.

—— Another edition. Milano, 1838, 12mo.

La Donna del Lago. The Lady of the Lake : a melodramatic opera in two acts. [Founded by A. L. Tottola upon Sir W. Scott's " Lady of the Lake."] *Ital.* and *Eng.* London, 1829, 8vo.

The Lady of the Lake. A Romantic Drama in three acts. (*Lacy's Acting Edition of Plays*, vol. xxxiii.) London [1858], 8vo.

The Lady of the Lake, plaid in a new tartan. An ephemeral burlesque by R. Reece. (*Lacy's Acting Edition of Plays*, vol. lxxi.) London [1866], 12mo.

Border Feuds ; or, the Lady of Buccleuch. A musical drama in three acts. Founded on Mr. S.'s poem of " The Lay of the Last Minstrel," etc. Dublin, [1811], 12mo.

The Spectre Knight. Songs and other vocal compositions, with an outline of the plot, and a description of the scenery, in the grand Caledonian aquatic romance (partly founded on Sir W. Scott's Marmion) called the Spectre Knight. By C. J. M. Dibdin. London, 1810, 8vo.

Marmion ; or, Flodden Field. A drama [in five acts, and in verse], founded on the poem of W. S. London, 1812, 8vo.

Montrose ; or, the Children of the Mist. A musical drama in three acts. Founded on the Legend of Montrose. By I. Pocock. London, 1822, 8vo.

L'Exilé, vaudeville en deux actes, tiré des Puritains d'Ecosse (Old Mortality) de Sir Walter Scott. Par Achille Dartois, Théodore Anne, et de Tully. Paris, 1828, 8vo.

Quentin Durward ; a drama [in three acts, and in prose] founded on the novel of the same name, by the author of Waverley. By James L. Huie. Edinburgh, 1823, 8vo.

Rob Roy ; a Drama by G. Soane, (*Cumberland's British Theatre*, vol. xxxvi).

Rob Roy Macgregor ; or, Auld Lang Syne ! A musical drama in three acts [and in prose, with songs]. Founded on the popular novel of Rob Roy. By Isaac Pocock. London, 1818, 8vo.

——Second edition. London, 1818, 8vo.

——(*Oxberry's English Drama*, vol. x). London, 1820, 8vo.

——(*Lacy's Acting Edition of Plays* vol. iii). London [1851], 8vo.

——(*British Drama*, vol. ii). London, 1864, 8vo.

Rokeby ; or, the Border Chief. A drama in three acts [and in prose], founded on Sir W. S.'s poem of Rokeby. By J. H. Thompson. St. Louis, 1851, 12mo.

The Knights of the Cross ; or, the hermit's prophecy : a romantic drama in three acts, from [the Talisman of] Sir W. S., by the

author of the Steward, etc. (*Cumberland's British Theatre*, vol. xxxiv).

Woodstock. A play in five acts [and in prose], founded on the popular novel of that name. By Isaac Pocock. London, 1826, 8vo.

Charles Stuart ; ou, le Château de Woodstock : mélodrame en trois actes tiré du roman de Sir W. S. Paroles de M. Félix D [e] C [roisy] and A. Béraud. Paris, 1826, 8vo.

SONGS AND OTHER MUSICAL COMPOSITIONS, FOUNDED ON, OR TAKEN FROM, THE WORKS OF SIR WALTER SCOTT.

The Overture, Songs, etc., in Guy Mannering composed by T. Attwood and Sir H. R. Bishop, 1816.

Les Normands (founded on *Ivanhoe*). By A. Casteguier, 1886.

La Donna del Lago. Opera, by Rossini, 1819.

Lucia di Lammermoor. Opera, by G. Donizetti, 1859.

Quentin Durward. Opéra comique, by Cormon and Carre. Music by Gévaert, 1858.

Alice Brand. Cantata, by H. Gadsby, 1876.

The Bridal of Triermain. Cantata, by E. Aguilar, 1884.

Same, by F. Corder, 1886.

The Lady of the Lake. Cantata, by Sir G. A. Macfarren, 1877.

The Lay of the Last Minstrel. Cantata, by T. M. Pattison, 1885.

The Lord of the Isles. A dramatic Cantata by H. Gadsby, 1879.

Albyn's Anthology; or, a select collection of the melodies and vocal poetry of Scotland and the Isles, collected and arranged by A. Campbell. The modern Scottish and English verses adapted to the Highland, Hebridean, and Lowland Melodies. Written by Walter Scott, etc., 1816.

The Centenary Souvenir. Six songs by Sir W. Scott. Music by G. Croal, 1871.

Gesänge von W. S. By A. Jensen, 1875.

Musical Illustrations of the Waverley Novels. By Eliza Flower, 1831.

Musical illustrations of the Waverley novels. By T. Eyton, 1840.

Norman's song, and the Coronach from the Lady of the Lake. By J. G. C. Schetky, 1810.

Thomson's Collection of the songs of Burns, Scott, etc., 1822.

Three Songs from Sir W. Scott's Lady of the Lake. By F. Schubert, 1861.

Vocal Sketches to words by Scott. By E. Masson, 1850.

Wilson's Songs in the Lady of the Lake, 1848.

"Adieu, jeunes filles" (from *The Pirate.*) By N. J. J. Masset, 1835.

"Ah! County Guy," from *Quentin Durward.* By Sir H. R. Bishop, 1823; C. G. C. Dick, 1885; E. F. Fitzwilliam, 1856; B. G. H. Gibsone, 1825; G. F. Graham, 1823; J. P. Hullah, 1871; E. A. Kellner, 1830; P. Knapton, 1825; Sir G. A. Macfarren, 1873 (*Choral Society.* No. 13); O. Peiniger, 1879; T. E. G. Rovedino, 1823;

B. B. Simpson, 1879; Sir A. S. Sullivan, 1867 and 1878; A. Voigt, 1823.

"Allen a Dale has no faggot" (from *Rokeby*). By J. Addison, 1813; J. Clarke, 1814; W. Gresham, 1815; W. Hawes, 1822; M. Hume, 1879; W. Russell, 1812.

"And said I that my limbs were old" (from *The Lay of the Last Minstrel*). By J. Clarke, 1810.

"And whither would you leave me" (from *Rokeby*). By J. Clarke, 1814.

"An hour with thee when earliest dawn." By C. A. Macirone, 1879.

"Anna Marie, love" (from *Ivanhoe*). By J. Clarke, 1820; J. Hunter, 1820; G. Kiallmark, 1819.

"As sunbeams through the tepid air"—The Mermaid's Song. By W. H. Longhurst, 1879.

"Ave Maria, maiden mild" (from *The Lady of the Lake*). By T. Attwood, 1810; Sir H. R. Bishop, 1810; N. Corri, 1810; W. Hills (trio), 1865; F. W. Kuecken, 1846; J. Mazzinghi, 1840; J. Ross, 1812; F. Schubert, 1859.

"Awake, my love, though 'tis not day." By W. W. Woodward, 1857.

"Behold me, sung Hassan"—Hassan the Brave. By J. Clarke, 1825.

"Breathes there a man" (from *The Lay of the Last Minstrel*). By J. Clarke, 1828.

"Bring the bowl that you boast". By C. A. Macirone, 1861.

"Call it not vain." By D. W. J., 1832.

" The dawn on the mountains was misty and grey " (from *Rokeby*). By S. Webbe, 1815.

" Donald Caird ist wieder da." By A. Jensen, 1875.

" Farewell, Farewell, the voice you hear "—The Pirate's Farewell. By Mrs. R. Arkwright, 1830.

" Farewell, sad field "—Waterloo. By J. W. Callcott, 1815.

" Farewell to Northmaven (from the *Pirate*). By J. Clarke, 1822; F. H. Hodges, 1864 ; Sir G A. Macfarren, 1869 ; S. Webbe, 1821.

" Fathoms deep beneath the wave" (from the *Pirate*). By A. Cowell, 1867 ; A. Fox, 1876 and 1885.

" For all our men were very, very merry." By P. Knapton, 1825.

" From the steep promontory " (from *The Lady of the Lake*). By A. Radiger, 1811.

" Full well our Christian sires of old "—Christmas Eve : a glee (from *Marmion*). By T. Attwood, 1810.

" Glowing with love " — The Troubadour. By F. J. Liddle, 1879 ; Sir G. A. Macfarren, 1852 ; Sir J. A. Stevenson, 1816.

" Go forth, my song." By J. Clarke, 1815.

" Hail to the Chief." By A. Affleck, 1879 ; Sir H. R. Bishop, 1864 ; H. D. Leslie, 1853 ; J. Mazzinghi, 1810 ; A. Meves, 1856 ; C. E. Tinney, 1876.

" Hail to thy cold and clouded beam " (from *Rokeby*). By J. Clarke, 1814 ; W. Hawes, 1822 ; W. E. Heather, 1820 ; R. H. Loehr, 1878 ; E. Prout, 1861.

" Hark ! the bell is ringing " (from *Guy Mannering*). By Sir J. A. Stevenson, 1817.

" The harp's wild notes, though hushed the song." By T. Attwood, 1815.

" Heap on more wood." By J. M. Bentley, 1876; A. Fox, 1875.

" The heath this night must be my bed." By T. Attwood, 1810 ; J. Clarke, 1806 ; J. Lacy, 1805 ; C. H. Osborne, 1870 ; Sir J. A. Stevenson, 1810 ; R. Zabel, 1867.

" He is gone on the mountain " (from *The Lady of the Lake*). By T. Attwood, 1810 ; J. Clarke, 1806 ; J. Mazzinghi, 1810 ; J. Ross, 1810.

" Hie away | hie away | " By E. J. Loder, 1844 ; A. Plumpton, 1870.

" Huntsman, rest, thy chase is done " (from *The Lady of the Lake*). By J. Clarke, 1810 ; J. Mazzinghi, 1815 ; F. Schubert 1874.

" Hush ! daughter, hush ! " By J. Hook, 1810.

" I have song of war for knight " (from *Rokeby*). By W. Russell, 1812.

" I'll give thee, good fellow, a twelvemonth or twain " (from *Ivanhoe*). By Kendryke, 1840 ; E. J. Loder, 1844 ; J. Monro, 1840 ; R. L. Pearsall, 1868.

" In peace love tunes the shepherd's reed." By T. Attwood 1820 ; J. Clarke, 1843.

" Is it the roar of Teviot's tide." By J. Clarke, 1835.

" It was an English ladye bright " (from *The Lay of the Last Minstrel*). By S. Bennett, 1807 ; E. Cunard, 1874 ; J. Fisin, 1820 ; C. Sloman, 1857.

16

" I was a wild and wayward boy " (from *Rokeby*). By J. Clarke, 1814 ; T. R. Hobbes, 1814 ; G. Kiallmark, 1815 ; J. Mazzinghi, 1815 ; W. Russell, 1812 ; S. Webbe, 1815.

" Joy to the Fair " (from *Ivanhoe*). By J. Beale, 1820.

" Look not thou on beauty's charming." By Sir H. R. Bishop, 1815.

" Love wakes and weeps " (from *The Pirate*). By C. B. Braham, 1881 ; J. G. Callcott, 1876 ; J. Clarke, 1822 ; F. Clay, 1874 ; J. Gledhill, 1875 ; H. Glover, 1847 ; J. Jackson, 1870 ; Sir G. A. Macfarren, 1874 ; J. MacMurdie, 1824 ; R. L. Pearsall, 1863 ; C. A. Ranken, 1876 ; F. G. Read, 1883 ; J. Thomson, 1861 ; S. Webbe, 1821 ; M. C. Wilson, 1821.

" March, march, Ettrick and Teviotdale " (from *The Monastery*). By T. Miles, 1827 ; W. T. Parke, 1820.

" The mass was sung " (from *The Lay of the Last Minstrel*). By G. W. Chard, 1841.

" Merrily, merrily bounds the bark " (from *The Lord of the Isles*). By J. Clarke, 1815 ; S. Glover, 1878, W. T. Parke, 1815 ; F. J. Read, 1886.

" Merrily swim we " (from *The Monastery*). By J. Clarke, 1820.

" Merry it is in the good greenwood." By J. Clarke, 1820.

" The Moon's on the Lake "—The McGregor's Gathering. By A. Lee, 1859.

" My hawk is tired." By J. Clarke, 1863 ; T. Macfarlane, 1878 ; F. Schubert, 1874.

" The news has flown." By M. C. Wilson, 1822.

" Not faster yonder rowers might "—The Lonely Isle, 1845 (from *The Lady of the Lake*). By G J. O. Allman, 1845 ; J. Mazzinghi, 1815 ; J. G. C. Schetky, 1810.

" La nuit de ses crèpes funèbres." By L. Bizot, 1835.

" O bold and true "—The Bonny Blue Caps. By T. Valentine, 1835.

" O Brignal Banks " (from *Rokeby*). By J. Clarke, 1814 ; W. E. Heather, 1820 ; J. M. Miles, 1825.

" Of all the birds on bush or tree "—The Bonny Owl. By G. Dance, 1825.

" Oh ! day of honour "—Waterloo. By W. H. Callcott, 1834.

" Oh ! low shone the sun on the fair lake of Toro "—The Maid of Toro. By J. C. Clifton, 1825 ; W. Horsley, 1811 ; E. Symthe, 1877 ; Mrs. Somerville, 1877.

" Oh ! poor Louise." By Mrs. R. Arkwright, 1845 and 1877.

" O hush thee, my babie." By G. Heuschel, 1879 and 1885 ; J. Hoffmann, 1880 ; A. H. Pearse, 1879 ; C. Sommers, 1858 ; Sir A. Sullivan, 1867.

" Oh ! who rides by night "—The Erl-King. By A. Cowell, 1835 ; A. R. Gaul, 1880.

" O lady, twine no wreath for me " —The Cypress Wreath (from *Rokeby*). By J. Clarke, 1814 ; M. Foote, 1820 ; W. Friedrich, 1870 ; W. Gresham, 1815 ; W. E. Heather, 1820 ; G. Kiallmark, 1815 ; J. Mazzinghi, 1815. W. Russell, 1812 ; Sir J. A; Stevenson, 1814.

" O lovers' eyes are sharp to see " —The Maid of Neidpath. By K. B., 1846.

"An hour with thee." By Mrs. R. Arkwright, 1835 and 1845 ; J. W. Lee, 1874.

"Our Vicar still preaches" (from *The Lady of the Lake*). By H. B. Richards, 1848.

"O Young Lochinvar" (from *Marmion*). By T. Attwood, 1844 ; Miss Hime, 1820 ; J. Mazzinghi, 1808 ; J. Whitaker, 1856.

"Pibroch of Donuil Dhu." By W. W. Pearson, 1878.

"Prenez un an"—Le Joyeux Frère. [Translated from "I'll give thee, good fellow," from *Ivanhoe*.] By L. Bizot, 1825.

"Proud Maisie is in the wood"— The Pride of Youth. By E. Hecht, 1876 ; A. O'Leary, 1875 ; R. L. Pearsall, 1864.

"The Rose is fairest" (from *The Lady of the Lake*). By R. Cooke, 1811.

"She may be fair." By Miss Lindsay, 1865.

"Soldier, rest, thy warfare o'er." By T. Avant, 1870 ; J. Hook, 1810 ; J. Kemp, 1856 ; J. Lacy, 1815 ; Nunes, 1879 ; P. Saxby, 1881 ; J. C. B. Tirbutt, 1884.

"Some feelings are to mortals" (from *The Lady of the Lake*). By R. Cooke, 1811.

"The sound of Rokeby's woods I hear" (from *Rokeby*). By J. Addison, 1813 ; J. Clarke, 1814 ; J. Mazzinghi, 1815.

"Summer eve is gone and past" —The Harper's Song (from *Rokeby*). By T. Attwood, 1815 ; J. F. Barnett, 1876 ; J. Clarke, 1814 ; W. Gresham, 1815 ; R. Hoar, 1876 ; T. R. Hobbes, 1814 ; W. Russell, 1812 ; Spiker, 1815 ; J. Whitaker, 1815.

"The sun shines fair on Carlisle Wall." By C. A. Macirone, 1864.

"The sun upon the lake is low." By F. A. J. Hervey, 1874.

"The tear down childhood's cheek that flows." By J. Parry, 1815.

"There came three merry men" (from *Ivanhoe*). By J. Clarke, 1820 ; J. Jackson, 1879 ; G. H. Rodwell, 1842.

"They bid me sleep, they bid me pray"—Blanch of Devan's Song. By J. Clarke, 1806 ; J. Kemp, 1815 ; Mrs. W. T. Tucker, 1863.

"They buried him at the mirk midnight." By J. Lodge, 1848.

"They came upon us in the night" (from *Waverley*). By J. Clarke, 1819.

"Thrice to the holly brake" (from *The Monastery*). By J. Clarke, 1820.

"'Tis merry, 'tis merry in Fairyland" (from *The Lady of the Lake*). By J. Mazzinghi, 1810.

"'Tis merry, 'tis merry in good Greenwood" (from *The Lady of the Lake*). By J. Mazzinghi, 1810.

"'Tis morning, and the convent bell." By J. Hook, 1810.

"To Horse ! To Horse !" By Miss Smith, 1834 ; J. E'Astes (Musical Sketches), 1857 ; C. H. Compton, 1855 ; J. D'Este, 1875 ; M. A. Scailes, 1874.

"The toils are pitched." By T. S. Cooke, 1810.

"To the Lords of Convention"— Bonnie Dundee. By W. M. Herbert, 1854.

"Twist ye, turne ye." By F. J. Klose, 1825.

"Wake, Allen Bane" (from *The Lady of the Lake*). By A. Radiger, 1812.

"Wake, Maid of Lorne" (from *The Lord of the Isles*). By W. Gresham, 1815 ; J. Mazzinghi, 1810 ; C. Jones, 1820 ; Sir J. A. Stevenson, 1815.

"Waken, lords and ladies gay." By E. H. B., 1870 ; G. Bairnsfather, 1871; Sir H. R. Bishop, 1840 ; W. Carter, 1876 ; W. A. C. Cruickshank, 1877 ; E. Hecht, 1876 ; A. Piatti, 1873 ; J. H. Sheppard (Four-part Song), 1862 ; H. Smart, (Choral Songs No. 3), 1864.

"Wake thy wild voice." By W. C. Macfarren, 1859.

"The war that for a space did fail" (scena, "The last words of Marmion)." By J. Clarke, 1866.

"The waves of slow retiring day" (*Li Donna del Lago*). By Rossini, 1856.

"A weary lot is thine, fair maid" (from *Rokeby*). By F. C. Atkinson, 1862 ; J. Clarke, 1814 ; W. E. Heather, 1820 ; W. Russell, 1812 ; Sir A. S. Sullivan, 1866; J. Waterson, 1880.

"Wert thou like me" (from *Montrose*). By W. Doyle, 1819 ; H. Fielding (Six Songs, No. 4), 1860 ; J. Goss, 1819 ; W. Hawes, 1820 ; G. Kiallmark, 1818 ; T. H. MacDermott, 1845 ; T. Miles, 1822 ; J. Monro, 1847 ; F. S., 1872 ; J. C. White, 1822.

"What makes the troopers' frozen courage muster ?" By J. Thomson, 1861.

"Where shall the lover rest" (from *Marmion*) ? By T. Attwood, 1843 ; D. Livius, 1810 ;

J. Clarke, 1810 ; L. Jansen 1815 ; D. D. Roche, 1815 ; C. H. H. Parry, 1885 ; T. Upward 1874.

"While the dawn of the Mountain" (from *Rokeby*). By J. Clarke, 1814 ; H. R. Couldrey 1880; J. Hunter, 1815; F. A. Jarvis, 1873 ; C. A. Macirone, 1874.

"Why sit'st thou by that ruined hall ?" By Miss Lindsay, 1862.

"Why then a final note prolong ?" (from *Marmion*). By J. Clarke, 1810.

"Why weep ye by the tide, Ladye ?"—Jock of Hazeldean, By M. A. Paton, 1825.

"Will Spring return ?" By M. W. Balfe, 1862.

"Woman's faith and woman's trust." By A. J. Caldicott, 1880.

"Yes, thou may'st sigh." By W. Horsley, 1835.

MAGAZINE ARTICLES.

Scott, Sir Walter. — Analytic Magazine, with portrait, vol. 8, 1816, pp. 105-123. — European Magazine, vol. 78, 1820, pp. 483-486. — New Monthly Magazine, vol. 10, N.S., 1824, pp. 297-304. — Fraser's Magazine, with portrait, vol. 2, 1830, p. 412.—North American Review, by W. B. O. Peabody, vol. 32, 1831, pp. 386-421.—New Monthly Magazine, with portrait, vol. 31, 1831, pp. 72-87.—Penny Magazine, vol. 1, 1832, pp. 297-304.—North American Review, by W. B. O. Peabody, vol. 36, 1833, pp. 289-315.—Selections from the Edinburgh Review, vol. 2, 1835,

Scott, Sir Walter.

pp. 209-216, 420-429.—West-minster Review, by Thomas Carlyle, vol. 28, 1838, pp. 293-345; reprinted in *Collected Works*, 1858.—North American Review, by W. H. Prescott, vol. 46, 1838, pp. 431-474.—Christian Examiner, by M. L. Hurlbut, vol. 26, 1839, pp. 101-122. —Eclectic Magazine, vol. 12, 1847, pp. 320-325.—Bentley's Miscellany, vol. 40, 1856, pp. 316-319. .North American Review, by S. G. Brown, vol. 87, 1858, pp. 293-320.—Fraser's Magazine, by W. F. P., vol. 61, 1860, pp. 35-38. Every Saturday, 1868, vol. 7, p. 586, etc.—Southern Literary Messenger, by G. W. Curtis, vol. 22, p. 291, etc.—North American Review, by H. James, Jun., vol. 99, 1864, pp. 580-587. —Blackwood's Edinburgh Magazine, vol. 110, 1871, pp. 229-256; same article, Eclectic Magazine, vol. 14, N.S., pp. 404-425; Littell's Living Age, vol. 110, pp. 579-599.—Broadway, vol. 4, 1872, 3rd Series, pp. 94-96.—Once a Week, vol. 8, N.S., 1871, pp. 136-142 and 160-164.—Nation, by J. R. Dennett, vol. 13, 1871, pp. 103, 104.—Harper's New Monthly Magazine (illustrated), by Mrs. Zadel B. Buddington, vol. 43, 1871, pp. 511-526.—Illustrated .Review, vol. 2, 1871, with portrait, pp. 97-103.—Cornhill Magazine, by Leslie Stephen, vol. 24, 1871, pp. 278-293.— Atalanta, by Andrew Lang, Oct. 1887, pp. 50-54.—Every Girl's Annual, by A. Haggard, 1888, pp. 337-350.

Scott, Sir Walter.

——*The Abbot.* Monthly Review, vol. 93, 1820, pp. 67-83. —London Magazine, vol. 2, 1820, pp. 421-437.—Edinburgh Monthly Review, vol. 4, 1820, pp. 691-717.—Portfolio, vol. 10, 4th Series, 1820, pp. 370-387.— Western Review, vol. 3, 1820, pp. 170-187, 255-260.—Eclectic Review, vol. 14, N.S., 1820, pp. 254-268. —European Magazine, vol. 78, 1820, pp. 241-246. ——*Achievements of the Genius of.* Tait's Edinburgh Magazine, by Harriet Martineau, vol. 2, 1833, pp. 445-460. ——*and Burns.* Macmillan's Magazine, by H. B. G. Frere, vol. 26, 1872, p. 168. ——*and Byron, and their Imitators.* Tait's Edinburgh Magazine, vol. 8, N.S., 1841, pp. 484-490. ——*and Fenimore Cooper.* Knickerbocker, vol. 11, 1838, pp. 380-386; vol. 12, pp. 508-520. ——*and his dogs.* Chambers's Journal, May 1877, pp. 273-276.—Sup. Popular Science Monthly, vol. 1, p. 233, etc. ——*and his Factor.* Gentleman's Magazine, 1869, pp. 586-595 and 680-692. ——*and his Imitators.* Fraser's Magazine, vol. 5, 1832, pp. 6-19, 207-217. ——*and his Literary Friends (with engraving).*—Eclectic Magazine, vol. 43, 1858, pp. 113-126. ——*and his Mother.* Good Words, by John Oldcastle, 1881, pp. 398-400; same article, Littell's Living Age, vol. 150, 1881, pp. 317-319. ——*and his Publishers.* Fraser's Magazine, vol. 9, N.S., 1874,

Scott, Sir Walter.
pp. 559-568.—British Quarterly
Review, vol. 59, 1874, pp. 330-
342.—Tait's Edinburgh Magazine, vol. 2, 1832, pp. 474-477.
——and *Lockhart, Ballantyne's
Controversy with.* Tait's Edinburgh Magazine, vol. 6, N.S.,
1839, pp. 657-672.
——and the *Regalia of Scotland.*
Victoria Magazine, vol. 17, 1871,
pp. 433-435.
——and the *Romantic Reaction.*
Contemporary Review, by Julia
Wedgwood, vol. 33, 1878, pp.
514-539 ; same article, Littell's
Living Age, vol. 139, pp. 298-
313.
——and *Scotland.* Art Journal,
1853, pp. 12, 314, 315 ; 1855,
p. 121 ; 1856, p. 361.
——and *Shakespeare, Parallel of.*
Monthly Review, vol. 2, N.S.,
1835, pp. 569-581.—Canadian
Monthly, vol 1, N.S., by D.
Fowler, vol. 1878, pp. 420-428.
——and *William Laidlaw.* Chambers's Journal, vol. 4, N.S.,
1845, pp. 49-53 and 72-74 ;
same article, Littell's Living
Age, vol. 6, pp. 609-717.
——*Anecdote of.* Antiquary, vol.
4, 1873, p. 163.
——*Anecdotes of, Hogg's.* American Monthly Magazine, vol. 3,
1834, pp. 177-184.
——*Anne of Geierstein.* Monthly
Review, vol. 11, N.S., 1829, pp.
288-301.—Westminster Review,
vol. 11, 1829, pp. 211-228.—
Southern Review, vol. 4, 1829,
pp. 498-522.—Edinburgh Literary Gazette, vol. 1, 1829, pp.
2-4, 41, 42.
——*The Antiquary.* Quarterly
Review, by W. Gifford, vol. 15,
1816, pp. 125-139. — Scots

Scott, Sir Walter.
Magazine, vol. 78, 1816, pp.
365-373. — Anti-Jacobin, vol.
50, 1816, pp. 625-632. — Monthly
Review, vol. 82, 1817, pp. 38-
52.—Christian Remembrancer,
vol. 5, N.S., 1843, pp. 576-580.
——*as a Novelist.* Edinburgh
Literary Gazette, vol. 1, 1829,
pp. 33-34.—Nineteenth Century,
by John Ruskin, vol. 7, 1880,
pp. 941-962.
——*as a Poet.* Edinburgh Literary Gazette, vol. 1, 1829, pp.
209-211. — Temple Bar, vol.
33, 1871, pp. 24-35.—Gentleman's Magazine, by T. H. L.
Leary, vol. 7, N.S., 1871, pp.
485-490.
——*at Work.* Chambers's Journal, 1869, pp. 721-726.
——*Autobiography of.* Monthly
Review, vol. 14, N.S., 1830, pp.
347-360.
——*Ballads and Lyrical Pieces.*
Monthly Review, vol. 53, N.S.,
1807, pp. 183-191.
——*Border Antiquities of.* Eclectic Review, by J. Foster, vol. 10,
N.S., 1818, pp. 305-322.
——*Bridal of Triermain.* Quarterly Review, by G. Ellis, vol.
9, 1813, pp. 480-497.—Scots
Magazine, vol. 75, 1813, pp.
282-286.
——*The Bride of Lammermoor.*
Blackwood's Edinburgh Maga-
zine, vol. 5, 1819, pp. 340-353.
—Quarterly Review, by A. W.
Senior, vol. 26, 1821, pp. 120-
126.
——*Byron and Wordsworth.*
Southern Literary Messenger,
vol. 4, 1838, pp. 268, 269.
——*Centenary of.* London So-
ciety, vol. 20, 1871, pp. 275-
280.—Harper's New Monthly

Scott, Sir Walter.
Magazine, by M. D. Conway, vol. 44, 1872, pp. 321-349.— Gentleman's Magazine, by C. Pebody, vol. 7, N.S., 1871, pp. 292-321.—Belgravia, by T. H. S. Escott, vol. 5, 2nd Series, 1871, pp. 382-388.—Tinsley's Magazine, vol. 9, 1871, pp. 83-88.— London Quarterly Review, vol. 38, 1872, pp. 35-59.
——*Characteristics of the Genius of.* Tait's Edinburgh Magazine, by Harriet Martineau, vol. 2, 1832, pp. 301-314.
——*Chronicles of the Canongate.* Blackwood's Edinburgh Magazine, vol. 22, 1827, pp. 556-570. —London Magazine, vol. 19, 1827, pp. 409-425.—Southern Review, vol. 2, 1828, pp. 216-263.
——*Cooper and Lockhart.* Lippincott's Magazine of Literature, by L. G. Clark, vol. 8, 1871, pp. 625-629.
——*Death of.* New Monthly Magazine, by Bulwer Lytton, vol. 35, 1832, pp. 300-304.— Niles' Register, vol. 43, 1832, pp. 203, 204, 218.—Fraser's Magazine, vol. 6, 1832, pp. 380-382.
——*Poem on Death of.* Glasgow University Album, 1838, pp. 152-154.
——*Diana Vernon.* Macmillan's Magazine, vol. 22, 1870, pp. 285-291 ; same article, Littell's Living Age, vol. 18, 4th Series, pp. 555-560.
——*Dirge on* (13 verses). Tait's Edinburgh Magazine, vol. 2, 1832, pp. 202, 203.
——*Domestic Manners of, by J. Hogg.* Fraser's Magazine, vol. 10, 1834, pp. 125-156.

Scott, Sir Walter.
——*Dramatic Powers of.* Blackwood's Edinburgh Magazine, vol. 19, 1826, pp. 152-160.
——*Early Days of.* Border Magazine, Nov. and Dec. 1863, pp. 257-267, Dec., 321-330.
——*Edition of Dryden.* Edinburgh Review, by H. Hallam, vol. 13, 1808, pp. 116-135. — Scots Magazine, vol. 70, 1808, pp. 355-359.—Analectic Magazine, vol. 2, 1813, pp. 139-146.
——*Edition of Swift.* Edinburgh Review, by F. Jeffrey, vol. 27, 1816, pp. 1-58.
——*Female Characters of.* Tait's Edinburgh Magazine, vol. 2, 1832, pp. 130, 131, 402, 403, 679.—New Monthly, by L. E. Landon, vol. 52, 1838, pp. 35-39.—New Monthly Magazine, by A. J. H. Crespi, vol. 7, N. S., 1875, pp. 259-272.
——*Field of Waterloo.* Christian Observer, vol. 14, 1815, pp. 750-760.—Monthly Review, vol. 78, N.S., 1815, pp. 251-260.— Anti-Jacobin Review, vol. 49, 1815, pp. 471-479, 521-528.
——*Fortunes of Nigel.* Edinburgh Review, by F. Jeffrey, vol. 37, 1822, pp. 204-225.—Quarterly Review, vol. 27, 1822, pp. 337-364. — Monthly Review, vol. 98, 1822, pp. 169-184.— Eclectic Review, vol. 18, N.S., 1823, pp.163-170.—New Monthly Magazine, vol. 5, pp. 77-81 and 172-178.—Blackwood's Edinburgh Magazine, vol. 11, 1822, pp. 734-735 and 747.— Scots Magazine, vol. 10, N.S., 1822, pp. 563-569.
——*Funeral of.* Tait's Edinburgh Magazine, vol. 2, 1832, pp. 196-202.

Scott, Sir Walter.

——*Genius of.* Tait's Edinburgh Magazine, by Harriet Martineau, vol. 2, 1832, pp. 301-314.

——*Gossip about.* New Monthly Magazine, vol. 82, 1848, pp. 250-257.

——*Guy Mannering.* Quarterly Review, by W. Gifford, vol. 12, 1815, pp. 501-509.—North American Review, by W. Tudor, vol. 1, 1815, pp. 403-436.— Scots Magazine, vol. 77, 1815, pp. 608-614.

——*Halidon Hill.* Eclectic Review, vol. 18, N.S., 1823, pp. 259-279.—London Magazine, vol. 6, 1822, pp. 174-181.—New Edinburgh Review, vol. 3, 1822, pp. 264-281.—Scots Magazine, vol. 90, 1822, pp. 27-37.

——*Harold the Dauntless.* Blackwood's Edinburgh Magazine, vol. 1, 1817, pp. 76-78.

——*Has History gained by his Writings?* Fraser's Magazine, vol. 36, 1847, pp. 345-351 ; same article, Littell's Living Age, vol. 15, pp. 49-53.

——*Heart of Midlothian.* Blackwood's Edinburgh Magazine, vol. 3, 1818, pp. 567-574.— Quarterly Review, by N. W. Senior, vol. 26, 1821, pp. 115-120.

——*History of Scotland.* Monthly Review, vol. 13, N.S., 1830, pp. 1-20.

——*Homeric Element in Poetry of.* Good Words, by J. C. Shairp, 1875, pp. 500-508 ; same article, Littell's Living Age, vol. 126, pp. 373-381.

——*Illustrations of Northern Antiquities.* Monthly Review, vol. 80, N.S., 1816, pp. 356-367 ; vol. 81, pp. 68-75.

Scott, Sir Walter.

——*Ivanhoe.* Edinburgh Review, by F. Jeffrey, vol. 33, 1820, pp. 1-54.—Monthly Review, vol. 91, N.S., 1820, pp. 71-89.— Blackwood's Edinburgh Magazine, vol. 6, 1819, pp. 262-272.—Edinburgh Monthly Review, vol. 3, 1820, pp. 163-199.— Quarterly Review, vol. 26, 1821, pp. 127-135. — Eclectic Review, N.S., vol. 13, 1820, pp. 526-540.—Portfolio, vol. 9, 4th Series, 1820, pp. 300-336.— British Review, vol. 15, 1820, pp. 393-454.

——*Dramatised Version of Ivanhoe.* London Magazine, vol. 1, 1820, pp. 437-440.

——*The original of Rebecca in Ivanhoe.* Century Magazine, by G. van Rensselaer, vol. 24, 1882, pp. 679-682.

——*Proposals for a continuation of Ivanhoe.* Fraser's Magazine, by W. M. Thackeray, vol. 24, 1846, pp. 237-245 and 359-367.

——*Kenilworth.* Blackwood's Edinburgh Magazine, vol. 8, 1821, pp. 435-442. — London Magazine, vol. 3, 1821, pp. 188-200.—Portfolio, vol. 11, 1821, pp. 161-193.— Monthly Review, vol. 94, 1821, pp. 146-161.—London Society, vol. 10, 1866, pp. 348-353 ; same article, Eclectic Magazine, vol. 5, N.S., 1867, pp. 35-40.—Western Review, vol. 4, 1821, pp. 154-176. —Edinburgh Monthly Review, vol. 5, 1821, pp. 324-353.— European Magazine, vol. 79, 1821, pp. 53-61.

——*Amy Robsart and Cumnor Place.* London Society, vol. 10, 1866, pp. 348-353 ;

Scott, Sir Walter.
same article, Eclectic Magazine,
vol. 5, N.S., 1867, pp. 35-40.
—— *Lady of the Lake.* Edinburgh Review, by F. Jeffrey,
vol. 16, 1810, pp. 263-293.—
Quarterly Review, by G. Ellis,
vol. 3, 1810, pp. 492-517.—
Eclectic Review, vol. 6, 1810,
pp. 572-602.—Christian Observer, vol. 9, 1810, pp. 366-389.
—European Magazine, vol. 58,
1810, pp. 363-369, 443-448.—
Scots Magazine, vol. 72, 1810,
pp. 359-364.— Monthly Mirror,
vol. 8, N.S., 1810, pp. 36-51,
256-258.—Universal Magazine,
vol. 15, N.S., 1811, pp. 393-
397.—Anti-Jacobin Review, vol.
38, 1811, pp. 239-248.
——*Lay of the Last Minstrel.*
Edinburgh Review, by F.
Jeffrey, vol. 6, 1805, pp. 1-20.
—Eclectic Review, vol. 2, 1806,
pp. 193-200.—American Review,
vol. 1, 1811, pp. 166-174.—
Monthly Review, vol. 49, N.S.,
1806, pp. 295-303.—Scots Magazine, vol. 67, 1805, pp. 37-45.—
Monthly Mirror, vol. 22, 1806,
pp. 385-395.
——*Letters of.* All the Year
Round, vol. 15, N.S., 1876,
pp. 229, 230.
——*Letters on Demonology and
Witchcraft.* Fraser's Magazine,
vol. 2, 1830, pp. 507-519.
——*Life of Napoleon Buonaparte.*
American Quarterly Review, vol.
1, 1827, pp. 578-605.—Monthly
Review, vol. 6, N.S., 1827, pp.
89-105.—Eclectic Review, vol.
28, N.S., 1827, pp. 148-162.—
New Monthly Magazine, vol.
20, N.S., 1827, pp. 104-112.—
Southern Review, vol. 1, 1828,
pp. 159-192 ; vol. 2, 1828, pp.

Scott, Sir Walter.
263-290.—Westminster Review
vol. 9, 1828, pp. 251-313.—
Christian Monthly Spectator,
vol. 10, 1828, pp. 32, etc.—
Foreign Quarterly Review, vol.
3, 1829, pp. 597-601.
——*Literary Character of.* Atlan-
tic Monthly, by T. S. Perry,
vol. 46, 1880, pp. 313-319.
——*Lives of the Novelists.* Quarterly Review, vol. 34, 1826, pp.
349-378.
——*Lockhart's Life of.* Monthly
Review, vol. 1, N.S., 1837, pp.
554-574 ; vol. 2, pp. 325-346,
607-610 ; vol. 1, N.S., 1838,
pp. 149-166 ; vol. 2, pp. 15-34.
—Tait's Edinburgh Magazine,
vol. 4, N.S., 1837, pp. 205-220,
467-487, 557-566 ; vol. 5, pp.
92-112, 307-327.—Dublin University Magazine, vol. 10, 1837,
pp. 142-156, 292-312, 385-402 ;
vol. 11, pp. 667-688. — New
Monthly Magazine, vol. 49,
1837, pp. 593-597.—American
Quarterly Review, vol. 22, 1837,
pp. 202-250. — Knickerbocker,
by J. F. Cooper, vol. 10, 1837,
pp. 259-264.—Scottish Monthly
Magazine, vol. 2, 1837, pp. 436-
454.—London and Westminster
Review, by T. Carlyle, vol. 28,
1838, pp. 293-345. — Dublin
Review, vol. 5, 1838, pp. 377-
407.—Christian Examiner, by
W. P. Lunt, vol. 25, 1839, pp.
340-366. — Quarterly Review,
vol. 124, 1868, pp. 1-54 ; same
article, Littell's Living Age,
vol. 96, pp. 451-480.—Month,
by H. J. Coleridge, vol. 4,
N.S., 1871, pp. 241-285.
——*Lord of the Isles.* Edinburgh
Review, by F. Jeffrey, vol. 24,
1815, pp. 273-294.—Quarterly

Scott, Sir Walter.
Review, vol. 13, 1815, pp. 287-309.—Eclectic Review, vol. 3, N.S., 1815, pp. 469-480.—North American Review, by W. Tudor, vol. 1, 1815, pp. 275-284. — Portfolio, vol. 6, 3rd Series, 1815, pp. 58-81.—Scots Magazine, vol. 77, 1815, pp. 42-49.—British Review, vol. 6, 1815, pp. 87-107.—Anti-Jacobin Review, vol. 50, 1816, pp. 105-127.

——*Marmion.* Edinburgh Review, by F. Jeffrey, vol. 12, 1808, pp. 1-35—Selections from Edinburgh Review, vol. 1, 1835, pp. 294-308.—Eclectic Review, vol. 4, 1808, pp. 407-422.—Monthly Mirror, vol. 4, N.S., 1808, pp. 85-92.—Scots Magazine, vol. 70, 1808, pp. 195-202.—Anti-Jacobin Review, vol. 38, 1811, pp. 225-238.

——*Meeting of Creditors of.* Tait's Edinburgh Magazine, vol. 2, 1832, p. 386.

——*Memorials of.* Chambers's Journal, Nov. 1878, pp. 705-707.

——*Minstrelsy of the Scottish Border.* Edinburgh Review, vol. 1, 1803, pp. 395-406.—Scots Magazine, vol. 64, 1802, pp. 68-71.

—— *Monastery.* Blackwood's Edinburgh Magazine, vol. 6, 1820, pp. 692 704.—Monthly Review, vol. 91, 1820, pp. 404-426.—Edinburgh Monthly Review, vol. 4, 1820, pp. 691-717.—London Magazine, vol. 1, 1820, pp. 565-568.—Western Review, vol. 2, 1820, pp. 341-354.—Eclectic Review, vol. 14, N.S., 1820, pp. 244-253.—British Review, vol. 15, 1820, pp. 393-454.

Scott, Sir Walter.
——*Monument to.* Tait's Edinburgh Magazine, vol. 2, 1832, pp. 237, 238.

——*Novels of.* Quarterly Review, vol. 26, 1821, pp. 109-146.—United States Literary Gazette, vol. 2, 1825, pp. 401-412.—American Monthly Review, vol. 4, 1833, pp. 429-440.—United States Review, vol. 2, 1853, pp. 238-247.

——*Paul's Letters to his Kinsfolk.* Monthly Review, vol. 80, N.S., 1816, pp. 337-355.—Scots Magazine, vol. 78, 1816, pp. 125-133.—Anti-Jacobin Review, vol. 50, 1816, pp, 661-679.

——*Peveril of the Peak.* London Magazine, vol. 7, 1823, pp. 205-210.—New Monthly Magazine, vol. 7, N.S., 1823, pp. 273-278. — Monthly Review, vol. 100, N.S., 1823, pp. 187-206.—European Magazine, vol. 83, 1823, pp. 169-174.

——*Pirate.* Blackwood's Edinburgh Magazine, vol. 10, 1821, pp. 712-728.—Quarterly Review, by N. W. Senior, vol. 26, 1822, pp. 454-474. — New Monthly Magazine, vol. 4, N.S., 1822, pp. 188-192.—Monthly Review, vol. 97, N.S., 1822, pp. 69-83.—Christian Observer, vol. 22, 1822, pp. 157-172, 237-250.—London Magazine, vol. 5, 1822, pp. 80-90.—Portfolio, vol. 13, 4th Series, 1822, pp. 73 85.—New Edinburgh Review, vol. 2, 1822, pp. 196-213.

——*Poetry of.* Retrospective Review, vol. 1, N.S., 1827, pp. 16-39, 436-438.—Edinburgh Literary Journal, May 1830, pp. 265-269, 280-282.—Glasgow University Album, 1869, pp. 234-242.

Scott, Sir Walter.

——*Provincial Antiquities of Scotland.* Christian Examiner, by F. W. P. Greenwood, vol. 6, 1829, pp. 170-173.

——*Quartet of Quarterly Reviewers.* Bentley's Miscellany, vol. 40, 1856, pp. 316-330 ; same article, Littell's Living Age, vol. 51, pp. 240-249.

——*Quentin Durward.* Eclectic Review, vol. 20, N.S., 1823, pp. 36-46.—Monthly Review, vol. 101, N.S., 1823, pp. 187-202.— New Monthly Magazine, vol. 8, N.S., 1823, pp. 82-87. — European Magazine, vol. 83, 1823, pp. 544-549.

——*Recollections of.* New Monthly Magazine, by J. H., vol. 42, 1834, pp. 208-213. — Fraser's Magazine, by R. P. Gillies, vol. 12, 1835, pp. 249-266, 502-515, 687-703 ; vol. 13, 1835, pp. 104-120. — Temple Bar, by Susan E. Ferrier, vol. 40, 1874, pp. 329-335 ; same article, Eclectic Magazine, vol. 19, N.S., pp. 434-438.

——*Redgauntlet.* Westminster Review, vol. 11, 1824, pp. 179-194.—London Magazine, vol. 10, 1824, pp. 69-78.—Portfolio, vol. 18, 4th Series, 1824, pp. 197-202.—New Monthly Magazine, vol. 11, N.S., 1824, pp. 93-96.

——*Reminiscences of.* Tait's Edinburgh Magazine, by John Morrison, vol. 10, 1843, pp. 569-578, 626-628, 780-786 ; vol. 11, pp. 15-19.

——*reviewed by himself.* New Monthly Magazine, vol. 46, 1836, pp. 79-85.

——*Rob Roy.* Edinburgh Review, by F. Jeffrey, vol. 29, 1818, pp.

Scott, Sir Walter.

403-432.—Analectic Magazine, vol. 11, 1818, pp. 273-311.— North American Review, by E. T. Channing, vol. 7, 1818, pp. 149-184.—British Review, vol. 11, 1818, pp. 192-225.— Scots Magazine, vol. 2, N.S., 1818, pp. 41-50, 148-153. — Anti-Jacobin Review, vol. 53, 1818, pp. 4 7-413.—Quarterly Review, by N. W. Senior, vol. 26, 1821, pp. 109-115.

——*Rokeby.* Quarterly Review, vol. 8, 1812, pp. 485-507.— British Review, vol. 4, 1812, pp. 270-282.—Scots Magazine, vol. 75, 1813, pp. 46-51.— European Magazine, vol. 63, 1813, pp. 223-226, 491.—Anti-Jacobin Review, vol. 44, 1813, pp. 377-390.—Portfolio, vol. 1, 3rd series, 1813, pp. 557-566 ; vol. 2, pp. 10-37.—Eclectic Review, vol. 9, 1813, pp. 587-605.

——*St. Ronan's Well.* Monthly Review, vol. 103, N.S., 1824, pp. 61-75.

——*Sir Tristrem.* Edinburgh Review, by G. Ellis, vol. 4, 1804, pp. 427-443. — Gentleman's Magazine, vol. 1, N.S., 1834, pp. 167-170. — Monthly Review, vol. 48, N.S., 1805, pp. 196-203.

——*State Papers of Sir R. Sadler.* Edinburgh Review, by E. Lodge, vol. 16, 1810, pp. 447-464.—Quarterly Review, vol. 4, 1810, pp. 403-414.

——*Subtleties of his Names.*— Knickerbocker, by Llwyvein, vol. 48, 1856, pp. 111-117.

——*Tales of a Grandfather.* Edinburgh Literary Journal, Nov. 1828, pp. 29-33 ; Dec. 1829,

Scott, Sir Walter.
pp. 405-407.—Monthly Review,
vol. 10, N.S., 1829, pp. 331-344.
—Westminster Review, vol. 10,
1829, pp. 257-283.
—— *Tales of my Landlord.* Scots
Magazine, vol. 78, 1816, pp.
928-934. — Quarterly Review,
vol. 16, 1817, pp. 430-480.
— Edinburgh Review, vol.
28, 1817, pp. 193-259. —
North American Review, by J.
G. Palfrey, vol. 5, 1817, pp.
257-286.—Monthly Review, vol.
82, N.S., 1817, pp. 383-391;
vol. 87, pp. 356-370 ; vol. 89,
pp. 387-403.—Eclectic Review,
vol. 7, N.S., 1817, pp. 309-336 ;
vol. 12, pp. 422-452.—Blackwood's Edinburgh Magazine,
vol. 3, 1818, pp. 567-574.—
Edinburgh Monthly Review,
vol. 2, 1819, pp. 160-184.—
Anti-Jacobin Review, vol. 56,
1819, pp. 507-514.—Edinburgh
Literary Journal, Dec. 1831,
pp. 317-321.
—— *Tales of the Crusaders.* New
Monthly Magazine, vol. 14,
N.S., 1825, pp. 27-32.—London Magazine, vol. 2, N.S.,
1825, pp. 593-599.—Monthly
Review, vol. 107, N.S., 1825,
pp. 160-174.
—— *Theatrical Apotheosis of.*
Tait's Edinburgh Magazine, vol.
2, 1832, p. 381.
—— *Two Drovers.* London Maga-
zine, vol. 9, N.S., 1827, pp.
341-360.
—— *Vision of Don Roderick.* Edin-
burgh Review, by F. Jeffrey,
vol. 18, 1811, pp. 379-392.—
Quarterly Review, vol. 6, 1811,
pp. 221-225.—Portfolio, vol. 6,
N.S., 1811, pp. 381-399.—
Christian Observer, vol. 11,

Scott, Sir Walter.
1812, pp. 29-33. — Eclectic
Review, vol. 7, 1811, pp. 672-
688.—Universal Magazine, vol.
16, N.S., 1811, pp. 126-134.
—— *Visits to, at Abbotsford.*
Broadway, vol. 4, 3rd Series,
1872, pp. 135-139. — Temple
Bar, by Susan E. Ferrier, vol.
40, 1874, pp. 329-335 ; same
article, Eclectic Magazine, vol.
19, N.S., pp. 434-438.—Old
and New, vol. 4, 1871, pp. 235-
241.
—— —— *Irving's Visit to, at
Abbotsford.* Tait's Edinburgh
Magazine, vol. 2, N.S., 1835,
pp. 414-417.—Monthly Review,
vol. 2, 1835, pp. 225-240.
—— *Walladmor. German Novel
attributed to Scott.* London,
Magazine, vol. 10, 1824, pp.
353-382.
—— *Waverley.* Quarterly Review,
by W. Gifford, vol. 11, 1814,
pp. 354-377.—Edinburgh Review, by F. Jeffrey, vol. 24,
1814, pp. 208-243. — Anti-
Jacobin Review, vol. 47, 1814,
pp. 217-231.—Analectic Magazine, vol. 5, 1815, pp. 89-110.
—— *Waverley Novels.* Portfolio,
vol. 13, 4th series, 1822, pp.
136-152. — London Magazine,
vol. 7, N.S., 1827, pp. 533-
535 ; vol. 3, 3rd Series,
1829, pp. 610-617. — North
American Review, by W. B. O.
Peabody, vol. 32, 1831, pp.
386-421. — Edinburgh Review,
vol. 55, 1832, pp. 61-79.—
National Review, vol. 6,
1858, pp. 444-472 ; same
article, Littell's Living Age,
vol. 57, pp. 563-570. —
Littell's Living Age (from the
Saturday Review), vol 76, 1863,

Scott, Sir Walter.
pp. 187-190.—Chambers's Journal, 1874, pp. 725-728.
—— ——*Authorship of Waverley Novels.* Blackwood's Edinburgh Magazine, vol. 8, 1821, pp. 355-358.—Irish Quarterly Review, vol. 7, 1857, pp. 469-503.—London Magazine, vol. 1, 1820, pp. 11-22.
—— ——*Dramas from Waverley Novels.* Dublin University Magazine, vol. 37, 1851, pp. 647-651.
—— ——*Heber's Letters on the Waverley Novels.* Monthly Review, vol. 97, N.S., 1822, pp. 356-364.
—— ——*Imitation of the Waverley Novels.* Christian Monthly Spectator, by L. Bacon, vol. 7, p. 80, etc.

Scott, Sir Walter.
—— ——*Landscape Illustrations of Waverley Novels.* Fraser's Magazine, vol. 6, 1832, pp. 600-604.
—— ——*Letter to the Author of the Waverley Novels.* Monthly Review, vol. 93, N.S., 1820, pp. 169-174.
—— ——*Poetry of the Waverley Novels.* Retrospective Review, vol. 1, 2nd Series, 1827, pp. 436-438.
—— ——*Sceptics in the Waverley Novels.* Continental Monthly, by C. G. Leland, vol. 3, 1863, pp. 439-450.
—— ——*Woodstock.* Monthly Review, vol. 2, N.S., 1826, pp. 73-96.—Westminster Review, vol. 5, 1826, pp. 399-457.—London Magazine, vol. 5, N.S., 1826, pp. 173-181.

- - - - - - -

VIII. CHRONOLOGICAL LIST OF WORKS.

State Papers and Letters of
Sir R. Sadler. [*Edited.*]   1809
Lord Somers' Collection of
Scarce and Valuable
Tracts. [*Edited.*] .   1809-15
English Minstrelsy. [*Edi-
ted.*]   1810
The Lady of the Lake: a
poem   .   .   .   1810
The Vision of Don Roderick:
a poem.   .   .   .   1811
Secret History of the Court
of James the First. [*Edi-
ted.*]   1811
Rokeby: a poem.   .   .   1813
Sir P. Warwick's Memoirs
of the Reign of King
Charles I. [*Edited.*] .   1813
The Bridal of Triermain:
or, The Vale of St. John.   1813
Works of Jonathan Swift.
[*Edited.*] .   .   .   1814
The Letting of Humours
Blood into the Head
Vaine. (*Edited*). .   .   1814
Waverley   1814
The Border Antiquities   1814-17
The Lord of the Isles: a
poem   1815
Guy Mannering   .   .   1815
The Field of Waterloo, a
Poem   1815
Memoirs of the Somervilles.
(*Edited*).   .   .   .   1815
Paul's Letters to his Kins-
folk.   1816
The Antiquary   .   .   1816
Tales of My Landlord.
—First series.   .   .   1816
(The Black Dwarf—Old
Mortality.)
Harold the Dauntless: a
poem   1817
Rob Roy   1818
Tales of my Landlord.
—Second series   .   .   1818
(The Heart of Midlothian)

Tales of my Landlord.
—Third series   .   .   1819
(The Bride of Lammer-
moor.—The Legend of
Montrose.)
The Visionary, Nos. 1, 2, 3   1819
Description of the Regalia
of Scotland .   .   .   1819
Ivanhoe   1820
The Monastery   .   .   1820
The Abbot   .   .   .   1820
Memorials of the Halibur-
tons (*Edited*)   .   .   1820
Carey's Trivial Poems and
Triolets (*Edited*) .   .   1820
The Novelists' Library
(*Edited*)   .   .   1821-24
Franck's Northern Memoirs
(*Edited*)   .   .   .   1821
Kenilworth   .   .   .   1821
The Pirate   .   .   .   1822
Chronological Notes of
Scottish Affairs, taken
chiefly from the diary
of Lord Fountainhall
(*Edited*)   .   .   .   1822
Halidon Hill, a dramatic
sketch   1822
Military Memoirs of the
Great Civil War (*Edited*)   1822
The Fortunes of Nigel   .   1822
Peveril of the Peak .   .   1822
Quentin Durward   .   .   1823
St. Ronan's Well   .   .   1824
Redgauntlet   .   .   .   1824
Tales of the Crusaders   .   1825
(The Betrothed—The
Talisman.)
Provincial Antiquities of
Scotland   .   .   .   1826
Thoughts on the Proposed
Change of Currency   .   1826
Woodstock   .   .   .   1826
Life of Napoleon Buona-
parte   1827

THE WALTER SCOTT PRESS, NEWCASTLE-ON-TYNE.

THE SCOTT LIBRARY.

Cloth, Uncut Edges, Gilt Top.　Price 1s. 6d. per Volume.

VOLUMES ALREADY ISSUED—

THE WALTER SCOTT PUBLISHING COMPANY, LIMITED,
LONDON AND NEWCASTLE-ON-TYNE.

THE SCOTT LIBRARY—continued.

THE WALTER SCOTT PUBLISHING COMPANY, LIMITED,
LONDON AND NEWCASTLE-ON-TYNE.

THE SCOTT LIBRARY—continued.

THE WALTER SCOTT PUBLISHING COMPANY, LIMITED,
LONDON AND NEWCASTLE-ON-TYNE.

THE SCOTT LIBRARY—continued.

THE WALTER SCOTT PUBLISHING COMPANY, LIMITED,
LONDON AND NEWCASTLE-ON-TYNE.

THE SCOTT LIBRARY—continued.

THE WALTER SCOTT PUBLISHING COMPANY, LIMITED,
LONDON AND NEWCASTLE-ON-TYNE.

THE SCOTT LIBRARY—continued.

THE WALTER SCOTT PUBLISHING COMPANY, LIMITED,
LONDON AND NEWCASTLE-ON-TYNE.

THE SCOTT LIBRARY—continued.

THE WALTER SCOTT PUBLISHING COMPANY, LIMITED,
LONDON AND NEWCASTLE-ON-TYNE.

EDUCATED WOMEN.

The object of this series of manuals will be to give to girls, more particularly to those belonging to the educated classes, who from inclination or necessity are looking forward to earning their own living, some assistance with reference to the choice of a profession, and to the best method of preparing for it when chosen.

Foolscap 8vo, Stiff Paper Cover, Price 1s.; or in Limp Cloth, 1s. 6d.

I.—SECONDARY TEACHING.

This manual contains particulars of the qualifications necessary for a secondary teacher, with a list of the colleges and universities where training may be had, the cost of training, and the prospect of employment when trained.

II.—ELEMENTARY TEACHING.

This manual sums up clearly the chief facts which need to be known respecting the work to be done in elementary schools, and the conditions under which women may take a share in such work.

III.—SICK NURSING.

This manual contains useful information with regard to every branch of Nursing—Hospital, District, Private, and Mental Nursing, and Nursing in the Army and Navy and in Poor Law Institutions, with particulars of the best method of training, the usual salaries given, and the prospect of employment, with some account of the general advantages and drawbacks of the work.

IV.—MEDICINE.

This manual gives particulars of all the medical qualifications recognised by the General Medical Council which are open to women, and of the methods by which they can be obtained, with full details of the different universities and colleges at which women can pursue their medical studies.

THE WALTER SCOTT PUBLISHING COMPANY, LIMITED,
LONDON AND NEWCASTLE-ON-TYNE.

IBSEN'S PROSE DRAMAS.

EDITED BY WILLIAM ARCHER.

Complete in Five Vols. Crown 8vo, Cloth, Price 3s. 6d. each.
Set of Five Vols., in Case, 17s. 6d.; in Half Morocco, in Case, 32s. 6d.

Vol. I.—"A DOLL'S HOUSE," "THE LEAGUE OF YOUTH," and "THE PILLARS OF SOCIETY." With Portrait of the Author, and Biographical Introduction by WILLIAM ARCHER.

Vol. II.—"GHOSTS," "AN ENEMY OF THE PEOPLE," and "THE WILD DUCK." With an Introductory Note.

Vol. III.—"LADY INGER OF ÖSTRÅT," "THE VIKINGS AT HELGELAND," "THE PRETENDERS." With an Introductory Note and Portrait of Ibsen.

Vol. IV.—"EMPEROR AND GALILEAN." With an Introductory Note by WILLIAM ARCHER.

Vol. V.—"ROSMERSHOLM," "THE LADY FROM THE SEA," "HEDDA GABLER." Translated by WILLIAM ARCHER. With an Introductory Note.

AN INTERESTING AND INSTRUCTIVE GIFT BOOK FOR EVERY ONE MUSICALLY INCLINED.

In One Volume. Crown 8vo, Cloth, Richly Gilt. Price 3/6.

MUSICIANS' WIT, HUMOUR, AND ANECDOTE.

Being *On Dits* of Composers, Singers, and Instrumentalists of all Times.

BY FREDERICK J. CROWEST,

Author of "The Great Tone Poets," "Verdi: Man and Musician"; Editor of "The Master Musicians Series," etc., etc.

Profusely Illustrated with Quaint Drawings by J. P. DONNE.

THE WALTER SCOTT PUBLISHING COMPANY, LIMITED,
LONDON AND NEWCASTLE-ON-TYNE.

Crown 8vo, Cloth, 3s. 6d. each; some vols., 6s.

THE CONTEMPORARY SCIENCE SERIES.

EDITED BY HAVELOCK ELLIS.

Illustrated Volumes containing between 300 and 400 pp.

CHATTERTON. With Engraving, "The Death of Chatterton."
COWPER. With Portrait of Cowper.
CHAUCER. With Portrait of Chaucer.
COLERIDGE. With Portrait of Coleridge.
POPE. With Portrait of Pope.
BYRON. Miscellaneous } With Portraits of Byron.
BYRON. Don Juan
JACOBITE SONGS. With Portrait of Prince Charlie.
BORDER BALLADS. With View of Neidpath Castle.
AUSTRALIAN BALLADS. With Portrait of A. L. Gordon.
HOGG. With Portrait of Hogg.
GOLDSMITH. With Portrait of Goldsmith.
MOORE. With Portrait of Moore.
DORA GREENWELL. With Portrait of Dora Greenwell.
BLAKE. With Portrait of Blake.
POEMS OF NATURE. With Portrait of Andrew Lang.
PRAED. With Portrait.
SOUTHEY. With Portrait.
HUGO. With Portrait.
GOETHE. With Portrait.
BERANGER. With Portrait.
HEINE. With Portrait.
SEA MUSIC. With View of Corbière Rocks, Jersey.
SONG-TIDE. With Portrait of Philip Bourke Marston.
LADY OF LYONS. With Portrait of Bulwer Lytton.
SHAKESPEARE : Songs and Sonnets. With Portrait.
BEN JONSON. With Portrait.
HORACE. With Portrait.
CRABBE. With Portrait.
CRADLE SONGS. With Engraving from Drawing by T. E. Macklin.
BALLADS OF SPORT. Do. do.
MATTHEW ARNOLD. With Portrait.
AUSTIN'S DAYS OF THE YEAR. With Portrait.
CLOUGH'S BOTHIE, and other Poems. With View.
BROWNING'S Pippa Passes, etc. ⎫
BROWNING'S Blot in the 'Scutcheon, etc. ⎬ With Portrait.
BROWNING'S Dramatic Lyrics. ⎭
MACKAY'S LOVER'S MISSAL. With Portrait.
KIRKE WHITE'S POEMS. With Portrait.
LYRA NICOTIANA. With Portrait.
AURORA LEIGH. With Portrait of E. B. Browning.
NAVAL SONGS. With Portrait of Lord Nelson.
TENNYSON : In Memoriam, Maud, etc. With Portrait.
TENNYSON : English Idyls, The Princess, etc. With View of
    Farringford House.
WAR SONGS. With Portrait of Lord Roberts.
JAMES THOMSON. With Portrait.
ALEXANDER SMITH. With Portrait.

THE WALTER SCOTT PUBLISHING CO., LTD.,
LONDON AND NEWCASTLE-ON-TYNE.